"Nothing wo̶̶̶̶̶̶̶̶̶̶ ̶̶̶̶̶̶̶ ̶̶̶̶̶ way you think it's going to when you're eighteen, Colt.

"At least, it hasn't for me. But that's okay. You know, when I think about it, not one thing has changed since that night in your pickup, and yet everything has changed. I'm a different person now, even though I'm still the smart girl who helps everybody with their algebra homework. I just get paid for it now. My life hasn't changed that much on the surface. I'm still in Aloma, still in the same house, still a—"

Becca broke off with a sharp intake of breath. She clamped her mouth shut and looked at him with wide eyes, her cheeks flushing. Colt thought for a second she was choking, but she'd just gone very, very still.

And in that moment the sentence completed itself in his head. He gaped at her.

"Becca, don't tell me you're still a *virgin?*"

Dear Reader,

The year is almost over, but the excitement continues here at Intimate Moments. Reader favorite Ruth Langan launches a new miniseries, THE LASSITER LAW, with *By Honor Bound*. Law enforcement is the Lassiter family legacy—and love is their future. Be there to see it all happen.

Our FIRSTBORN SONS continuity is almost at an end. This month's installment is *Born in Secret,* by Kylie Brant. Next month Alexandra Sellers finishes up this six-book series, which leads right into ROMANCING THE CROWN, our new twelve-book Intimate Moments continuity continuing the saga of the Montebellan royal family. THE PROTECTORS, by Beverly Barton, is one of our most popular ongoing miniseries, so don't miss this seasonal offering, *Jack's Christmas Mission*. Judith Duncan takes you back to the WIDE OPEN SPACES of Alberta, Canada, for *The Renegade and the Heiress,* a romantic wilderness adventure you won't soon forget. Finish up the month with *Once Forbidden...* by Carla Cassidy, the latest in her miniseries THE DELANEY HEIRS, and *That Kind of Girl,* the second novel by exciting new talent Kim McKade.

And in case you'd like a sneak preview of next month, our Christmas gifts to you include the above-mentioned conclusion to FIRSTBORN SONS, *Born Royal,* as well as *Brand-New Heartache,* award-winning Maggie Shayne's latest of THE OKLAHOMA ALL-GIRL BRANDS. See you then!

Yours,

Leslie J. Wainger
Executive Senior Editor

Please address questions and book requests to:
Silhouette Reader Service
U.S.: 3010 Walden Ave., P.O. Box 1325, Buffalo, NY 14269
Canadian: P.O. Box 609, Fort Erie, Ont. L2A 5X3

That Kind
of Girl

KIM McKADE

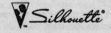

INTIMATE MOMENTS™

Published by Silhouette Books

America's Publisher of Contemporary Romance

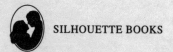

SILHOUETTE BOOKS

ISBN 0-373-27186-7

THAT KIND OF GIRL

This edition published by arrangement with Harlequin Books S.A.

® and TM are trademarks of Harlequin Books S.A., used under license.
Trademarks indicated with ® are registered in the United States Patent
and Trademark Office, the Canadian Trade Marks Office and in other
countries.

Visit Silhouette at www.eHarlequin.com

Printed in U.S.A.

Books by Kim McKade

Silhouette Intimate Moments

A True-Blue Texas Twosome #915
That Kind of Girl #1116

KIM McKADE

came out of the womb knowing she was going to be a writer. She was also convinced she would someday be a gourmet chef (at last count she's destroyed two blenders, three mixers and innumerable pots and pans), dreamed of singing like Wynonna (but has the vocal talent of Alfalfa) and at one time aspired to be a dancer (but was born with the legs of a coffee table). She has persevered in her dream to write, however, and today spends happy hours concocting stories in the Texas home she shares with her husband and her daughter, who is inarguably the world's cutest kid.

For my biggest fans and staunchest supporters,
Kelly and Kathy.

For Darryl.
Everything good in my life started with you.

And with special thanks to Brenda Ash,
for getting me started down this road.

Chapter 1

He had a body that belonged on one of those beefcake calendars. Clothed now in faded jeans and a white undershirt that had seen better days, he had broad shoulders, a narrow waist, and everything in between...well, everything in between was just where it should be.

He hunkered down over the broken board on the front porch—the board she'd almost fallen through one day when she'd come to look in on his father. His black hair had been raked back with his fingers, ruffled across his forehead in an unruly wave. He pounded on the board, loud enough to drown out the sound of her arrival. No photographer could have set up a better shot to showcase masculinity at work than Colt Bonner hefting a hammer.

Becca had fantasized—a million years ago when she was young and held out hope that fantasies came true— that Colt was Heathcliffe and she was Catherine, and he would sweep her across the dry west Texas plains as if they were the moors of Scotland.

Fat chance.

Back then, she'd been about as desirable as a box of rocks. And the only sweeping being done was with the handy O'Cedar.

But she had changed. She chanted those words like a mantra as she drove down the road to the Bonner house, and even as she climbed from the car and closed the door softly behind her. From her long red hair pulled back in a shower of curls, to the crisp teal-green suit she wore, she'd changed her style. True, she wasn't a siren in red leather, but at least she'd made an improvement on the shapeless, drab dresses Mama had always insisted she wear.

She'd changed on the inside, too. She'd worked hard over the past few years cultivating a sense of self-esteem, a sense of herself. Wasn't she proving that right now? If she wasn't confident in herself, would she ever be able to come here? After all, Colt was the one to whom she'd offered her virginity, a dozen years ago.

Colt was the one who had turned her down.

The reminder had her nerves jittering. This was a bad idea. She closed her eyes and took a deep breath. He hadn't seen her yet. She could tiptoe away and he'd never be the wiser.

"You okay?"

Becca gulped and opened her eyes. Colt studied her frankly over his shoulder.

"Fine," she said brightly. Too brightly. She forced some moderation into her smile and stepped toward the porch. "I'm Becca Danvers. We went to school together." So much for making him guess who she was.

Colt snorted. Actually snorted. "I know who you are, Becca. I haven't been kicked in the head that many times."

"Of course not," she stammered. "I just thought that since I—well, people say I've changed a lot. I didn't know if you would recognize me."

"Haven't changed a bit to me," he said, turning back to the porch.

Her smile fell. "Oh. Well, good. Good."

Wonderful. She was really impressing him with her cool sophistication now. He'd noticed her for all of three seconds. She reminded herself why she was here. The man had just lost his father—well, not *just;* Doff Bonner had passed on two months ago—and Colt had come back to a town he'd avoided for over a dozen years. It was bound to be a hard time for him.

"I stopped by to see if you needed anything. I heard you got back in town last night—" Actually, she'd seen his pickup pull up, but she wasn't going to let him think she sat around staring at his house.

"I see the Aloma gossip mill is still in business." He didn't bother to look up. "Everybody's already worried what that degenerate Bonner is up to now."

She pursed her lips and moved closer to the porch. She should have known Colt would be angry. She hadn't seen him in over twelve years, but she remembered enough to know that anger was his first line of defense. She wasn't put off by it any more now than she had been when she was ten.

She stepped onto the porch and leaned against the rail, crossing her ankles. "Yes, the entire town was peeking through their curtains when you drove past the city limits sign. We held a town meeting this morning to decide how we're going to run you out. Someone suggested calling in the National Guard. But me? I prefer a good old-fashioned stoning any day." She smiled and raised her eyebrows at him.

Colt sat back on his haunches, his forearms across his knees, and gave her a rueful half-smile. Her heart did a slow flip.

"Okay, your point is made. I guess you could say I'm not exactly glad to be back in Aloma County."

"I can't say I blame you, considering everything that happened before you left." She folded her arms across her middle, careful to make sure the Santa Fe Sand she wore on her perfectly manicured fingertips—which were probably still a little wet, anyway—didn't smudge against the teal of her power suit. She was doing a pretty good job, she thought, pretending the sight of him didn't make her breath come short and her heart pound. "And considering what's brought you back. I'm sorry about Doff, Colt."

Colt's eyes narrowed, and he waved away that consideration with his hand. "Don't be. He brought it on himself."

She raised her eyebrows but didn't say anything. There was no love lost between Colt and his father; everyone knew that. She'd grown up a hundred yards from Doff Bonner's violent temper. She knew what the man was capable of, including turning his own son against him. As Colt said, he brought it on himself.

Colt stood and walked across the porch, his boots clopping softly on the wooden boards. She watched him until she realized with a jolt that he was moving toward her, his eyes dark with intent.

Her mouth went dry. The memory of the last night she'd seen Colt came to her in excruciatingly vivid staccato flashes. Kissing him, holding on to him for dear life. The feel of him beneath her as she sat on his lap; feeling closer to him in that moment than she'd ever felt to anyone, before or since.

Her ridiculous offer of a dozen years ago hung foremost in her mind, and she realized with mortification that he was probably remembering it, too, more clearly than she.

His eyes were steady on hers, brooding. He meant to kiss her again. She could see it in the way he honed in on her. She regained enough presence of mind to close her mouth.

He moved toward her with a tangible sense of purpose, his jaw set with determination. His gaze held hers with an intensity that had her heart stuttering. He stopped inches from her. She could smell the scent of hard work. In a delicious panic, her eyelids fluttered closed.

He was silent for a moment, then cleared his throat. "'Scuse me, Becca. You're leaning on my shirt."

She opened her eyes a fraction, to see him watching her with barely disguised amusement. She willed the porch to open up and swallow her whole. When it didn't, she sighed and moved aside.

Once again, she'd made a colossal fool of herself in front of Colt Bonner.

He picked up the shirt from the porch rail and slipped his arms into it, leaving the buttons undone. Then he moved to the opposite rail and leaned against it, hooking his thumbs in his pockets. "So, what do you think I need?"

She blinked rapidly a few times. "What?" Her voice quavered.

He ducked his head, but she saw his grin, anyway. Oh, well. If she couldn't be cool and sophisticated, she could console herself with the knowledge that she was amusing.

"You said you came by to see if I needed anything. What did you have in mind?"

Since her vivid imagination had deserted her, she told him the truth. "Dinner," she said. "I didn't know if the electricity was turned on yet, and I didn't think you would want to eat at the Dairy Queen your first night back in town."

"Electricity got turned on this morning."

"Oh. Okay." She walked slowly around the porch, deciding that she couldn't have made a bigger failure of this visit if she'd tried. She'd wanted to comfort him over the loss of his father, which he obviously didn't need. She'd wanted to show him that she wasn't that same mousy, shy wallflower, and instead she'd proved conclusively that she was a nut. He didn't even want her dinner.

"Okay, then. I need to be going. I have papers to grade and—"

She heard his shout of warning at the same time the porch decided to finally open up and swallow her. Not whole, though. Just her left shin.

Jagged wood bit into her leg as she pitched forward, and she slammed her hand against the wall to regain her balance. Cold air under the porch brushed against her skin, and her foot thudded against solid ground.

Colt leapt across the porch and grabbed her before she fell on her face. His hands under her elbows, he brought her against him.

Becca pulled frantically on her leg. It was stuck.

"Stop, Becca!" Colt said sharply. "You keep pulling like that and you're going to make it worse."

She stopped. Colt leaned over the splintered wood, one hand cupping her leg behind her knee. Becca bit her lip and looked down at his dark head bent over her leg. Physical pain began to seep past her hurt pride.

Colt cursed, then tilted his head to offer her a curt apology. "This place is a disaster. I should just pay to have the place bulldozed and sell the land. It's going to take a month or more to get it livable again." He muttered something under his breath and sat back on his heels. "Don't move. I'm going to have to get the hammer and pry some of this loose before you can pull your leg out."

She stood there, lopsided, while he picked up the hammer and fit the claw end into the hole beside her leg. "I hope this doesn't hurt," he said as he gave it a mighty tug. The muscles of his shoulders flexed as he worked the wood free. The entire board popped up with a screeching groan.

It did hurt, a little. She asked through gritted teeth, "You're going to remodel the house?"

He shrugged and put his hand on her calf, helping her out of the hole. "I'm going to try— How does it feel? It looks pretty scraped up."

The Silky Sheer Precious Ivory panty hose she'd bought early that morning before school were ruined, of course. A big ugly hole opened around the scrape, and three different runs inched from the hole toward her skirt. She managed to nod, as he ran his fingers down the abrasion.

"It's fine, really." She drew her leg away from his fingers. "You're not staying, are you?"

"I'm going to get the house livable again, and sell it as quick as I can. Right now, it ought to be condemned." He cursed and shook his head.

"Damn old drunk, I'm surprised he didn't break his neck in this dump." He knelt in front of her and looked up, grim faced. "Do you want to see a doctor?"

She shook her head and smiled. "Of course not. It's just a little red." It stung mightily, and her shinbone ached. She resisted the urge to bend over and blow on it. "A little soap and water, and it will be fine."

Colt stood and took her hand, leading her away from the hole. "Lazy, worthless drunk. I can't believe he let the place go like this." He scowled at the piles of junk in the yard, the tangles of weeds and dried grass, the gray weathered wood that had once been painted white.

Because it felt a little too overwhelming, Becca withdrew her hand from his. If he noticed at all, he didn't acknowledge it.

Becca took off her bone-colored flat and shook out dirt. "He had a few other things on his mind the past few years. Like maintaining a constant state of inebriation."

"So, nothing's changed. You're the one who left those Alcoholics Anonymous pamphlets for him, aren't you."

Becca nodded.

Colt shook his head. "Still the champion of lost causes,

Becca? You know he was using them as coasters for his beer, don't you?''

"I know. And I don't think anyone is a lost cause."

"He is," Colt said grimly. "He is now."

Becca rolled her lips together and locked her hands behind her back. Despite his attitude, she knew Colt was upset over his father's passing. Or maybe that was just her, needing to see the best in him. "We tried to get hold of you when he died, Colt. We knew you were in Wyoming, because I—we saw you on television. The bull rides were televised. But by the time we got word to you, you were gone."

She didn't want to talk about that day, and knew Colt wouldn't, either. That morning she'd found Doff passed on in his armchair, and that evening she watched Colt take the hardest toss she'd ever seen, off the back of the bull and into the wall. The bull had charged after him and dug a horn into Colt's back. She'd thought she was witnessing the death of the entire Bonner family, then.

But the announcer said, as they carried Colt out of the ring on a stretcher, that he'd just had the wind knocked out of him. And though she was sorry for the circumstances, her heart had leapt at the knowledge that Colt was finally coming home.

Except, he hadn't come home. She, Toby Haskell and Luke Tanner, Colt's best friends, had buried Doff Bonner. Two months passed, and this was the first any of them had seen of Colt.

"I got your message," Colt said shortly. "I was tied up at the time. Couldn't get away."

Becca nodded. "Have you been to the cemetery yet? We picked out a marker, I hope you approve of it. We didn't know what—''

"I'm sure it's fine. How's your leg?"

She smoothed her skirt and looked down at the ugly red scrape and gaping hole in her hosiery. Lovely. "It's fine. Don't worry about it.'' If she left right now, she might be able to get away without adding another insult to her injury. Why, she asked herself, did she still have this ridiculous crush on Colt Bonner? He wasn't *that* good-looking.

Liar, she answered herself.

"I've got to go," she said firmly. "If you need anything, just give me a call." She limped down the steps.

"Becca—"

She turned her head, and he was there, close. Before she could react, he kissed her.

It was warm and soft and firm, invasive and overwhelming and delicious, all at once. And over before she knew how to react. He drew his head back, his eyes unreadable. If she hadn't just felt his lips against hers, she would almost believe it hadn't happened.

She touched a finger to her lips. "Why did you do that?" The question came with the thought, and she immediately wished she hadn't voiced it.

He was silent for a long time, his face closed. "Because I'm a damn fool, I suppose."

She didn't know what to say to that, so she just said, "Oh."

Not her most brilliant response, but then, the past ten minutes had been one big blow to her ego, so why worry about it now? She moved to the bottom step of the porch and smoothed her hair back from her forehead. "Yes, well—"

"Look, Becca." He put his hand high on the porch rail, and his undershirt rode up slightly. Becca caught herself staring at the sight of his flat stomach peeking from underneath. *You'd think I'd been brought up on a planet without men,* she thought. Feeling her cheeks grow warm, she dragged her eyes back to his.

"I appreciate your coming over here. But I really don't have time to be...well, I'm just going to get this dump livable again and get the hell out of Aloma County. I don't really want to be around anyone right now."

She heard the hum of a motor, and looked up to see dirt billow as the sheriff of Aloma County drove down the dirt road.

"It looks like you're not going to get your wish. There's Toby Haskell. Sorry, Colt. You have people who care about you here, whether you want them to or not." She gave him a sad smile. "I'll go so you two can catch up."

Colt's eyes focused on the sheriff's Jeep pulling up in front of the house. He took a deep breath as if to brace himself, and nodded, not looking at her. "Yeah. I'll see you later."

Becca drove down the road seconds later, watching in her rearview mirror as the men pounded on each other in welcome. Despite the obviously jovial meeting, she couldn't help but wonder what would make a man need to brace himself for a reunion with an old friend.

"Hoss!" Toby grabbed Colt's hand and pulled him into a bear hug, thumping him on the back. "It's about time you got your scrawny carcass back to Aloma."

Colt pulled away with a wince and patted Toby on the stomach. "Can't call you scrawny, can we? Matter of fact, you're getting downright plump. So you're the sheriff now, huh? How'd a clown like you manage that one?"

"My stunning good looks and charming personality," Toby answered with a shrug and a grin. "Becca told me you got in last night."

"I figured I couldn't be in town for fifteen minutes before some busybody alerted the law."

"Becca's not a busybody. Hell, I wish there were more people like her in this county. She just got into the habit of looking out for the place, that's all. She kept an eye on your dad, before…before—"

"Before he died," Colt said flatly.

"Yeah," Toby said quietly with a nod. "She brought him groceries, made sure his electricity didn't get cut off, made sure he didn't burn the house down."

"Or drink himself to death," Colt muttered. "Doff needed someone to look after him. He sure didn't do it for himself— How about something to drink? It's hot out here."

The men crossed the cracked linoleum floor into the kitchen. Colt looked around. "I forgot, all Doff had on hand was coffee. And Wild Turkey." He held up the coffeepot and cocked an eyebrow.

Toby nodded and picked up a cup from the counter. He eyed it, then turned on the faucet and rinsed the inside. "Times like these, I'm glad I'm not a bachelor anymore." He held the cup out, and Colt poured. "That was Becca who was just leaving, right? She's changed a lot, huh? She's gorgeous now."

"She was always pretty."

"How could you tell? She always wore those thick glasses, always had her head ducked down so you couldn't even see her face. But the past few years…she's changed a lot. Come out of her shell, I guess." He shook his head. "If I weren't such a happily married man…"

"Bull," Colt scoffed. "You never had eyes for anyone except Corinne, since we were seven years old. I heard you two finally got married. Congratulations."

Toby grinned. "Thanks. Took us ten years, but we finally did it. How about you? I know you're still riding the bulls, but did you ever find anyone who would settle for you, anyway?"

Colt ducked his head and decided to change the subject. "Nah," he said simply. "What about Luke? He still hanging around?"

"Hell, he's my deputy now."

"You're kidding." Colt laughed. "You and Luke Tanner in charge of the law and order around here? I guess he's probably settled down, too.''

"Nah, he's still hounddogging all the ladies. Teases me about getting old and fat, too. Man, it's good to see you, Hoss.''

Colt took a step back and frowned. ''You're not going to hug me again, are you?''

"I'm not *that* glad to see you. I'm real proud of you, man. One more win and you take Doff's record. The whole town's kept up with your career, you know, watching the bull riding competitions on television. But it's not the same as having you here. I'm sorry it had to be under these circumstances.'' He nodded vaguely at the filthy, broken-down house around them.

"Yeah'' was all Colt said. ''I got the message. I just, uh, I just couldn't really turn loose of my schedule right then. You want some more coffee?''

"Hell, no, not this sludge. So,'' Toby said, slapping his hands together and rubbing his palms, ''how long are you staying?''

Colt shrugged. ''A few weeks. I plan on selling the place, so I have a few things to fix before I can put it on the market.'' He looked around the kitchen, at the torn linoleum, the cabinet door hanging on one hinge, the bare lightbulb sagging from the stained ceiling. ''A few weeks. Maybe a month.''

"Great. The longer it takes, the longer you'll be around. Right now, I have to get back to the station. Corinne made a coffee cake this morning, and Tanner is liable to eat the whole thing before I get back.''

"Yeah, if you don't have your afternoon snack, you might dry up and blow away.'' Colt eyed Toby's belly as he walked by.

"Say what you like. Corinne thinks I'm sexy. And she's a hell of a lot prettier than you are.''

"And more diplomatic. Tell her I said hi." He followed Toby back to the Jeep.

"Tell her yourself. Come by the house and have dinner with us."

"Sure," Colt said, looking down the road.

"If I have to hog-tie you to get you there, I will," Toby promised, pulling on his hat.

"I'll be there. Just give me a few days to get things going around here."

"Tanner and I are already planning our first poker game."

Colt grinned. "Good. I can pick up a few extra bucks."

"We don't play for money anymore, being the responsible pillars of the community that we are now."

"Corinne put a stop to it, huh?"

Toby shrugged. "She said it was 'morally reprehensible' of me to be engaging in illegal acts while I was the elected sheriff. Corruption of power and all that. So now we play for Tootsie Rolls."

Colt laughed and shook his head. For the first time he was actually a little glad he was back in Aloma. Friendship…he'd forgotten what it tasted like. "Okay, whatever. I'll still win."

Toby opened the door to his Jeep and shrugged. "Probably. Of the three of us, you're the only one with a poker face. Listen, go over and see Becca while you're here, okay?"

"She already asked me over for dinner tonight. I told her no."

"Then, change your mind."

"Why?"

Toby turned the key. "No reason, except she looked after your old man and you owe her. She cared about Doff, even though he was an ass to her."

"I can't imagine anyone wanting to be around Doff for more than five minutes."

"Becca likes to take care of people."

"Sounds like someone else I know," Colt said, looking pointedly at Toby.

Toby grinned. "So let her take care of you a little. It'll make her happy."

"I wasn't planning on doing a lot of socializing while I was here."

"You never planned on socializing, Hoss. If you ever went to a party, it was because I dragged you. And I'll do it again if I have to. Go have dinner with Becca." He put the Jeep into reverse and tugged his hat low. "It's your duty. A home-cooked meal with a pretty woman. Not a bad deal, as duties go."

In the end, it wasn't duty or Toby's request that made Colt decide to go to Becca's house. He was simply sick of his own company. He'd been angry with Doff for two months—actually, it was more like two decades—and coming back to see the mess the old man had left him just angered him more. His nerves hummed like live wires all day, and work had done nothing to take the edge off.

Anger had always been his tool, something he pulled out of his pocket and swallowed down before he climbed onto the back of a bull. Thinking about Doff before a ride could get his blood pumping and his nerve sharp. The determined adrenaline stayed with him through the ride.

But out here, there was nothing to climb on and ride the anger out. He'd been practically vibrating with it, until the moment he looked over his shoulder to see a pretty woman standing in his front yard. And in that moment, a thought had popped into his head.

Now, I could ride that.

He almost laughed to think what prim and proper Becca Danvers would think about *that*. She'd actually invited him to do so, a lifetime ago. Of course, she wouldn't have offered if she hadn't been stone drunk, and she obviously didn't remember the incident.

But it wasn't that memory that had him knocking off work earlier than he'd planned. What Toby had said, about Doff being an ass to Becca, kept running through his mind. Of course, Doff was an ass to everyone. But Becca, being Becca, had turned the other cheek and kept coming back. She had come today, and he had been barely a notch or two above jerk-level to her.

He'd spent his whole life—or at least his adulthood—proving to himself he was better than that washed-up drunk. But times like these, he cursed Doff because he knew he carried some of dear old Dad's quality traits. Like picking on those weaker than himself.

So it was a guilty conscience and determination to prove he wasn't the jackass Doff had been that had him searching for a bar of soap in a filthy house. He took one look at the bathtub and decided he'd have better luck with the water hose in the backyard.

Half an hour later, his blood cooled to the point of civility by his makeshift cold shower, he pulled on clean jeans and a shirt and headed across the field to fulfill his "duty."

Chapter 2

Becca flipped the stick of graphite between her fingers and used the wide edge to shade the bell of the wedding dress on her sketch pad. Her brow furrowed as much in consternation as concentration, she tried to ignore the voice that echoed spitefully through her head.

Haven't changed a bit to me.

She closed her eyes and blew a gust of breath at her bangs. Of course, he was right. Oh, she'd worked hard to change her outward appearance. And at the risk of sounding vain, she'd made some major improvements. But then, there had been a lot to improve upon.

Trust Colt to see right through the new hairstyle, the hours spent at the makeup counter at the department store learning how to make the most of her "natural attributes," the constant inner reminder to hold her chin up, to look people in the eye, to speak clearly.

Trust Colt to see immediately what she had forgotten. That she was really, underneath it all, still the same old Becca Danvers.

Who had she thought she was kidding? Certainly not herself, though she'd tried hard enough. She'd tried this morning, when she pulled her special-occasion-only suit out of the closet, telling herself there was no sense in owning a power suit if it never saw the light of day. And again this afternoon, when she stopped by Dottie's Nails & More for the second manicure of her life. And even this afternoon when she'd actually looked herself in the eye in the rearview mirror and said, "I believe I'll just stop by and see if Colt Bonner needs anything." As if she hadn't been planning it from the moment she saw him pull up in front of his house.

She'd deserved what she got, too, she decided as she dropped the graphite stick on the tray in disgust. She tucked her feet up on the stool and examined the red scrape on her shin. Her power suit was back in the closet where it would be until the next open house at school. Her demolished Silky Sheer Precious Ivories were wadded in the wastebasket. She'd come home, humiliated, and changed into flannel boxers and a white tank top.

She gathered her hair into a ponytail and wound it on top of her head, jabbing a pencil into the mass to hold it in place. It had been a long time since she'd felt like such a fool. But then, it had been a long time since she'd tried to be something she wasn't.

She went into the kitchen and opened the fridge, the cold air chilling her bare toes. At least she no longer had to waste hours of her life, imagining ridiculous scenes of how Colt would react when he saw her again. At least she no longer had to wake up at night visualizing something out of a movie—Colt taking one look at her, being instantly bedazzled and setting out in pursuit of her like a man possessed.

He'd seen her—and been terrifically underwhelmed. And in her power suit and manicure, no less!

She pulled a pitcher of iced tea from the fridge and told

herself again that it served her right. What was she expecting? That when Colt realized it was she standing there, he would confess that he'd traveled the world in an attempt to get her out of his mind, that he couldn't forget the taste of her, the feel of her? And that now that he'd come to her again, he would never let her go?

Come *on.*

She frowned and poured a big glass of tea. Okay, so maybe that was a little over the top, even for her. But would it have killed him to say she looked nice?

But she had learned the lesson years ago and, except for this one crucial day when, apparently, she was hell-bent on humiliating herself, she'd lived by the wisdom of it.

She bent and made a face at her reflection in the chrome toaster. "Accept who you are," she said firmly. "Accept what you are."

"What was it trying to be? A can opener?"

Becca shrieked, jerked and spun. She splashed frigid iced tea all over herself at the same moment she saw Colt standing at her open kitchen window.

She tried to draw breath to speak, but all she could manage was a series of shallow gasps and then a noise that came out sounding like "Uhhuhhh."

"Sorry. Did I scare you?"

She nodded, openmouthed.

"I only meant to surprise you."

"Yes, well…you did that, too." She finally got some air into her lungs and stepped up to the screen.

"Cold, huh?"

To his credit, Colt did make an attempt to hide the grin that crept up his cheeks.

She nodded again. "What are you doing here?"

"You invited me, remember?"

"Yes, and I—I also remember you declined."

"I reconsidered. Is the offer still open?"

"Of course it is."

"Um, Becca?"

She cocked a brow.

"That was really cold tea, wasn't it."

"Yes." Hadn't he already asked that? She looked down and wished this time for the floor to open up and swallow her whole. Her white tank top—now virtually transparent—tented out under the hard buds of her nipples.

She grabbed at the shirt with both hands and pulled it away far enough that he could probably see down the neck as well. "I'll just—I'll just go change." She backed away, picturing how she must look with her pencil-eraser nipples, scraped shin and gaping mouth. Quite lovely, to be sure. She kept backing, and bumped into the doorjamb.

"That'd probably be a good idea," he said.

"The front door's unlocked. Make yourself at home. I'll just be a second."

In her bedroom she stripped down to her underwear, wondering what had changed his mind. Certainly it hadn't been her cool, sophisticated poise. And he'd told her to her face that her looks hadn't made an impression. That left the power suit and the Precious Ivories. Or maybe it was the ingenious way she had of falling through his porch that won him over.

One day back in town and the man already had her mind twisted in knots. She didn't know what to think about that kiss. In fact, every time her mind even barely brushed up against the thought of it, she got even more confused. So she told herself she just wouldn't think about it. Which, of course, she recognized as a lie as soon as she thought it. She hadn't forgotten their last kiss, and that had been twelve years ago. She could still feel his hands and lips on hers, without even trying. The kiss today hadn't shared that same unharnessed passion, but it did share the same barrier-shaking intimacy.

She walked into the adjoining bath and wiped off her

midriff with a warm washcloth. She caught her reflection in the mirror, and her hand slowed, then stopped. Her cheeks were flushed, her eyes as bright as if she had a raging fever.

Why was she doing this to herself? What was it going to take for her to learn?

She'd worked hard to build her self-esteem. It had taken years of conscious effort for her to accept herself, to even like herself. It had not been easy; she had a lifetime of feeling like a freak to wipe away. But she'd done it. And now she was champing at the bit to let it be brushed aside by a few careless remarks and a kiss that obviously meant nothing to Colt.

She put her palms on the counter and faced her reflection sternly. It was time to be perfectly honest. The truth was, she'd always had a bit of a soft spot for Colt. Okay, a *big* soft spot. A ridiculous crush, in fact. And maybe a part of her had always wondered whether if she *looked* different, and *acted* differently, he would *see her* differently. Less as the weirdo girl who lived down the road and made up stories to tell him when they were kids. Less as the bookish wallflower in high school, and more as...well, as more.

But the fact was—aside from falling through his porch and splashing iced tea all over herself—she hadn't done anything overwhelmingly embarrassing. At least she hadn't thrown herself at him—again. And if there was a God in the sky, Colt would not remember that night and she could go on pretending it had never happened.

The only real injury today had been to her pride, and she was an old hat at rebuilding that. So there was no reason she could not go out there as Colt's old friend, have dinner with him, catch up on old times, and act like a normal person. If she stopped behaving like an imbecile *right this second.*

Whatever had changed Colt's mind about dinner, it

surely involved little more than an empty stomach. And if she had any brains at all—which she knew she did; they were in there somewhere—she would go out there and quit reading something into every little move he made. She would relax and enjoy herself.

Just to prove to them both that she really didn't care if Colt found her attractive or not, she left her hair piled in a messy nest on top of her head. She dragged on baggy sweatpants, topped off with a T-shirt that announced "Math is Power." Then she faced her reflection again and nodded. Now, there was a woman who was truly comfortable with herself, in all her nerdiness.

When she went back to the kitchen, though, he wasn't there to test her indifference. Neither was he in the living room. She slumped against the arm of the sofa and made a face. She scared him off already. This had to be a new record for her—

"This is really good. Did you do it?"

She grinned. He was in her office.

He stood in front of the mural she'd painted on the south wall, his thumbs in his back pockets.

"Yes, I did it."

"It's great. When I came in I thought it was a real window."

"Yes, well, the light is dim. Of course, if it were a real window, the light would not be dim," she said inanely. She flipped the light switch and moved to stand beside him, noting the way his hair, still damp from his shower, curled at the back of his neck.

"This is incredible. You've caught it all, just as if there *was* a window here." He reached up to trace a blunt finger over the telephone pole beside the dirt road, the tumbleweeds built up along the barbed-wire fence.

"Thank you."

"It's great." He turned to face her. "Mind if I ask you a question?"

"Shoot."

"If you were just going to paint what's really there—
I mean, it's really good and everything—but if you were
just going to paint what you would see if there *was* a
window there, why not just put in a window?"

"I turned out to be a lot handier with a paintbrush than
I am with a saw."

"You could get someone else to do it. I'd do it, if you
want. It'd take about half a day—"

"I don't want. Why would I want you to destroy my
mural? It took me months to finish. And besides," she
said with a sniff, "this is far superior to an actual window.
It never needs cleaning. It won't let in dust, no matter
how hard the wind blows. And if I ever get the urge to
move, all I have to do is drag out the brushes and paints."

"But seriously, Becca, you could have the real thing."

"And look at this—" Ignoring him, she stepped up to
point out the giant mulberry tree. "This is the tree that
grows beside the elementary school. You remember that
tree, out at the west edge of the playground?"

"Sure, I remember. I stared at it all the way through
the third grade, wishing I was out in that tree instead of
inside trying to figure out fractions."

"I used to sit under it and read all through recess."

"I remember. You sat on this root right here, the big
one that grew up through the sidewalk."

She looked at him and blinked. Told herself there was
nothing touching or heartwarming about his remembering
her in elementary school. They had, after all, been friends.
Just friends. "Yes, well…" She scratched under her ear.
"I wanted it in my window here. So I put it here."

"You could plant a mulberry tree, you know. You
could have a real tree and a real window."

"Not a tree that's thirty feet tall and has branches thick
enough to swing from and roots big enough to sit on."

"Well, not for a while."

"Admit it. My window is superior."

Colt shook his head. "If you say so." He looked up at the stand of mesquites that bordered the quarry in the distance. "But doesn't it bother you that it's just...just pretend?"

She faced him and smiled. For the first time since he'd pulled up to his house, she didn't have to tell herself she was glad to see her old friend. She didn't have to remind herself that she cared for him as the person she'd grown up with, had once been close to. She didn't have to remind herself, because she just was.

"No," she said simply. "It's real enough for me."

"But I'm telling you, in a matter of hours—"

"Still the same old Colt. Always ready to rip everything apart and put it back together again."

He rubbed his chin and nodded. "Well, I suppose I come by the urge to knock holes in things honestly enough. But you have no room to talk, you know. You haven't changed that much, either."

She focused on the bird's nest she'd added in the crutch of the telephone pole, and told herself she didn't care. "I know," she said quietly.

"Oh, don't get mad. I'm not talking about your looks. Sure, you look a lot better with your hair all—" He made a vague motion in the general direction of her head. "All up and out of your face. At least people can see how pretty your face is now. And you dress better, that's for damn sure. But I'm talking about the way you always felt just fine living in your little fantasy world. If you couldn't have what you wanted, you just pretended like you did. Or pretended like you didn't want it." He shook his head and stepped back. "That always confused the hell out of me."

Since she couldn't have spoken coherently to save her soul, Becca just stared at him.

"What's this?" he asked, pointing at the drawing on her easel. "Your idea of the perfect pretend couple?"

Becca cleared her throat and blinked, moving around to face the easel. "Not hardly," she said. "This is a drawing I'm doing for Dunleavy's Department Store ads." She picked up the graphite stick and fiddled a little with the guy's tux. "They're far from perfect."

Colt grunted. "The guy looks like a real wuss."

"Oh, he is." She motioned to the bride with her chin. "She's got him completely whipped."

"Probably reads his horoscope daily and has his remote controls color-coded. His chin is weak."

Becca grabbed her eraser. Within a few minutes the groom's chin could have broken granite. "That's better. But still, he's not quite…" She picked up her thinner pencil and sharpened it. A few strokes later, the groom had a thin scar threading below his eye.

"Bar fight?" Colt asked.

"An unfortunate accident with the weed trimmer. He keeps an immaculate lawn, you know. Won an award from the neighborhood association."

She glanced at Colt and saw that he was grinning. A real grin—not the one he dragged out that was supposed to make people think everything was okay.

She tapped the pencil against her chin. "I know what's missing." She stepped up to block Colt's view and spent a few moments working on the groom's hair. With a satisfied sigh she stepped back. "One lock of hair, falling rakishly over his forehead."

"Rakishly?"

"It's a word. There now. The perfect groom."

"And that's the standard? Rakish hair?"

"Of course. A lock of hair falling rakishly over the forehead signals the perfect balance of vulnerability and masculinity. Very sexy, don't you think?"

He shrugged. "Doesn't really do anything for me. Sorry. What are we going to do about her?"

Becca sighed. "There's not a lot we can do, unfortunately. The dress is far too frou-frou my taste. But since the dress is the whole reason for the ad, it's got to stay—I'm going to start dinner. Hungry?"

"Always. What are we having?"

"I'll let you know as soon as I know. Your hesitation has cost you one of my world-famous lasagnas, I'm afraid. I don't have time now. But I'll dig up something."

"Are these yours, too?" He motioned to canvases stacked against the wall.

She nodded.

"Mind if I take a look?"

Actually, the idea held the same level of appeal as if he'd asked to look through her underwear drawer. But since she couldn't think of a logical reason to tell him no, she simply nodded. "Go ahead. I'll be in the kitchen."

Colt watched her go, chewing the inside of his lip. He still couldn't decide if it had been a good idea to come over here tonight. The live wire of anger still fizzled in him. He'd even argued with her over her painting on the wall, though she hadn't seemed to mind. She didn't seem to mind anything, really.

But then, that was Becca. Everything pretty much rolled off her back, always had. He was still a little disappointed she hadn't made it out of Aloma. Not surprised, but a little disappointed, for her. He figured that night twelve years ago was the only time she'd ever allowed herself to admit that she had dreams, that she wanted more than what she had.

He flipped through the stack of canvases, remembering the last night he'd seen her, the night of high school graduation. She'd been desperate to get out of town then, desperate to get away from her mother. Desperate enough to offer herself to him as a way out.

He cleared his throat as that particular memory took its effect on him. On more than one occasion he'd regretted the necessity of telling her no that night. No to taking her with him, and no to taking her to bed. But it didn't take a genius to know he'd made the right decision. Still, if things had been different...

If things had been different, she wouldn't have given up and resigned herself to a lonely life in the back of nowhere. And he wouldn't be here cleaning up after the mess of a drunken bum.

He let the stack of canvases fall back against the wall, sick of his own thoughts. It was the real reason he'd come over, he reminded to himself. He was tired of his own company. And Becca was one hell of an improvement.

She didn't hear him step up to the kitchen door. She stood at the counter slicing mushrooms, humming softly to herself. Her slender bare feet poked out beneath the shapeless sweats, and she reached up to brush away a strand of hair that had fallen and lay at her neck.

Colt stepped up to her and pulled at the pencil that held her hair up. "What's this—uh-oh," he said as her hair came tumbling down. "Sorry."

Her hair fell, and his hand fisted loosely in it. Becca looked at him over her shoulder, and for a moment their eyes met, and held. Colt rubbed the slippery strands of hair between his fingers, then shifted his hand to cup the back of her neck. The cords of it felt fine and delicate beneath his fingers. Her eyes grew wide—dark green pools that looked bigger now that they weren't hidden behind glasses. For an intense flash, Colt remembered what it had been like to kiss her, to have her on his lap, offering him everything. His eyes drifted down to her lips and watched them part almost imperceptibly.

Then she drew away, smoothing back her hair. "That's

okay," she said. She fumbled with it, then finally let it drift loose down her back. She looked at the counter, the piles of chopped vegetables in front of her, anywhere but at him. "I hope omelettes are okay."

"Anything sounds good to me right now," he said. "Been a while since I've had a decent meal at all."

He leaned back against the doorjamb and crossed his arms over his chest. What the hell had that been about?

Becca continued to move around the kitchen, chattering as if the moment hadn't happened, chopping her vegetables. He hadn't meant to scare her. But then, he hadn't really meant to touch her. He had to admit, though, it had felt nice.

The last time he'd seen Becca, she'd been sitting on his lap, kissing him almost past the point of no return. It was hard to look at her now and not think of that night. He had assumed all these years that she wouldn't remember; she'd been pretty drunk. But the look in her eye had him wondering.

He picked up the hunk of cheddar she'd set out, and the grater in the dish drainer, and began grating cheese into a bowl. "So, I thought you were going to Paris?"

"Who told you that?"

"You did, graduation night. You said you were going to New York to art school, then to Paris, because that was where all artists went."

Becca made a show of concentrating on the eggs she was beating. She poured them into the hot skillet and tilted the pan to let the eggs spread evenly. "I said a lot of things that night. People do that when they're drunk. They blather."

"Sure they do," he allowed. "And sometimes being drunk makes them relax enough to really speak the truth."

"I wouldn't know. That was the first and last time I ever enjoyed that particular experience— Do you like mushrooms?"

He nodded, and she sprinkled them in, along with a bit of chopped ham. She took the bowl of cheese from him and dribbled cheese in, too.

"So, what happened?"

"You know what happened. I didn't get accepted into the art school. I believe I told you that."

"Yeah, I remember."

She looked at him then, and her face went still. "You do remember, don't you. I was hoping you didn't."

"It's not the kind of night a guy is likely to forget." He couldn't help the grin that started to creep up.

She mumbled something and turned back to her omelette, folding it over with a spatula.

"I figured *you* wouldn't remember," he said. "You were pretty wasted."

"You don't know women that well, Colt. Our most humiliating moments are the ones we remember most clearly. Wasted or not."

She slid the omelette onto a plate and returned to work on the next, not looking at him.

"It wasn't humiliating," he said. "At least, it shouldn't have been."

"Come on, Colt. I acted like a fool." She faced him, one hand gripping the spatula, the other on her hip. "I practically begged you to take me away with you. And I—I…" She sighed and turned back to the pan. "You know what I did."

Oh, yeah. He knew.

He stepped up and took the plate she held out to him. He wanted to touch her again, but got the feeling he'd get a fork speared in his hand if he tried. Instead he rooted around until he found the silverware drawer, and carried two forks and knives to the small table in the dining room.

Becca followed with a tray containing her own plate, a smaller one with a stack of toast, two glasses and a pitcher of orange juice. Her face was flushed, but he didn't think it came from standing over a hot omelette pan. He decided the gentlemanly thing would be to change the subject.

"The house looks nice. You've done a lot with it."

"Thanks."

"Did you do all the work yourself?"

"What I could. I had this window enlarged, and I hired Pete Huckaby to do it. He moved to Aloma after you left, I think. He just finished a few months ago. And there was some plumbing that needed to be redone, which I couldn't do, of course."

She tore off a bit of toast, but he noticed she didn't eat it. She looked around the room.

"It was mostly cosmetic work. Paint and paper, and changing the furnishings. But it makes a lot of difference."

He forked a bite of omelette and studied her as he chewed, thinking of the "cosmetic work" she'd done to herself. "Yeah, it makes a difference in the appearance. But underneath, it's still the same house."

She faced him head-on, and he knew from the steely glint that came into her green eyes that she caught on immediately. He knew, and was impressed when he saw her chin lift.

"Yes, it is. But then, the house was basically a good house, solid and strong. All it needed was cosmetic work and a little attention to make it a home again. So why not take it and make it into the home I always knew it could be?" She lifted one brow and almost defiantly stuffed a forkful of omelette in her mouth.

And for some inexplicable reason, that made him want to jump across the table and kiss her.

Instead, he just grinned and shrugged. "No reason I can think of." He looked around at the design she'd painted on the dining room wall; deep green vines and morning glory climbing over a trellis. She was right—it

did feel more like a home than it ever had when old lady
Danvers lived here with all her dark, stuffy furniture.

"So you decided to just paint the house instead of
painting the world."

"I paint," she said defensively. "I haven't bowled the
art world over with my talent the way I'd planned, but I
do paint. And you saw the ads I draw for Dunleavy's.
That actually pays a little."

"I suppose that's enough, then."

She glared at him, then sighed. "Yes, Colt, it's enough.
I didn't go out and set the world on fire like you did, but
it's fine. I have a good life. And my painting may be more
of a hobby than a profession, but it's still mine." She
closed her eyes for a second, then shook her head and
looked at him again. "Nothing works out the way you
think it's going to when you're eighteen, Colt. At least, it
hasn't for me. But that's okay. You know, when I think
about it, not one thing has changed since that night in
your pickup, and yet everything has changed. I'm a different person now, even though I'm still the smart girl
who helps everybody with their algebra homework. I just
get paid for it now. My life hasn't changed that much on
the surface. I'm still in Aloma, still in the same house,
still a—"

She broke off with a sharp intake of breath. She
clamped her mouth shut and looked at him with wide
eyes, her cheeks flushing. He thought for a second she
was choking, but she'd just gone very, very still.

And in that moment the thought followed itself through
in his head. He dropped his fork to his plate and gaped
at her.

"Becca, don't tell me you're still a *virgin?*"

Chapter 3

He shouldn't have laughed, he decided later. He was justified in being surprised, even shocked. She'd just admitted to being a thirty-year-old virgin, for Pete's sake. Surprise was to be expected.

But really, he should not have laughed.

The clock on the wall behind him had ticked loudly in the silence that had echoed his question. She'd sat, her face flushed, and stared back at him. As soon as it dawned on him what she'd just said, or had tried *not* to say, he felt a grin start to build like he hadn't felt in a very, very long time.

Becca Danvers, with her sweet kisses and carefully banked desires, was still untouched.

The thought had filled him with so much pleasure, in fact, that he laughed. Out loud.

He wasn't laughing now.

Now he was trying unsuccessfully to stop the scene of the previous night from replaying itself in his head. Now he was working like a demon, hauling off old furniture and ripping rotten carpet from the floor of Doff's house, in the hopes that hard work would erase the memory of Becca, her face a mask of complete humiliation, from his mind.

It wasn't working.

Colt stood and rubbed at his aching back, surveying the damage he'd done to the house today, and thinking about the damage he'd done to Becca last night.

Many times over the years he'd imagined what it would have been like if he hadn't turned Becca down when she offered him her virginity. Imagined it in vivid, Technicolor detail. But he'd assumed, of course, that someone else had eventually taken what he'd declined.

"Stop looking at me like I'm some kind of freak," she'd said as she stabbed her fork in her omelette.

He couldn't help himself, though. The only coherent words he'd been able to form, after he regained his voice, were, "How the hell did that happen?"

"It's actually a matter of something *not* happening, Colt."

She'd sniffed and swallowed, and he felt like a jerk. But still, the thought kept running through his head that no one had touched her. No other man had touched her. And the urge to laugh again welled dangerously close to the surface.

It was a wonder she hadn't tossed him out on his butt. But then, that was Becca. Even when she was humiliated—or thought she was—she maintained that cool pride. It might have hurt to think he was laughing at her, but she'd manage to get over it quickly enough.

Even so, the memory felt sour in his stomach today. "Are the guys around here nuts?" he asked the empty room. He got a rumble in response, and noticed for the first time that the light outside had grown dim. He crossed the room and looked out the window; storm clouds were building in the west.

"Damn it." He rubbed the small of his back and contemplated his options. He'd decided to tear out the old carpet—it was filthy and had probably been butt-ugly even when it was new—and refinish the wood floors underneath rather than replace it. The gleam of polished wood would help sell the house, but it was hell on his back.

It was a habit now to curse Doff when the pain in his back got bad. The pain was going to force him to call it quits for the day. His career was hanging by a thread as it was; he wasn't going to jeopardize his recovery—and his chance to beat Doff—for the old man's mess.

The thing was, he was loath to stay in the house one second more than necessary. He ate his meals, and even slept, on the back porch. With the rain coming, he wouldn't be able to hang out there. And he sure as hell wasn't staying in Doff's house.

He didn't realize he'd focused on the hole in the living room wall until he'd stared at it for several minutes. He'd put that hole there a dozen years ago. The last time he'd been in this house. The last time he'd seen Doff.

He reached for a cigarette, cursed again when he remembered he'd quit two months ago, and walked slowly into the kitchen. Out of spite—whether to himself or to Doff he didn't know—he turned back to the living room and stared again at the hole in the wall.

Doff had been three-quarters of his way into a bender the day Colt walked home from a two-day stint in the county jail—another pleasant memory for his mental scrapbook, courtesy of Doff Bonner. The old man had been happy to gloat over Colt's time behind the bars, had thought it was a good way to teach him a lesson. He'd been too drunk and giddy to coherently say exactly what lesson Colt was supposed to learn from going to jail over something that was Doff's fault.

But Colt felt that he had, indeed, learned his lesson. If

he was old enough to go to jail, he was old enough to stand up to Doff.

Maybe he shouldn't have egged Doff on, Colt had thought since then. Maybe he should just have told the old fart to shut up, and kept walking. But something in him wanted revenge. So he stood up to him. Told the old man how being in jail was a damn sight more fun than being in the rat hole they lived in. How his friends had come up to the jail and played cards with him. How the sheriff's wife—Toby's mother, back then—had taken pity on him and baked more food than he could possibly eat.

That hadn't been enough to coax more than a little frustration out of Doff, though. Colt found that once the hateful flow of words started, he couldn't stop them. Or maybe he could have, but it made him feel powerful to be the one hurling the abuse for a change.

So he kept it up. Told the old man all the things he'd wanted to say for eighteen years. Told Doff what a sorry bum he'd always been, how Colt hated him and was ashamed of him. Still it wasn't enough to make Doff unleash that fury that was usually so close to the surface.

So Colt pulled out the one weapon he knew he had.

"You're a joke, and always have been. World Champion bull rider, my foot. You cheated. Everyone knows you bought the vote. Even today you're the biggest joke on the circuit."

That had done it. As soon as Colt saw Doff's fist coming at him, he knew that was what he'd been pushing for. And he swung back.

He should have known what would happen. He outweighed the old man by a good forty pounds, and all of it muscle. And he had eighteen years of being on the receiving end of the punch. He had plenty stored up to unleash.

Doff crashed into the wall, so hard he knocked a hole

in it. He'd slumped to the floor, his hands up in defense instead of attack, and looked up at Colt, fear in his eyes.

That was the last time Colt had seen his father. The shame had grabbed him by the throat in that moment and had not let go. He hated Doff Bonner for making him what he was, hated him for teaching him to use his fists as weapons. Hated him for giving him the knowledge of what it was like to be on both sides of that equation.

And hated himself for following in dear old Dad's footsteps.

He'd run. Run from the house, into town and straight to the Haskell's house, which was the closest thing to a home he'd ever known. He'd tried to run from the shame, but it was always there, in the memory of a pitiful old man's fearful eyes and trembling hands.

Of course the bum hadn't patched up the hole. Doff probably didn't even notice it, in his constant drunken state. But that was okay with Colt. He didn't need the past to be patched up and glossed over. He would leave that hole there until it was the finishing touch on the house. Because the ache was like a sore tooth, and he needed to know it was there. He needed to remember.

He paced, edgy. The room had darkened with his mood, and he stood in front of the window, watching clouds build on the horizon.

It irritated him that his injured back slowed him down, and resentment made him want to work harder. But he knew that, for today at least, he was done.

He walked out to the back porch, a fresh wind stirring the grass. The ball of rage that sat constantly in his gut— sometimes a dull glow, sometimes a hot flame—flared as lightning slashed a vertical rip in the sky a few miles away. Once again, Doff had the last laugh. Colt had been close—so *close*—to beating Doff's record, to proving he was the better man, the better athlete, when he'd been tossed from Rascal's back. He could swear that in his dying moment Doff had possessed Rascal's body and dug that horn into his back, just to get in the last word. Thunder rolled overhead, and the temperature of the wind dropped noticeably. It chilled the sweat on Colt's neck and tossed his hair. Lightning cracked. He could see the rain line just a few miles away now.

It wasn't much of a surprise that his mind drifted south, to Becca's house. He'd heard her car drive by a few hours ago, when she came home from school. He could go there.

He *should* go there. He'd left things in a bungle last night. But hell, what did she expect, dropping a bomb like that on him? He stuffed his hands in his pockets and scowled. He'd handled the news badly.

But a *virgin?* He'd known Becca's life was sheltered, but for crying out loud. How in the world did someone as pretty and sweet as Becca get to be thirty years old and remain a virgin?

Not that he was going to ask her, not after last night. But in his gut he knew he'd made the right choice twelve years ago. It had been hard as hell, but he'd done the right thing by telling her no. She would have ended up hating him.

And that was one thing he didn't think he could take.

He rubbed his jaw and looked over at her house. She'd turned on the kitchen light, and the welcoming glow caused a shifting somewhere in him, a lump in his throat that he swallowed against.

Funny, he'd forgotten that he'd always gone to Becca, when they were kids. When things got rough with Doff, rougher than normal, and it was either clear out or get killed, he'd always found some way to get to Becca. She'd developed a signal for him to send her, an old tractor tire someone had left out in the fields behind their houses, and he rolled it over by the big cottonwood that bordered her yard. She explained it all like some kind of secret spy adventure, but they both knew it was a desperation call.

When things got to be too much, and he needed her, that was his way of calling her.

And she always came. He waited out by the old quarry, pitching stones and dreaming about another life, and she always came. She made up stories to tell him. Nonsense, fanciful tales where kids ruled the world and had all kinds of fantastic adventures conquering demons and trolls. And for a few hours, he forgot what waited for him, and she forgot what waited for her.

So it wasn't a surprise to find his feet headed across the field that separated their houses. It was an old habit, one that he hadn't thought about in many, many years, but one that came back to him with ease. Things were getting to be too much, and maybe now he didn't need her, but he sure as hell wanted to see her again.

Becca laid the stack of papers she had to grade on the table beside her favorite wicker chair on the screened-in porch. Pewter clouds built high in the sky; the storm was only minutes away. She didn't want to miss it.

Lightning cracked again, thunder rumbled immediately after, and the sky broke. The rain came thick and heavy right away, and immediately the world shrunk down to a few dozen square yards. Her little house was the universe, and she alone lived there. She smiled.

She heard the teakettle shriek on the stove at the same instant she saw the dark gray form moving across the field. She knew it was Colt by the walk, even before she could make out the features.

She opened the porch's screen door. "Hurry," she called above the downpour. "You'll get soaked."

As he jogged up the steps, she saw that it was too late. His entire body was already streaming with wet.

She stepped back and let him in. "People get killed by lightning, you know. Don't move. I'll get a towel."

She flipped off the burner under the screaming teakettle

on her way through the kitchen. In the bathroom she grabbed two towels and a quilt. On the way back outside, she stopped, watching Colt pace up and down her porch. She set the quilt and towels on the kitchen table and took two tea bags from the cabinet. Chamomile and hibiscus. She and Colt could both use the calming.

She tossed the tea bags in a teapot and added boiled water, then tucked the quilt and towels under her arm, kicked the door open with her toe, and carried the hot tea outside.

"Hold these," she ordered, in the same tone she'd learned to use on errant students.

He took the cups from her, sniffing rainwater off the end of his nose.

She dropped the towels on the chair and took the cups from him. "Okay, strip down and wrap up in this quilt. I'll throw your clothes in the dryer."

"No, that's okay—"

"Colt, you have chill bumps the size of marbles on your arms, and you're trying so hard not to shiver, you're about to crack in two. Now strip, and I'll throw your clothes in the dryer."

At his hesitation, she raised an eyebrow. "You don't honestly think this is my way of making a pass at you, do you? I tried that already, remember? Now strip. I'll wait inside. Lay your clothes on the table inside the door, and knock when you're decently covered. Okay?"

He gave her a sheepish grin that made her heart do a slow flip, and started working the buttons to his shirt. Becca beat it inside before she made a fool of herself by staring.

He did as he was told. She joined him on the porch a few minutes later, but only after giving in to ridiculous curiosity. Powder-blue boxers.

He sat in her favorite chair, one hand clutching the quilt closed at his neck, the other curled around her china cup.

His bare white feet and shins poked out from the bottom. He was doing a pretty good job, she decided, of looking like he didn't feel ridiculous.

He had toweled his hair, and it stood out in unruly black curls around his head. Becca sat down opposite him and tried not to laugh.

"Okay, want to tell me why you're here?"

"Just thought I'd stop in and say hello."

"Sure. In a thunderstorm. I believe that."

Colt sighed and hitched a shoulder. "I couldn't get any more work done today, and I couldn't—didn't want to just hang around there. And I didn't have anywhere else to go."

"Now there's an answer I believe." She sipped her tea, telling herself that it didn't bother her to be the last resort. What else were friends for? She openly studied the haunted look in his eyes, the dark circles underneath. He hadn't shaved that morning, either. "It's hard for you to be in that house," she said.

He drew his head back. "It isn't hard. It just hacks me off to have to clean up after his mess."

"Why don't you cut your losses, then? You could sell the house like it is, even if it doesn't bring much. I know you don't need money. I've seen your face endorsing everything from work gloves to shaving cream."

"No, I don't need the money."

"Then, why are you doing it if it makes you so angry that you grind your teeth? Why not just pay someone else to deal with it, and get back to your life?"

"I keep asking myself the same thing."

He stared at the hot tea cupped between his palms, and she could see his mind working.

Then he said quietly, "I may not have a life to go back to."

She leaned forward, more alarmed by the tone of his voice than his words. "What do you mean?"

"I mean, I banged up my back. I got tossed…"

"By Rascal. At Jackson Hole."

He nodded.

"I saw on television. The announcer said you'd just had the wind knocked out of you. But I wondered."

"I asked them not to let anyone know. I didn't want everyone knowing Doff had done it to me again."

Again, Becca asked, "What do you mean?"

But instead of answering, he stood and paced, clutching the quilt in front of his chest. "I don't know for sure that I won't be able to ride again. There was a surgeon in Portland I went to, and they say he's really good. He gave me a lot of exercises to do, and I do them—" his upper lip curled "—most of the time. But he said my spine was like a stack of wooden blocks right now. Another toss could put me in a wheelchair. And wouldn't Doff just love that."

Becca didn't know what to say to that, so she sat quietly, letting him talk. And hurt for him.

He stopped and blew out a gust of breath. "So, there's your answer. The only one I have, anyway. It's not as if I have a long list of pressing engagements waiting for me elsewhere. Until I get the okay from the doctor, I might as well keep busy. Because I'm not going anywhere."

He stopped, then turned to face her, his brow drawn low. "I don't know how you do it, Becca. I know you wanted to get away from Aloma as much as I did. But you stayed, here in this house. Doesn't it all bring back memories that—" He clenched his jaw and made a fist. "That just make you crazy?"

She hadn't intended to stand, didn't realize she was doing so until she was before him, one palm against his stubbled cheek. His eyes met hers, and for what felt like a long moment she saw something there, something desperate, and pitifully grateful. And she allowed herself the thought that he was here because she was here.

Then they shifted, and the moment was gone. He took her wrist and pulled her palm away.

"I don't need your sympathy, Becca. And I don't want your comfort."

"What *do* you want, Colt?"

"I want—" He broke off and looked out at the pouring rain. "Damn it, I *wanted* revenge."

"You got your revenge, Colt. You were successful. More successful than he ever dreamed you'd be, I'm sure."

"I wanted to beat him. And I wanted him to watch me beat him."

"And that would have made a difference? That would have taken back every hateful thing he ever said? Every punch he ever threw?"

He shook his head and rubbed his jaw. "I guess I'll never know, now."

The rain slackened, tapering to a steady pour that patted on the grass beyond the porch. Thunder rolled again, softer and more distant. Inside, she could hear the metallic clink of the buttons on Colt's jeans as they tumbled in the dryer.

"No. You won't ever know. Not for sure."

He turned and leaned against the porch rail. The blanket drooped, and he pulled his arms free and balled it at the center of his chest. "You didn't answer my question. How can you stay here? Why did you even come back?"

"Mama got sick right before I got out of college. She needed someone to take care of her. I tried hiring people, but she kept running them off." She tilted her head and wrinkled her nose. "She could be a little hard to get along with at times."

Colt snorted but refrained from comment.

"So I moved back home and took care of her. When she died, she left the house to me."

"Didn't you want to sell it and get the heck out of here?"

"This is my home, Colt. By the time she died, I had a job, friends here. And while I grant you I have a few unpleasant memories of my childhood, they're really not any worse than the average, I think."

"Still, when we were kids you said you were going to see the world."

"Which is a great dream for a kid to have. I'm not a kid anymore, Colt."

His gaze stayed on hers for a moment, then drifted to her lips and back up again. "Yes, I noticed. Still, you could have—"

"Colt." Becca laid her hand on Colt's arm. "Just because you went out and pursued your dreams doesn't mean it was that easy for the rest of us. For some people it's just not meant to be."

"Who decides what's meant to be? There are always choices."

"What choice was I supposed to make, Colt? To abandon my own mother? I know she wasn't easy to get along with. She had problems of her own that made her difficult at times. But she was my mother. She was all I had."

"And she's been gone, what—two years now?"

"Almost four," Becca said quietly.

"Don't you think it's time you get a life of your own, instead of—"

"What are you doing, Colt?" She drew a deep breath in through her nose and blinked hard. "Who are you arguing with? Me, or yourself? What is so bad about my life that you feel the need to come in and show me all its flaws? Am I so pathetic that you have to save me from myself before I end up a shriveled old—"

"God, no." He put a hand on her shoulder and squeezed. "Aw, I'm sorry, Becca. Of course I didn't mean that. I didn't mean—it's just that, when you said…" He closed his mouth and frowned.

"When I said I was still a virgin—" Her voice cracked, and she swallowed hard and narrowed her eyes. "When I said I was still a virgin, you decided I had wasted my life and you were going to be the one to shove me into what you think my life should be."

"I hate to see you end up—"

"An old maid schoolteacher?" She put her hands on her hips and bumped her chin up, taking a few steps back. "I've got news for you, Colt. I'm *already* an old maid schoolteacher. An old maid *math* teacher at that. Not even a class that anyone likes."

"You're not—"

"Oh, stop." Becca hugged herself and turned away from him. "Just stop it. You said you don't want my sympathy. Well, I don't want yours. I'm not like you, Colt. I don't go around railing over all the ways that life has treated me badly." She was surprised by the anger in her voice but unable to stop it. From the look on Colt's face, he was shocked, too. "I've found that my life is a lot easier when I quit wishing for what I don't have and focus on what I do have. When I quit wondering why things turned out the way they have, and just accepted that they *did,* my life became a lot more peaceful. Things happen for a reason, Colt. I know they do. And who the hell are you to come here and point out all the ways you think my life should be different?"

"I'm your friend, that's who." He stepped away from the rail and made a movement toward her. "I want to see you get what you want out of life."

She put her hands back on her hips and glared at him. It wasn't his fault, she told herself, even as she wanted to slap him for making her feel this way. "I told you what I wanted," she said quietly. "I told you twelve years ago. And you left."

"You mean…" His voice tapered off and he stared at her. "You don't mean Paris."

She found she couldn't answer, couldn't even move her head in affirmation or denial.

"Becca, you don't still want me to…" He took a step toward her. "You're not seriously saying you still want me to make love to you, are you?"

Words stuck in her throat. Rather than speak them, she swallowed them down.

"Good God, Becca, what are you trying to do to me here? Do you have any idea how hard it was for me to walk away last time? It almost killed me."

"You managed."

"Just. Becca, I'm naked under here. You don't want to say things like that to me."

"I'm not drunk," she said, quietly but with force. "If I made the offer again, and you said no, you wouldn't have that as an excuse. Your only excuse would be that you just don't want me."

He took another step, stood in front of her now. She could see the stubble on his chin, the lines around his eyes from worry and lack of sleep. She could see where the shadow of his tan carved down to a *V* over his chest.

"Are you offering?" His voice was so gruff, he sounded like someone else, a stranger.

She lifted her eyes to his, and the moment stretched between them, heavy with the knowledge of what could be.

"Becca, are you offering?" He emphasized each word.

She swallowed and opened her mouth to answer.

The buzzer on the dryer went off.

She didn't know he'd been holding his breath until he blew it out in a gust. She lowered her head, looked at his hands, the floor, the rain outside.

"Bit of a cliché, isn't that? Except, it's a buzzer that's saved you and not a bell."

She moved to step around him. He put a hand out to stop her. "Wait—"

She kept moving. "I'll get your clothes, Colt."

She could feel his eyes on her as she walked across the porch and opened the door. Could feel them, though she didn't turn back to see.

Chapter 4

Colt scraped putty from the edge of the new window and rubbed a knuckle into his back. This was the last of the three windows he'd had to replace; he couldn't for the life of him figure out how Doff had managed to break them all. Not that it mattered now.

He groaned, flexed his shoulders and looked at the sky. Judging both from the low sun in the west and his aching back, it was time to knock off for the day. His eyes drifted downward, and he saw Becca walking toward the quarry, a canvas and easel under one arm and a small tackle box in the other hand.

It irritated him, seeing how serene she looked walking across the field, when he'd felt like chewing nails all day. His eyes were gritty from lack of sleep. He'd lain awake, stiff as a rod all night because he couldn't get her off his mind. And *she* was out for a stroll without a care.

He dropped the putty knife into his toolbox and closed the lid with a satisfying *bang*. Was she *trying* to drive him crazy? Was she trying to tease him until he was ready to pull his hair out? Because if she was, she was doing a damn fine job.

But he knew she wasn't. Becca wasn't a tease. She was naive, and so genuinely good that it was almost unbelievable. It wasn't her fault he wanted to drag her to the ground.

He felt like an idiot, tagging after her. But he did it, anyway. He told himself he wanted to see what she was painting. And he actually did ask about the painting, when he joined her at the quarry.

She cast a quick glance at him over the edge of the canvas. "It's the quarry, of course."

Of course. She was as breezy as if the previous day hadn't happened. He stuffed his hands in his pockets and fidgeted around behind the easel. She went back to painting.

"So…" He kicked a small stone into the quarry.

"Yes?"

"How's school going?"

"It's almost gone, thank goodness. The spring gets longer every year and the summer gets shorter."

"Hmm." Fascinating conversation. He bounced on his heels a few times and turned back to her.

"I was wondering…I mean, if you don't want to talk about it, that's okay. But I'm curious. How is it that you're—"

"Still a virgin?"

"Yeah."

"Maybe I was waiting for marriage."

"Are you?"

"Maybe I'm toying with the idea of becoming a nun, but I just can't commit to the black habit."

"Is joking about it your way of saying you don't want to talk about it?"

Becca faced him, and he could see what a struggle it was for her to look him in the eye.

"Yes, it is. It's an embarrassing subject."

"I don't mean to embarrass you, Becca. I just—"

"Then, let's not talk about it. I've worked really hard, Colt, to overcome the person I used to be. And…I don't know, seeing you again…for a while it was like I was back in high school again." She swirled her brush in a dab of paint before she met his eyes again. "For some people, that's a pleasant trip down memory lane. For me, it's not. I don't want to go through all that again, and I don't want to think about it. The past is the past, and I can't undo it. I'd really rather just not talk about it."

He was silent for a moment, then picked up a rock and tossed it into the quarry. It arced and seemed to hang, then finally went down with a *plop*. "So, you'd rather I just keep away from you while I'm here."

"No." She looked at him, her brow furrowed. "No, I would not rather you do that."

"You said seeing me made you feel like you were in high school again. If I bring back bad memories for you…"

"You make me remember what a fool I made of myself. That's not your fault, it's mine. But you bring back good memories, too. Like now, here in the quarry. Some of my fondest memories from growing up were right here. No, I don't want you to stop coming to see me. I just don't want to talk about the state of my nonexistent sex life anymore."

He reached over and rubbed a finger lightly over her collarbone. The surprisingly intimate contact made her jump. He felt the corner of his mouth twitch, and he drew his hand back and pulled her sweater closer around her neck. "Sounds fair enough."

Colt arched suddenly, pressing his fist into the small of his back.

"You okay?" Becca asked.

He nodded, looking around as the rising dark drifted

almost imperceptibly up from the quarry, turning the bottom a dark, dusky pink, the sides a golden rose. "It's not bad. Just a little stiff. You remember those stories you used to make up when we came out here?"

"Sure. Parts of them, at least. Why, you want me to make up a story for you now?"

He smiled and shook his head. "I was just thinking you should try to sell those. You know, write them down. You could do the artwork, too. Have your own series of picture books."

"Yeah, that would be nice." She sat on the boulder between them and tucked her feet up beside her.

"Seriously, you should. Why not?"

"Only about a jillion reasons. I have no education in writing or art. The stories were just fanciful things I made up."

"I liked them."

"You were nine. Book editors are a little older than that."

"Their readers aren't. Look, who cares if you have formal education or not?"

"It must be somewhat important. Everyone else who writes children's books gets an education. You can't believe how stiff the competition is in that field, Colt. I wouldn't stand a chance."

"How do you know until you try?"

Becca looked away and tucked a strand of hair behind her ear. The breeze was picking up, rustling through the trees and waving in the tall grass. "I know."

"You already tried."

"Yes, I did. A few years ago, when I first started painting again. It got rejected."

"And that was it?"

"There's not much you can say after that."

"How about 'try again'? Becca, no one would get anywhere if they gave up after the first try."

"Maybe I don't want it bad enough to try again." She moved her shoulders.

Colt was silent a moment, then stepped in front of her. The setting sun shone behind him, a red ball on the horizon at his back. The wind blew his dark curls, and his brown eyes looked intently at her. "But you do want it."

"Yes," she whispered. "I really do."

Colt sighed, then squatted in front of her. "Okay, the thing to do, when you're faced with an obstacle, is list the things you have to overcome, then figure out how you're going to overcome them, one by one. You said there were a jillion reasons, and the first one is your lack of education."

"And how am I going to overcome that? Run off to art school now?"

"Not a bad idea. But no." He stood and sat down on the rock beside her, taking her hand. "I don't think that's necessary. How long has it been since you sent that first book in?"

Becca shrugged. "Almost four years ago. Right after Mama died."

"And since then you started painting again, right? And you're doing the drawings for Dunleavy's, too. So you have more experience, and therefore more education. You've learned things."

"I suppose I have learned a few things, but—"

"No 'buts.' You're better now than you were four years ago. So that problem is taken care of. Now, what's the next?"

Becca shook her head and smiled. "I don't know. A lot of publishers accept only computer artwork now. I don't even have the programs on my computer. My old computer probably wouldn't handle the programs even if I did have them."

"But that problem could be solved pretty easily, with a little money."

"Oh, yeah, a new computer and software. I'll just run down to Circle D and pick those up."

"What I'm saying is that it's not impossible."

"Spoken like someone who is not on a teacher's salary. Do you have any idea how much computers cost?"

He ignored the question. "Okay, so what's our next obstacle? That's only two out of a jillion."

Becca drew her head back and sighed. "Colt, seriously—"

"I am serious, Becca. What's the next problem?"

She studied their fingers linked together. How was it, she wondered idly, that he felt so comfortable just picking up her hand, when she couldn't seem to drag her mind away from the feel of his palm against hers, his fingers twining around her own?

"Come on, what is it?"

Becca raised her chin and looked Colt in the eye. "I really don't think I can do it. I mean, I know I can write the stories, and I can do the art. I just don't think I can do a good enough job that anyone would actually pay for them."

"Oh, well then." Colt stretched out his legs and smiled. "That's not a problem. Because I think you *can* do it. Matter of fact, I think it enough for both of us. So don't worry about that. You don't have to believe in yourself. I believe in you."

Becca stared at Colt, her breath caught in her throat, unable to speak. She had never realized that she had missed hearing those words in her life, never realized what a hole there was in her until Colt filled it, and so easily that it appeared effortless. She found herself blinking back hot tears.

"That—that might be the nicest thing anyone's ever said to me," she whispered.

He turned to face her, his mouth open to speak. He looked into her eyes and closed his mouth again. His thumb moved over hers softly. "Well, I wasn't going for that. I was just telling you the truth."

"I know. That's what makes it so special. You'd better watch it, Colt. A few more words like that, and I might not believe you're the bad guy you keep trying to convince me you are."

She wished the comment back as soon as she'd said it, because his face got that hard look she was coming to recognize and despise.

"That would be your mistake." He released her hand and stood. He stuffed his hands in his pockets. "You should know as well as I do what I'm capable of."

He was trying to push her away. She recognized it, and refused to let him. "I know what you're capable of. You're capable of encouraging me like no one ever has."

"How do you know I didn't just say that out of guilt?"

"Guilt over what?"

"Over not taking you with me when you asked me. For leaving you here to waste your life."

Waste her life. The words swirled in the wind around Becca. She told herself that he didn't really mean it, that he was just trying to push her away because she'd said something nice about him.

And knew it was working, after all. "Is that why you said that? Because you feel guilty?"

He didn't answer. He stood before her, jaw clenching and releasing, and looked at the horizon.

Becca closed her eyes and looked away. She would not let him do this to her. He only had the weapon if she handed it to him, and she would not do that.

"If it is, then let me just ease your conscience. You did the right thing when you refused to take me with you. It would have been a colossal mistake, and I'm grateful that you had sense enough to see that at the time. And as for me wasting my life..." She sighed and raked a hand through her hair. "You haven't *wasted* your life, have you, Colt? You pursued your dreams and became very successful. And what good has it done you? You're still the same bitter, hateful person you were when you left Aloma. Only now, I believe you're even harder than you used to be. The boy I knew would never have deliberately tried to hurt me the way you just did.''

She stood and brushed off the back of her dress. Her voice quiet, but steady, she said, ''Damn you, Colt. Damn you for saying that. And damn you for thinking it.''

She gathered her equipment, refusing to give in to the tears that built behind her eyes.

Colt grabbed her arm as she moved by him. ''Becca, wait.''

She faced him, her teeth clenched, determined that he wouldn't see a trace of hurt in her eyes, would only see the anger she was fully justified in feeling.

''Damn it,'' he said softly. He kissed her, hard, and she could feel the frustration vibrating off him. She let him, because she knew he was looking for a fight and she refused to give it to him.

When he drew his head away, she met his gaze squarely. ''Was that guilt, too, Colt?'' She was fiercely proud that her voice, if soft, at least didn't tremble.

He scowled and backed away, wiping his mouth with the back of his hand.

''Well, was it? If you're going to do that, at least don't be a chicken about it. Was that guilt, too?''

He shook his head slowly. ''No. It wasn't guilt.''

She opened her mouth to ask what it was. But she decided she didn't want to know. Was better off not knowing. So instead of asking, she said, ''I don't want to play this game anymore, Colt.''

He cleared his throat. ''And what game is that?''

She whirled around, her arms out, frustrated and angry at them both. ''*This* stupid game. From the moment you came back into town, I've flirted with the idea of picking

up where we left off that night. And you've thought about
it, too—I can see it in your face when you look at me.
But we both know it's not going to happen. It won't happen, and shouldn't happen. It was a mistake before, and
it would be even more of a mistake now, when we're both
old enough to know better.''

She stopped, hands on her hips. ''I just—this is so *stupid,* Colt. You and I are never going to be together, so
why can't we both just—just—''

''Just what?'' He stepped up, close, and took her by
the wrist. ''Why can't we just…what?''

''Just forget about it. Forget about the whole thing and
be like we used to be.''

He spoke through a clenched jaw. ''Don't you think
I've tried? For twelve years I tried, and I did a pretty good
job of forgetting about it. Until I saw you again. I only
thought of it once or twice a day up till then. Now I think
about it all the time. I can't forget about it, because twelve
years ago you asked me to make love to you. And all
these years later, I still wish I could.''

Becca swallowed, staring into his eyes. She would have
liked to speak, but her mind wouldn't form the words.

''Did you hear me?'' he demanded.

She nodded.

''I still want to. And you saying it will never happen,
that doesn't seem to change one bit the fact that I still
want it to happen, so bad it's making me crazy. You want
me to quit playing games? Well, little girl, I want you to
quit haunting me. I want you to quit being there every
time I turn around, with that—'' he stepped back and
dropped her hand, waving at her ''—smile, and those eyes
that look right through me. I want to quit seeing you when
you're nowhere near me. Just stop.''

''I *haunt* you?''

''Damn right, you do. How could you not, standing
there, looking at me like that? Yesterday it was all I could

do to keep from throwing you down on the porch and taking you right there. And you want us both to just *forget* about it. Forget about it and be friends. And I guess that's what we'll have to do. Because any fool knows you don't save something for thirty years, just to blow it on some bum passing through town. That's the kind of thing that has to wait for Mr. Right. And we both know that's not me.''

The bell over the door dinged as Colt pushed through it. Frank's Barbershop still looked much the same as it had when Colt had gotten haircuts here as a boy, but it sure didn't smell the same. Ever since Barbara Foust married that boat salesman and moved to Houston—closing down Aloma's only beauty shop—Frank had been doing double haircare duty for the citizens of Aloma county. Or—as Frank liked to put it with a wink and a grin, as if he were saying something risqué—*unisex* styling.

Now, the small building was divided clearly. The men's haircuts were done on the left side, with a red-and-white barber pole and fishing-and-hunting magazines beside the waiting area. On the other side, Hollywood lights surrounded the mirror, and pictures of pouting models' faces lined the walls, giving examples of the latest hair fashions from New York and Paris. The old familiar smells of hair tonic and aftershave were now overpowered by the ammonia-laden odors of permanent waves and peroxide bleach.

Toby Haskell was just sitting down—on the men's side, of course—for his monthly trim, when Colt walked in.

''Hey, Hoss!'' he called as he saw Colt. ''I haven't seen you for a few days. I was afraid you'd taken off already. Corinne will skin me if I don't bring you over for dinner before you go.''

Colt nodded. ''Be happy to.''

''How about Sunday night? Frank, you be careful back

there.'' Toby twisted in his chair and looked back at the barber. ''Don't be cutting off anything I might need.''

''Turn around and quit telling me how to do my job,'' Frank said congenially. He palmed the top of Toby's head and faced it forward for him. ''How much do you want off?''

''Just a trim. With me being a figure of public authority and all, it wouldn't do to make me look too pretty. Might lose some of my menacing influence.''

Frank snorted and Colt laughed.

''Why don't you invite me over for dinner, too, Sheriff?'' Frank asked as he snipped at Toby's hair.

''You don't look like you've missed too many meals lately,'' Toby said with a pointed look in the mirror at the small roll of Frank's belly over his waistband.

''I'm starving to death,'' Frank complained. ''That daughter of mine is eating me out of house and home. I thought once she got married, I'd have a few extra dimes to rub together, but she just started bringing that dimwit she married over to eat my food, too. And now that she's pregnant, she's decided to up her intake a little. She must be having a multiple birth, because she's eating for at least five.''

Toby laughed. ''I'll have Corinne throw an extra steak on the grill for you. How's the house coming along, Hoss?''

''Fine, fine,'' Colt replied. Actually, he'd worked almost around the clock for the past three days. But all the sweat and labor had done little to get his mind off Becca. He picked up a six-month-old copy of *Field & Stream*, in the hope that a picture of a flopping bass on the end of a string would take his mind off Becca's lips. Off the hollow at her throat. Off the way her sweater lay against her collarbone. Off the way he'd really wanted to push that sweater back a little—just a little—to see more of her soft skin, to follow that delicate line with his fingertip—

"Your turn, Colt," Frank said, breaking into Colt's reverie. Colt looked up to see both Frank and Toby watching him quizzically. He realized he'd been caught daydreaming again.

"Don't worry, Hoss," Toby joked as he combed his fingers through his hair. "Frank's old and shaky and his eyesight's not so great anymore, but he likely won't cut you bad enough to sever any major arteries."

Colt let the men's banter cover up his own lack of participation in the conversation. As soon as Toby left, he could talk to Frank about what he wanted.

Except, Toby didn't leave. He picked up a magazine, plopped down in a cracked leather waiting chair and crossed one ankle over the opposite knee.

Colt frowned. He didn't think the taxpayers of Aloma County were paying Toby to sit there and stare at him while he got his hair cut. Besides, he couldn't tell Frank what he needed to tell him, with Haskell sitting right there listening in.

To make matters worse, Bobbie Pinkett walked in, spit tobacco into the spittoon by the door and began to complain loudly about the price of diesel fuel.

Great. Just what he needed—an audience.

"How d'you want your hair cut, Colt?" Frank asked. He combed through the back of Colt's hair and waited.

Colt cleared his throat. "Just—just a little off the back, I guess."

Frank raised an eyebrow at his hesitation, but began silently snipping. Toby and Bobbie got into an argument about which direction the economy was headed, and which politicians were likely to send them all into the quickest ruin, come the next election.

"And, on the top," Colt said quickly, while the other men's attention was diverted. "On the top, make it so that it would—you know—fall…rakishly, over my forehead."

Frank froze, his comb in one hand and his scissors in the other. "What?"

"You know—rakish. On my forehead."

"What is that supposed to mean?"

Toby and Bobbie looked up from their debate. Colt glared at them.

"Just don't take too much off the top, okay?" he snapped.

"I won't. I just don't get what you mean—'rakish.' Like a comb? You want me to get some of that mousse or something, from the other side?" He motioned with his head to the women's section of the shop, and the shelf full of mysterious perfumed haircare products.

"No!" Colt said, exasperated. "Just—can't you do something to where it's not such a—such a *bush* here on the top of my head?"

All three men were now staring at him like he'd lost his mind.

"You don't just want a regular haircut?" Frank asked, obviously trying to return some normalcy to his day.

"This is a normal haircut!" Colt insisted. "Where have you been, under a rock? For crying out loud! *This is normal.*"

The other men looked at each other. Bobbie cleared his throat and looked out the window.

"Can't you just—" Colt scrubbed at his hair and looked at Frank in the mirror in frustration. "Can't you just make it do *something* besides sprout around up there like a bunch of wild snakes?"

Bobbie snorted, Toby glared at him, and Frank raised an eyebrow. "What do you want it to do, Colt?"

Colt sighed. "Nothing. Just a regular men's haircut, Frank."

Frank nodded his approval. "Coming up."

Colt sank into the chair and wished he'd gone into Abilene to get his hair cut.

"You know," Frank said as he snipped, "you boys always wear those darn cowboy hats. That's your problem. You've got a permanent case of hat-head."

Colt muttered something and sank a little lower in his chair.

"If you'd leave your head alone, I might be able to do something with it, when you come in. But when you come in spouting nonsense like 'rakish' and complaining about snakes and wild bushes…well, the situation is pretty much out of my hands."

"Sorry I asked," Colt mumbled.

Toby waited until Frank was finished with Colt, then walked outside with him.

"So, how's the house going?" he asked Colt as they walked down the sidewalk.

"You already asked me that."

"I know. But I figured it would be rude of me to come right out and ask how you're doing, staying in Doff's house. Seeing as how you haven't been back to see him or talked to him in twelve years. I figured to ask that would be nosy and interfering and might make you mad."

Colt allowed a slight smile. "Yeah, I can see your predicament."

"So I figured I'd be kind of subtle and ask about the house—that way we could kind of talk *around* the thing with Doff, and nobody gets embarrassed." Toby grinned crookedly at him.

Colt nodded. "That's why you're the diplomat here, Haskell. The house is going fine."

Toby cocked his head. "Really? Been a long time since you've been there."

"I know how long it's been. It's not my favorite place in the world. But I don't hate the house as much now as I did when I left it."

Toby nodded. "Good."

And that was the extent of their heart-to-heart talk.

"So, seriously, come over for dinner Sunday night. And bring your girlfriend."

"I don't have a girlfriend."

"Bull. No man gets weird about his hair unless there's a woman involved."

Colt opened his mouth to deny, but Toby cut him off. "There's no way in hell all that wasn't about some woman. Bring her. I'd like to meet the girl who's got Hoss so worried about his silky tresses. Sunday night." He moved to cross the street and head to the courthouse. "See ya then."

When Corinne Haskell poked her head around Becca's classroom door, Becca had been staring at the papers in front of her for twenty minutes. She had not graded one of them.

"Geometry theorems finally rot your brain?" Corinne asked. She crossed the room on long legs.

They were deep in the middle of final exams. Becca's head pounded and her back ached. She was sure her frazzled nerves perfectly matched her frizzled hair. But of course her best friend Corinne looked as cool and impeccably tailored as she had when she walked through the doors of Aloma High that morning. Becca started to ask Corinne if she'd sold her soul to Christian Dior to look so perfect all the time. Instead, she cocked her head and said, "Why do you ask?"

"You look…how shall I put this?" Corinne propped a hip on the corner of Becca's desk.

"Like I'm beset with confusion over which direction my life is headed? Or maybe I'm disgusted that it's not headed anywhere? Like I'm wondering how I got to be thirty years old without ever *doing* anything? Is that how I look?"

"I was going to say 'befuddled.' Call me Jessica

Fletcher, but I get the feeling this isn't about finals. Want to tell me what's going on?''

Becca sighed and sat back in her chair, her legs flopped out in front of her. "I don't know. I'm acting like a child, that's what's going on.'' She sat up and smoothed her hair back from her forehead. "Okay, enough of that. How are finals going for you?''

"Do you remember when I first came back to Aloma, and was having trouble with my classes?''

"I remember.''

"And when everything in my life was turned upside down because I had fallen in love with Toby and I didn't know what to do about it? And again, when I was struggling with my own school work and trying to get my teaching certificate and worried about finding a job? And again, when they changed my curriculum halfway through the school year and I panicked because I didn't know if I could handle the change? Do you remember all those times?''

"Of course I remember, Corinne. I was there.''

"Exactly. You were there for me. And now, it's my turn.''

"Corinne, you don't have to be—''

"You owe me.''

Becca cocked an eyebrow.

"That's right, you owe me,'' Corinne insisted. "I'm seriously overdrawn at the friendship bank. You owe me the opportunity to dig myself out of this hole at least a few inches. Tell me what's got you chewing the inside of your lip.''

"Corinne, you don't owe me—''

"I know it. You owe me. I thought we were clear on that. Now, what is it? Is it man trouble?''

Becca rolled her eyes. "There has to be a man before there can be trouble.''

"Then, it has to be something here at school. Is it Mr. Sammons? One of the students?"

"Corinne, really. It's nothing. A blue mood, that's all. It's gone now, so there's no point in worrying about it."

"Fine." Corinne stood and moved toward the door. "See if I come running to you next time I have a crisis. I'll be forced to go to Mrs. Meddlar for advice, and you know what a disaster that will be."

Becca watched her friend walk toward the door. "Corinne, wait. It's nothing, really. It's just this guy—"

"I knew it was man trouble." Corinne spun on her heel and scooted back to the desk. "You have that shell-shocked look. Okay, who is it? It's not that guy who applied as the new football coach, is it?"

Becca wrinkled her nose and picked up a stack of papers. "No."

"I didn't think so. He didn't seem like your type."

Becca laid the papers back down and looked at Corinne. "What is my type, exactly?"

"You would know that better than I would."

"Evidently not. The—the guy who's making me looked shell-shocked says he's not my type, either."

"Oh, honey. I'm sorry."

Becca waved her hand in dismissal. "Don't be. He's probably right. Though, I think what he meant was that I am not *his* type."

"I'm sure what he meant was that he knew he wasn't good enough for you and he would only break your heart."

Becca knew Corinne was joking, but she let the words dwell in her mind a few moments, anyway. "You know, I really think he may have." She stood and slipped geometry finals into her satchel. "At any rate, there's no real trouble. Just me, wondering when my life is going to start."

"And what is this you're living now?"

Becca shrugged. "I don't know. Like I said, it's probably just a blue mood."

"Then, as your best friend it is my duty to snap you out of your blue mood. Let's go to the drugstore, buy double dips of mint-chocolate-chip ice cream and a pickle, and then sit there and watch everyone speculate which one of us is pregnant."

"Thanks, but I have finals to grade."

"So do I. What better reason is there for procrastinating? Come on, it'll be fun. I haven't started a good scandal in so long. And you can tell me all about this guy who obviously doesn't deserve you."

Becca gave Corinne a wan smile. "You know, that's really sweet. But I really want to just go home and get my grading done. Take a rain check?"

Corinne sighed. "You're making this very difficult. Okay, a rain check, then. Valid only for dinner on Sunday night, though. I was going to ask you, anyway. Toby and I are having a little get-together for Colt, kind of a welcome-home thing. You guys could ride in together."

Becca cleared her throat and studied the latch on her satchel with inordinate interest. "Oh, Sunday—"

"No." Corinne placed both palms on the desk and narrowed her eyes at Becca. "Whatever excuse you're about to give, it won't work. You're coming over for dinner Sunday night, and that's all there is to it. Colt will be there—and Luke and his girlfriend, if they haven't broken up yet. Toby said Colt might bring his girlfriend."

Becca's fingernail broke off against the latch. "Colt has a girlfriend?"

"Apparently. Toby saw Colt in the barbershop and said he was mooning over some girl. Toby told Colt to bring her to dinner. I have to admit, I'm kind of curious to see what she's like."

"Mmm." Becca studied her torn nail, knowing that if

she raised her head Corinne would see how red her face was.

"Of course, Toby could have been exaggerating. He does that sometimes. But he said Colt was looking a little shell-shocked himself."

Becca stopped digging through her purse for an emery board and looked at Corinne. "Really?"

Corinne nodded. "Of course, Colt denied he was with anyone. He's always been such a private person. And Toby doesn't know the meaning of privacy. But he got the feeling that if Colt wasn't with someone, there was someone he really *wanted* to be with."

Becca bit her lower lip. "Hmm. Well..." Not really knowing what to say, she handed the emery board to Corinne. "Here you go."

"Becca." Corinne cocked an eyebrow at Becca. "You're the one with the broken nail."

"Oh!" Becca snatched it back and stuffed it back in her purse. "See, I need to get home and get some rest. I guess those theorems *have* rotted my brain."

"I guess so."

Corinne peered at her, and Becca offered what she hoped would pass for a smile.

"So, we'll see you Sunday night?"

"Sure," Becca said, her voice too bright. "Sunday night."

A few moments later, Becca dropped her satchel onto the car seat beside her and let out the breath she'd been holding. Now why, she wondered, should she feel as if she'd been caught in some lascivious act?

A *foolish* act was more like it. She had a crush on Colt Bonner. It was as plain as the nose on her face, and she was so aware of it that she thought everyone else could see it, too. Surely Corinne was smart enough to figure it out. And when she did...well, when she did she would know what a fool Becca was. Because anyone with half a brain could see that even if Colt *was* acting shell-shocked over her—which he probably wasn't—anything between them was a losing proposition. She'd told Colt just that, the other day at the quarry.

Stop haunting me, he'd said.

Colt was looking a little shell-shocked himself, Corinne had said.

Becca dropped her head against the steering wheel and groaned. Which was she more afraid of? That Colt wasn't attracted to her? Or that he *was?*

Chapter 5

Becca debated asking Colt if he wanted to ride with her to Toby and Corinne's house, but finally decided against it.

Stop haunting me.

She'd never been so confused in her life. Things were much easier when she knew beyond a doubt that she was ugly. There had been no possibility then, and therefore no room for questions. Now all she had were questions.

Corinne said Toby thought Colt had a girlfriend. Maybe she should ask Toby to try to get more information from him. Maybe…

Maybe she should pass a note to him in study hall and see if he *liked* her liked her, or just liked her. Becca rolled her eyes at her reflection and applied mascara. She was acting like a sophomore. Like an eighth grader, even.

Still, she couldn't help but think…maybe she had gotten her wish. Maybe Colt really did see her as more than he once had. But if that was the case, he certainly wasn't happy about it.

He'd been angry when they'd talked at the quarry. She'd seen him angry before, but never with her. He had been hurtful and insulting, then he'd kissed her with a desperation that tore at her.

She haunted him? That didn't even make sense. If he was so struck by her, why did he keep walking away?

She groaned as she poked earrings into her earlobes. It didn't matter. She couldn't take it anymore. Every minute with him had her either flying high because he'd said something that melted her heart, or crashing to the ground because he'd said something that broke it. She'd told him that being around him made her feel as if she was in school again, but this was worse than school. She'd been the school outcast, but at least she'd been sure of that spot. She hadn't been happy with it, but she had been comfortable.

She wasn't comfortable with anything anymore. And that had started the minute Colt Bonner walked back into her life.

So in the end, she grabbed her purse and decided to pretend surprise when Colt showed up at the Haskell's house.

She got her surprise a little early, however, when she opened her front door and saw Colt coming up her porch steps. So surprised, in fact, that she started to slam the door and hide.

As usual, though, her mind raced while her body froze, giving him time to say, "Haskell said you were going to their house for dinner, too. I thought we might ride in together."

"I—um—sure. Okay. Just let me get my keys."

He nodded toward her hand. "Those look like keys to me."

She looked down. Sure enough. *Keys.*

"Yes, they are. Of course. Okay. I suppose I'm ready, then."

She stepped out, turned and locked the door behind her, not looking at Colt. She walked down the steps beside him, pretending great interest in the boxwood bushes beside the porch. When she got to the pickup, she reached for the door handle—and jumped six inches when Colt beat her to it.

She gave him a nervous smile over her shoulder. He frowned and opened the door for her.

"Look, Becca, I'm not going to jump you. I just thought we could ride into town together."

"I know you're not going to jump me." She laughed, too high and too hard. "Who said you were going to jump me? Certainly not me. I never said that. Just a ride into town. That's all I was expecting." *Shut up and sit down,* she thought.

She shut up and sat down.

"Then, why are you so jumpy? Do you really feel that unsafe around me?"

She took a deep breath and decided to be honest. "I really feel that confused around you."

One corner of his mouth tipped up—not quite a smile. "Confused, huh? I thought you were the one who knew what was going on here."

Before she could think of a more ladylike response, she snorted. "Hardly."

He put a hand on the roof of the pickup and grinned. A real grin, charming because it was so unrehearsed, treasured because it was so rare.

"Well, that's not good," he said. "Somebody needs to have a plan."

"Oh, I have a plan, all right. It just goes out the window every time I see you."

He leaned into the pickup. "Sounds familiar."

Becca's heart raced at the intent look in his eye. She opened her mouth to speak but didn't have the faintest idea what to say.

"Matter of fact," he said, leaning closer until his nose was inches from hers, "I didn't plan on kissing you. I didn't plan on kissing you that first day on the porch. Or the other day out by the quarry. And I sure didn't plan on kissing you now."

She tore her gaze away from his eyes and looked at his lips. Her heart thundered in her ears.

"But you're going to, aren't you?" The words floated somewhere between query and a request.

"Oh, yeah," he whispered, right before his lips touched hers.

It was a soft kiss, full of tenderness and yearning. She slid her hand up to cup the back of his head, fully aware that the previous hours spent telling herself this was the very thing she was *not* going to do had been a waste of energy, and equally aware that she didn't care.

He pressed her back into the seat, continuing the deep kiss, focused completely on her mouth. Becca relaxed and enjoyed the sensation, reminding herself to feel guilty about how easily she had changed her tune. Later.

He pulled away with a moan and lay his forehead against hers. "God, what are we doing?"

"It's called kissing," she said calmly, if a little breathlessly. "Even I know that, and I'm the inexperienced one."

He took her hand in his and brought it to his lips. "This is the game you were talking about, isn't it? Do you feel okay with this?"

"What I feel is dizzy and short of breath. And a little hypocritical. If you're asking if I want you to stop kissing me, the answer is no."

He kissed her knuckle, his eyes steady on hers. He brought it into his mouth, moving his tongue slowly around her finger until she felt as if every bone in her arm had melted.

"You know where kissing leads, though."

"I'm inexperienced, Colt," she said when she managed to get her breath back. "Not stupid."

He drew her hand away and kissed her again. "You really want to go to Haskell's?"

"They're—" She drew in a sharp breath when his teeth closed over her ear. "They're expecting us."

"And it's the right thing to do," he murmured against the pulse point at her throat.

"Definitely." She ran an indulgent hand through his hair. She'd always wanted to touch his hair, to see what it felt like. In a way she couldn't put into words, it felt as shiny as it looked.

He moved his lips to her collarbone, and she knew without a doubt that if she didn't stop him right then, she wasn't going to.

"Colt."

"I know," he said as he dragged his head away. "Any more of this and it's going to be too late." He backed up, her hand in his, and gave a lopsided grin. "We can pick up later where we left off."

She swallowed. "I'd like that."

He narrowed his eyes and cocked his head. "Would you? The other day you said I was bitter and hurtful."

"You were upset—"

"Don't make excuses for me. I am bitter, and I can be hurtful. Doesn't that scare you?"

"No." Not in the way he meant.

"I can't stop thinking about you. About being with you. If I start kissing you again, I'm not going to stop. I keep thinking that if we went ahead and made love, maybe I could get it out of my system."

"That's very romantic, Colt." She wrinkled her nose.

"I'm not romantic, Becca, and I won't ever be. You should know at least that much."

"I know more about you than you want me to, Colt."

At least, that was what she told herself. "Let's think of some excuse to leave dinner early."

He grinned then, and what hesitation she had was gone.

"That's my girl," he said. As he walked around to the driver's side, she heard him say, "This is going to be one uncomfortable ride."

When they pulled up in front of Toby and Corinne's house, there was a red-and-silver double-cab pickup parked at the curb.

"Did Toby get a new pickup?"

"No, that looks like…" His voice trailed off as he got out of the cab.

Becca followed him up the sidewalk, and saw his face split into a wide grin when Toby's front door opened and a tall, skinny man walked out.

"There's that lazy bum!" the man cried. He was laughing, though, when he shook Colt's hand so hard that Becca thought he might dislocate something.

"Lazy bum? And what are you doing here when you should be in Nevada?"

"I had a few weeks' vacation coming," the man said with a defiant tilt of his chin.

Colt laughed. "You got into a fight and got suspended, didn't you." Without waiting for an answer he turned to Corinne, Toby and Luke, who were on the sidewalk behind the stranger, and said, "I take it you've already met these guys."

"I found him wandering around downtown looking for you," Luke said. "I brought him over here."

"Downtown? Is that what you call that building? I saw a badge and knew he'd know where to find you, Bonner."

Colt took Becca's elbow and brought her up even with him. "So, the only one you haven't met is Becca. Becca Danvers, this is Jasbo Malone, the craziest bullfighter you'd ever care to meet. Jas, this is Becca."

Becca extended her hand, telling herself she must be imagining whatever pride she thought she heard in Colt's voice.

"I think I've seen you on television," Becca said. "Though, it's hard to tell without the makeup and red-and-white polka-dot boxers."

Jas laughed. "I'm out of costume for dinner. No wonder you ran home, Bonner, if this was what was waiting for you. A little TLC from a pretty girl like that ought to heal your back up real good."

Ignoring—or unaware of—the awkwardness that comment brought, Jas entertained them all with stories of bull rides and escapades on the professional bull riding circuit, as they went back into the house.

As dinner parties went, it was a rowdy one, mostly due to Jasbo's input. He had an endless stream of tales of his and Colt's life on the road, and Becca was fascinated by this man who'd spent so much more time with Colt than she had. She forgot to eat as she listened to one after another of the adventures they'd gotten into. She would have been concerned about the wildness of it all, except she noticed that in most of the stories Jasbo told, Colt was the one who ended up putting a stop to any trouble, rather than starting it.

Jas fell into the easy insulting-joking camaraderie the other men shared, as if he had grown up beside them. And Becca watched, amused and a little wistful at how at home Colt seemed to be with Jas.

This was the world he was used to, she thought as he and Jas traded insults. A world filled with men, one in which he could relax and be himself. A world that didn't include her.

She told herself that she was glad for him, glad that he had this place to go when he left Aloma, and she meant it. If she was a little sorry for herself that she would be left here in a lonely world of her own making, that was her own foolishness.

"Sweetheart, Hoss says I'm getting fat," Toby said.

"He's just jealous of your well-toned physique, dear," Corinne said blandly as she watched him spoon another helping of mashed potatoes onto his plate.

Toby smiled smugly at Colt and sprinkled salt and pepper on the potatoes.

"You mean, you weren't intending to get fat?" Luke asked, his blue eyes innocently wide. "I thought you were trying to bulk up."

"One more word from you and you're fired."

"Fat chance. Who else can you find to put up with your attitude?"

"I could replace you in a minute. JoAnn Huckaby would be happy to be my deputy. And her coffee's a lot better than yours."

"How is it working out with JoAnn?" Corinne asked, her chin on her hand.

"She's the best. Matter of fact, the only reason I haven't fired Luke is out of pity. JoAnn has the office organized and running like a machine."

"Yeah." Luke snorted a little unhappily. "We're organized, all right. Now everything has its proper place and there's hell to pay if it's anywhere else. It's like being in school again." He looked quickly from Corinne to Becca. "No offense."

"None taken," Becca said quietly, suppressing a smile. She turned to Colt and explained. "JoAnn Huckaby just started as the secretary and part-time dispatcher for the Sheriff's Office. I'm sure she is organized. She's got two sons. At least now Pete is home to help her out a little."

"Yeah, he's helping out around the house. He's having a hard time finding a job," Toby said, frowning. "I wish we could afford to pay JoAnn a little more, but it's just not in the budget."

"It's going to be difficult for him," Corinne said. "No one is willing to take a chance with him again. No matter how reformed he is, no one's going to forget." She turned to Colt and Jasbo. "Her husband just got out of the penitentiary a few months ago. It's been difficult, getting started again since he got back."

"I hope they don't have to leave Aloma. I'd hate for Bradley to have to leave now, when he just has two more years of high school left. He's such a good student. He doesn't have the attitude his older brother had," Becca said.

Toby shrugged. "They may have to move if Pete can't find work. JoAnn barely held it together while he was gone. With Jeremy in college, they're having a rough time of it."

"I thought he got a scholarship."

"He did, but it was just for books and tuition. He still has to pay his housing. If he plays his cards right, he might be able to do better next year. He showed me some of his grades so far for this semester, and they're pretty good. He's working hard."

"Abilene's not that far. He could live at home."

Toby shook his head. "He refuses to be in the same house with Pete. He's still furious with him. It's going to take some time."

Colt cleared his throat, and Becca realized they were talking around him and Jas. It was so easy to see them all together again, she'd almost forgotten Colt had been away. It was strange to think she was the one on the inside now.

"Jeremy is Pete and JoAnn's oldest son. Corinne and I both taught him, and he really got a chip on his shoulder when Pete was arrested for selling drugs a couple of years ago."

Colt looked at Toby, who nodded grimly. "Yeah, I arrested him. He was a truck driver, selling out of his truck. Jeremy was there when I busted him.''

"I can't say I blame the kid for being mad.''

"Me, either. It was a stupid thing to do. But Pete's doing everything he can think of to make it up to him. He and JoAnn just want to try and get past it, be a family again. It's tearing JoAnn apart. She's happy Pete's out, but there's this big cloud still hanging over the family. Not to mention, there's not enough money coming in.''

"He can't get his old job back?''

"Not a chance. I don't think he wants to drive trucks anymore, anyway. He told me he thought that was a lot of the problem in the first place. Being away from home all the time, kind of losing touch with his foundation, you know.''

"Sounds like a cop-out excuse to me,'' Colt said.

Becca noted the stern line of his mouth and the anger in his eyes, but didn't say anything.

Toby just shrugged one shoulder. "Maybe. But whatever led him to it, he's sorry now. He's done his time, and he wants to do whatever he can to bring his family back together again. JoAnn and Bradley stood by him, but Jeremy sure hasn't.''

"He'll come around,'' Corinne said. "It'll take a couple of decades, but he'll come around.''

"Why should he?'' Colt asked. "The guy screwed up his life. I'll bet everyone in town knew about it, didn't they?'' He looked at the faces around the table. "Yep. Everybody in Aloma County was talking about it.''

"You can't blame people for talking, Colt. It's just human nature. No one intended to make Jeremy feel any worse about the situation.''

"I'm not blaming people for talking. Hell, I ought to know you can't stop the small-town gossips.''

"It wasn't gossip, I think, as much as it was just concern for him, for the whole family. Certainly everyone knew about it. And everyone talked about it. Because they cared about the two boys and JoAnn, even if they were horrified at what Pete was doing. You can't keep a thing like that secret. But Jeremy got such a chip on his shoulder, he made things worse. He got into trouble every chance he could, to get back at Pete. He's straightened out his own life now, but he's still so angry with Pete."

Colt shook his head. "Why shouldn't he be? I don't think the kid ought to be pressured into making nice with his dad, just because the guy's out of the joint now and wants everything to be okeydokey. It was…what's his name? Pete? It was his decision to do something that would screw up his whole family. He made that choice. He doesn't get to decide how they're all going to deal with it and when they should forgive him, too."

"Everyone makes mistakes, Colt," Becca said quietly.

"And everyone has to pay for their mistakes," Colt said, his chin out. "I don't know the guy but I think he got what he deserved."

They sat in awkward silence, until Luke joked, "I hope that doesn't happen to me. If I ever get what I deserve, I'm in big trouble."

Toby took Corinne's hand in his and kissed it. "I got a hell of a lot better than what I deserved."

"And don't you forget it," Corinne said, leaning in to kiss him back.

"How can I, with you reminding me all the time?"

Luke groaned. "I'm begging you not to start that again." He turned to Colt. "He's like this all the time. It's disgusting. Almost married two years now, and still acting like an idiot."

"Like my beautiful wife said, you're just jealous."

Luke snorted. An awkward feeling still hung in the air after Colt's remarks, but Luke's joking had provided them with a way past it.

"I'll get some coffee." Corinne rose from the table.

"I'll help," Becca offered.

In the kitchen, Becca put cups on a tray, while Corinne poured coffee from the maker to a ceramic pot. Becca had fought all evening to keep her mind off the kiss she and Colt had shared, and the promise of what was to come, hoping Corinne wouldn't pick up on anything.

She should have known better.

"I'm sure you know what you're doing, Becca," Corinne said as she poured milk into the creamer.

There was no point asking what Corinne was talking about. Becca opened her mouth to toss off something casual, but she couldn't do it. If ever she needed a friend, now was the time.

"I hope so, too." She smiled ruefully.

"When I suggested you two ride together, I had no idea you'd come in with the air crackling around you. Sowing some wild oats?"

"I'm trying."

Corinne sighed and edged to the door, watching the four men around the table. "I grant you, he's certainly easy on the eyes."

Becca tiptoed over beside her, and watched Colt as he ducked his head and gave a halfhearted laugh at one of Luke's remarks. He passed a hand over his hair, in an unconscious and fruitless attempt to smooth it. It was a characteristic he'd had since she could remember; he had never liked the waves that ran through his black hair.

"Mmm," she agreed with Corinne. "He is that."

"Yes, he is. But he's going to be very hard on the heart."

Becca turned away and got spoons out of a drawer. "Yes, well, I suppose I'll just have to keep my heart to myself, then, won't I."

Corinne studied Becca. "You're already in love with him, aren't you."

"Of course not."

"Yes, you are. You should see how your eyes shine when you look at him."

"It's a crush. I've had a crush on him for as long as I can remember. But I'm smart enough not to fall in love with someone like Colt." As she said the words, she wished fervently for them to be true. She wasn't really in love with Colt. Not really. "It's just a crush," she said to reassure them both.

"What are you going to do when he leaves?"

Becca bumped the drawer closed with her hip and shrugged. "The same things I did before he came back, I suppose. I've missed a lot of things, Corinne. Lots of things that most people experience and take for granted, long before they're thirty years old. I've always been the one to watch. Never to do."

"I know. Maybe that's why I'm worried about you. You haven't built up any defenses like other people have."

"You're worried about me because you're a good friend. And because I am undoubtedly making a great fool of myself."

"No, you're not."

"Regardless, I'm going to do it, anyway. I'm tired of watching and missing opportunities. This is my time to do." She lifted a hand as if she were talking about something no more important than a new hairstyle. "Don't worry about me, Corinne, okay? I'm not going to *let* him be hard on my heart."

"You may not have as much say in that as you think."

"Of course I do. If I don't expect anything, I can't be disappointed, can I? Now stop looking at me like that and be happy for me that I'm finally getting to sow what little oats I have left."

Corinne sighed and gave her a quick hug. "I am happy for you. Anything that has put that light in your eyes can't be all bad. But just in case, if you do get your heart just a tiny bit smushed, I'll stay up and eat chocolate-chip ice cream with you, and you can cry on my shoulder.''

"I told you, you're a real friend.''

"I know. Go ahead and take this tray out. I have to open a bag of sugar.''

Becca reached the door in time to hear Luke announce, "Colt and I have to maintain the bachelor status, after your betrayal to the other side.''

"Don't worry,'' Jas reassured him. "I'll get him back to the bulls where he belongs, and marriage will be the last thing on his mind.''

Colt just smiled and studied the scuffed boot that rested on his other knee. But he wasn't really listening; she could tell by the way the vein jumped at the side of his throat. He was still thinking about Pete Huckaby, though he was trying not to show it. Her heart ached for him. She was probably the only one in the room who understood how he could be angry with someone he'd never met.

Becca took a deep breath and entered with a tray of coffee. When she glanced at Colt, she saw him looking at her speculatively. She quickly looked away.

When Corinne came in a few moments later carrying the sugar bowl, Toby said, "You know, sweetheart, I had the best idea. Why doesn't Colt hire Pete Huckaby to help him fix up his house?''

"That is a stupendous idea, Toby. You're brilliant,'' she said blandly, and kissed him on the cheek.

"Okay, it's settled.'' He turned to Colt. "I'll send him out to your place tomorrow.''

"Hang on,'' Colt protested. "This is the drug dealer, right? Do I have any say in this?''

"No,'' Toby said cheerfully. "Why would you? He's not a drug dealer anymore. He's done some work for you, hasn't he, Becca? And, Colt, you need the help.''

Colt wrinkled his brow. "If I need help, I'll hire someone myself. Someone without a record. Besides, Jas is here. He can help me.''

"Yeah, sure. Be happy to. And I'm flattered, by the way, that you're not holding that unfortunate incident in Rochester against me." Jas turned to Toby. "The last time we did a construction job together on the off-season, a guy accidentally got his pinkie finger cut off." At the look Colt gave him, he protested, "Hey, I warned him to move back. You can't baby-sit everybody, you know."

"It sounds as if you might need a backup plan, Hoss," Toby said.

"I'm managing fine on my own."

"You got a permit for the work you're doing on that house, Bonner?" Luke asked, leaning back in his chair.

Before Colt had a chance to answer, Toby joined in. "Probably not. And that pile of tin you're driving can't be up to inspection, either."

"The sticker's on the window," Colt said.

"I mean *my* inspection," Toby said. "I'm sure if I look hard enough I can find all kinds of things to toss you into jail for."

"It wouldn't be my first visit to the Aloma County jail."

"Besides," Toby continued, ignoring his words, "with two people the work will go twice as fast, which means you can get out of here and back to competing that much quicker."

That would be the deciding factor for Colt, Becca thought, looking away from Colt, and reaching for milk to pour in coffee she normally took black.

"Yeah," Colt said. He drained off his coffee and turned to Becca. "Are you about ready?"

The ride out of town was a quiet one. Colt knew beyond a doubt that the Huckaby guy would show up at Doff's house first thing in the morning; Haskell was the most stubborn son of a gun when he got an idea in his head.

Well, Colt would just have to send him back home. He wasn't running a halfway house. And besides, he didn't want to lay eyes on the lowlife. What kind of idiot sacrificed his family like that, put them through pain and humiliation, and then just decided he'd done his time and it should all be over?

It would never be over for that guy's family. What they'd gone through would stay with them for the rest of their lives. He could imagine those kids, knowing every person in a fifty-mile radius was talking about them, suspecting them—or pitying them, which was just as humiliating.

He tried to block Doff out of his thoughts, but it was a losing battle. The thoughts of Huckaby and the sympathy for his son tangled with his own unwanted memories. Scenes flashed without order through his mind as he turned onto the dirt road he and Becca lived on. Drunken rages, the solid smack of fist on face, roared rantings and accusations. Looks of pity and whispers behind his back from well-meaning townspeople. And quieter than the rages and the whispers, but nonetheless painful, the constant derision. Always criticism. Always mockery. Never praise. Never a kind or civil word spoken.

He wrenched the wheel more roughly than he had intended and bounced up the drive to Becca's house. She clutched at the seat beside her as he brought the pickup to an abrupt halt.

He clamped his teeth together, trying to get a handle on the anger that had nothing to do with her, that she didn't deserve to see. It was the legacy that Doff had left him; the short fuse that burned too brightly.

He swallowed and turned to her, fighting for control. "I'll walk you up," he said, punching the release of his seat belt.

She did the same, her gaze steady on him. In the dim glow of the dash, he searched for pity in her eyes.

"Colt," she said, placing her hand on his arm.

There it was, in her voice.

He couldn't stand it. Didn't want to hear it. He wasn't a victim. He wasn't.

He shook off her hand, and the words were out of his mouth before he knew it. "This is a bad idea, Becca. One of us needs to have the sense to stop it, and I guess it's going to have to be me, again."

Her eyes narrowed and her chin lifted, and he knew he had hurt her.

Better now than later, he told himself, even as he fought the urge to scoot across the seat and take her in his arms. Better to hurt her now, and hurt her badly enough to scare her off completely, than to wait until it was too late. Because she would be hurt—of that he had no doubt. A guy like him didn't know how to do anything else. He'd forgotten that, for a while. But his common sense had been restored.

"You were the one who kissed *me*," she reminded him.

"I know that. I guess you don't understand guys very well. Sometimes we'll do just about anything when the mood strikes us. It doesn't mean a thing to us." The lie tasted bitter, but it was necessary.

She popped open the door, and light flooded the cabin. Her face was washed out, a pale mask of shock and hurt. "I can walk myself up," she said steadily. "Thanks for the ride."

As the door was closing behind her, he heard her mutter, "Damn you, Colt Bonner."

After she was inside, he put the pickup in reverse and drove the few yards back to his house, thinking the whole way, *Yes, damn me. Damn me.*

Chapter 6

The first thing Colt thought when he saw Pete Huckaby was that the man *looked* like he'd just gotten out of jail. He hunched his shoulders a little and eyed everything warily—as if braced for attack. His wore his short black hair slicked back, and a black T-shirt tucked into jeans that had seen better days. He was thin. Too thin, Colt thought, to be much good. But on closer examination, he saw what he'd seen on so many bronc riders: wiry, ropy muscles that carried more than their weight.

Pete nodded a greeting. "Sheriff Haskell said you might need some work done around the place."

Colt propped the ladder he was carrying against the side of the house with a satisfying *thud*. He didn't feel like talking to anyone right now. He'd sent Jasbo to Abilene on an errand, to get his friend out of his hair. But during the night he'd had second thoughts about Huckaby. Haskell was right. The sooner Colt got this house done, the sooner he could get away from Aloma. And away from Becca.

"I might. You know how to drywall?"

Pete nodded. "I know just about everything about contracting."

"Roofing?"

He nodded again. "Brother-in-law's a roofer, down around Beaumont. Did some work for him a couple—a few years back."

"Anything here you *don't* know how to do?" Colt squinted and put his hands on his hips.

"If I tried to do any electrical work I'd more than likely get us both fried." He attempted a smile.

Colt didn't return it.

"I'm hiring an electrician to get all that up to speed. So far it looks like a couple of outlets need to be replaced, but everything else works okay."

Pete nodded. "Sounds good."

"I can't pay much."

Evidently Huckaby didn't do much aside from nod. "Didn't expect a lot."

"The job's only for a few weeks."

Again with the nod. He reminded Colt of the little bobbing dog Jasbo had on the dash of his car.

"I'm hoping to get on at the cotton gin when ginning season starts."

Colt didn't comment on that. They both knew his chances were slim.

"Haskell told you I been in prison?" Pete asked, a silent challenge underscoring his words.

Colt was still two-thirds of a mind to turn him down. Instead he said flatly, "Yeah, he told me."

"Just got out about six months ago."

"He said you were selling drugs. You planning on selling drugs on my property?" Colt asked.

"Wasn't plannin' on it."

"Good. Let's get to work. There's a set of gloves by the back porch rail."

They tackled the roof first, working silently as the early summer sun beat down on them. The rip of shingles torn from tarpaper, the flat crash of them thrown to the ground, and the grunts and sighs of effort were the only noises for several hours. Colt kept waiting for Pete to suggest a break, but finally he had to give in and take one himself.

"I'm gonna grab a—" He started to say "smoke," remembered with faint regret that he didn't anymore, and said "drink" instead. "Come on down."

"Be there in a minute," Pete said, still pulling up old shingles. Colt was halfway through a bottle of cold water before Pete came down. Colt stripped off his shirt and stuck his hands under the faucet on the side of the house, then dumped the water over his head. He paced around the yard, rubbing his back and slinging water out of his eyes.

"You ought to try some massage for that back," Pete offered, then raised his own cup of water to his lips and drained half of it.

Colt grunted irritably.

"Rascal dug you pretty good, huh?" Pete nodded at the triangular scar on Colt's lower back.

Colt acted as if he hadn't heard. He didn't want to get into a lengthy discussion about it, especially with this guy.

"I saw you get tossed. Right into the fence, wasn't it?"

"You were there?"

He shook his head. "Saw it on TV. Sometimes they broadcast the bull rides on the sports channel."

Colt nodded noncommittally. Becca had said the same thing. It didn't sit well with him to know anyone around Aloma knew about it.

"It was the talk of the town for a while." He went on as if reading Colt's thoughts. "Everybody worried about how bad you were hurt."

"I'll bet they did," Colt said dryly. "I'm a real local hero."

"Yeah, you are," Pete said simply. "Edging up on the world record. Everybody's real proud."

Colt snorted. "Attitudes change when the town can get some publicity. A dozen years ago most everybody in town couldn't wait to see me leave."

"I know how that feels." Pete grinned. "Local bad boy, huh?"

"You could say that. Didn't spend time in the pen, though." He nodded respectfully in Pete's direction. "Just a few nights in the county jail. Might as well have been a convicted felon, though."

"What'd you do?" Pete asked frankly. Apparently that wasn't the taboo question Colt thought it was.

Colt didn't care. It wasn't like he'd been selling drugs. "Stole the old man's pickup. At least, he said I stole it. I borrowed it to go to a rodeo."

"He thought it was stolen?"

"He knew I had it—that's why he reported it stolen. Haskell's old man was sheriff then. He had to arrest me. Didn't have much choice. Doff said I didn't have permission to take it, even though he'd given me permission earlier in the day. So I spent two days in the county jail 'cause he wouldn't bail me out."

"That's tough."

Colt bent to turn on the water again, filled his bottle and drank deeply from the fresh flow. "Actually, you know, it wasn't that bad. The sheriff brought Luke and Toby down there, and we all camped out in the cell. Played poker and smoked cigarettes. Thought we were real rebels." He scrubbed both hands through his wet hair, sending tiny droplets flying. "I got out of school for two days, and added another stripe to my reputation."

Ridiculous as it sounded, being in jail was one of his fondest memories. He and Haskell and Tanner, swapping lies and insults, eating the mounds of food Mrs. Haskell and Mrs. Tanner felt compelled to bring. But then, he always had fun with Luke and Toby. The Haskells always treated Luke and Colt like their own kids. Colt felt like he was part of a real family when he was around them. Just a regular guy.

Pete shrugged. "Never knew a boy who didn't have problems with his old man at some point. Know I did, when I was young." He turned and narrowed his eyes against the sun, not saying anything about the problems he was having with his own son. "I guess your dad was trying to teach you a lesson."

Colt bent to pick up his shirt from the porch and curled his lip. "Yeah, he was a great one for the lessons." Over a decade later, the anger shouldn't come back so hot and sharp.

"It's hard to imagine a father deliberately hurting his own son," Pete said quietly.

Colt narrowed his eyes. "Yeah, hard to imagine anybody being so low. Because all fathers are good fathers," he said stonily. "Knocking a girl up automatically makes you caring and wise." Before he said anything he might or might not regret, he jerked his thumb toward the ladder. "Let's get back to work."

Colt worked like a man with a deadline for the rest of the day. They stopped briefly for lunch, then climbed right back up.

He barely noticed—yeah, right—when Becca drove past late that afternoon, the windows on her car rolled down, her hair flying around her head like a glorious cloud a man could tangle his hands in and hang on to. She got out in front of her house, wearing a turquoise silk tank top and a long flowing skirt, bangle bracelets on her slim arms. She reached into the car to take out her satchel.

Colt tossed a chunk of old shingles, missing the pile they'd built by a good twenty feet.

Later, he stomped around the roof, testing for rotten spots, ignoring the sight of Becca in shorts and one of those damn tiny tops she wore, when she came out to work in her garden. She had on that ridiculous baseball cap, like she was a teenager. She didn't glance over his way once. Not once.

"This is going to have to be replaced," Pete announced, pulling Colt out of his thoughts.

"What?" He clomped across the roof and shoved his boot heel at the spot Pete indicated. It sank into the soft wood.

He let loose with an oath and headed for the ladder. "We'll have to go to the lumberyard."

Pete followed him down the ladder without a word. Colt was tugging his shirt over his head when he realized how hard the man had been working all day. Pete's shoulders slumped and his feet dragged a little, though he didn't complain.

"It's getting late. Let's shut it down for today. I can handle getting the lumber myself. We'll patch it up tomorrow."

"You got a phone? I need to call my wife and have her pick me up."

"Don't worry about it. I'll take you home."

"I live on the other side of town."

"No problem."

Pete hesitated. "It's a couple miles out."

"I said it's no problem." Colt opened the driver door and climbed into the pickup.

After a moment, Pete followed. "I'll give you some gas money when we get there."

Colt sighed and started the engine. "If it'll make you feel better."

They didn't speak on the way to the Huckaby house, but when they got there Pete hurried inside, came back out with a few dollars and handed them to Colt through the window.

"You going to need me tomorrow?"

From the braced look on his face, he clearly expected Colt to say no. "Yeah, be there about eight."

"I can be there at seven-thirty."

"Suit yourself. I'll see you tomorrow."

But when he got back to town and should have turned right to the lumberyard, there he turned left instead, toward Abilene. He told himself the lumberyards had a better selection and better quality than the one in Aloma. He told himself he needed to get out of town.

He made all kinds of excuses to himself, but he knew good and well where he was going and why. The idea had come to him when he'd been trying not to watch Becca out in her garden, an idea that latched on and refused to let go. And though he was ten kinds of fool for doing what he was about to do, he was going to do it, anyway.

Becca dropped her keys on the coffee table, her purse on the floor and her body into a dining room chair. She groaned and dug the heels of her hands into her eyes. She'd made it through yet another year of teaching high school math and, wonder of wonders, only two students would be repeating classes next year.

Her hands froze in midair. She could just see around the hall corner into her office. And that was *not* her computer.

She stood slowly and walked to the office, wondering if Corrine was right and theorems finally had rotted her brain. What other explanation could there be for a new computer in her office? The Computer Fairy?

No. *Colt.*

Becca read the note he'd scribbled and left on the keyboard. *You're running out of excuses.*

Several boxes lay on the table beside the computer. Word-processing programs, drawing programs that she couldn't begin to know how to use. Everything she would need to get started creating her own book for submission. Her finger itched to turn the computer on, to start playing and exploring, and it was all she could do to hold back.

She stared at the note, then at the computer, then back at the note, wondering what to do. She couldn't keep it, of course. A gift this extravagant…well, it wouldn't be right. No matter how badly she wanted to.

But telling him so would lead to a confrontation. And after the way he'd made her feel the last time she'd talked to him…

She let the options roll around in her head until she thought the top of her head would pop off. With a sigh, she accepted that, ugly confrontation or no, she would have to give the gift back.

She found Colt on the roof of Doff's house, pounding shingles with a hammer. She looked up at him, shielding her eyes from the sun with one hand.

Colt saw her, set the hammer down, and came to stand at the edge of the roof, his hands on his hips. "I take it from that look that you've already been home."

"Yes. We need to talk."

"Not if you're going to tell me you won't accept it."

"I *can't* accept it, Colt."

"'Course you can. You don't even have to do anything. Just turn it on."

"It's too much."

"Too much what? Too much money? I've got money, Becca. I'm not Donald Trump, but I've got enough to spare on a computer."

Becca toed a line in the dirt and decided that if things were going to get ugly she might as well get it over with. "It's too much money to spend on a guilt present."

Colt narrowed his eyes, muttered an oath and moved to the ladder. He climbed down quickly and grabbed a bottle of water from the shade beside the porch.

"It isn't a guilt present. I can see already how you're

going to play this. You're going to use this issue as yet another excuse to avoid going after what you really want."

"How am I supposed to see it, then, Colt? One day you do your best to scare me off, and the next thing I know I find a new computer in my office. I'd consider that a guilt present. I'd consider that your way of apologizing. Well, there's nothing to apologize for. You were right."

He frowned and rubbed his chin. "Consider it a challenge. I challenge you to quit hiding and finally pursue something worth pursuing."

"What I do is very important, and you have no right to say my job as a teacher isn't worth pursuing."

"It isn't worth spending your entire life on if it isn't what you *want*. If you didn't have dreams and enough talent to sink a ship, it wouldn't matter at all." He took a long drink of water, then wiped his mouth with the back of his hand. "But you do have dreams. And you do have talent. Or are you saying now that you don't really want other people to see your work, read your stories?"

"I've never denied that it would be nice—"

"Nice? For Pete's sake, Becca, are things ever anything more than 'nice' or 'okay' with you? What does it take to get you excited about something?"

"I don't really think I could—"

"*I* know you could. I know what I saw, stacked against the walls of your office. And I know what's up here—" He tapped his forefinger lightly against her forehead. "I know you can do it. And it infuriates me that you just sit in that house year after year and let all your work pile up in the corner where no one can see it. It's a waste, Becca."

Whatever she'd been about to say was long gone, and she found she couldn't speak past the sudden lump in her throat.

He stopped and rubbed his jaw, looking off in the distance. "You can't devote your whole life to one thing if it isn't the one thing you dream about, Becca."

He leaned back against the porch rail. "There are people in the world who don't have dreams. Or who have dreams about everyday kinds of things—having a family, a home, maybe their own business. Attainable dreams. And then there are people who have big dreams and are afraid to put themselves on the line for them, so they live their lives pretending the dreams don't exist or don't matter. I don't want you to be that kind of person.

"One day you'll wake up, and it won't matter how great a teacher you are. It won't matter how many kids you've taught or if you've won the highest award a teacher can win. None of it will matter, because all you'll be able to do is wonder what would have happened if you'd poured all that time and energy into what you truly wanted."

Becca threw up her hands. "I came over here prepared to fight with you. But I don't have the faintest idea how to fight with that."

"Then, don't."

"How did you know what I needed?" For a moment she wasn't sure if she meant the computer and programs, or the words he'd just spoken.

His gray eyes remained steady on hers for a heartbeat, and something flickered inside there, something she was sure she wasn't meant to see, something that wasn't for her. Then he blinked, and it was gone.

"I made a few phone calls. A buddy of mine writes cowboy poetry, and he knows a guy who writes westerns. And that guy, in turn, knows an agent. And the agent just happens to be a fan of bull riding. He gave me some information, and told me which programs to get."

"That's a lot of trouble to go to, Colt. I'm in your debt."

"No, you're not. You still have to do all the work."

"I don't have the faintest idea how to get started."

"You know what you have to do when you don't know what to do, right?"

She wrinkled her nose and gave a short laugh. "What?"

"When you don't know what to do, you pretend like you do."

"Oh, that's a good answer."

"I'm serious. If you don't know, and there's no real way for you to find out except just doing it, you pretend like you do know. Pretend like you're already a published author and artist. What would someone like that do?"

"I don't know, Colt."

"Well, I'd bet money they wouldn't stand here and argue with me."

"Probably not."

"So pretend like you've already sold four books. What would you do now?"

"Besides faint at the very thought? I don't know. I guess I'd...well, I guess I'd get to work on the next one."

"There you go." He grinned at her and reached to take her hand before he stopped himself and stuck it back in his pocket. He nodded toward her house. "You get over there and start to work on your fifth book."

"Colt, this is silly—"

"I haven't told you the best part. I convinced the agent to take a look at your stuff after it's done."

"But—but I haven't even started yet. I've never touched that program. I'm not ready to submit anything."

"Which is why you need to get started. Don't panic. He said whenever you had something, just send it in."

Nerves danced in Becca's stomach. "You don't understand. I can't just whip up something and send it off. This is a big step."

"I do understand. Big steps take a lot of work. So what are you doing standing here arguing with me?"

"Oh, Colt..." Becca didn't know what else to say—panic, gratitude and fear warred inside her. On impulse she stood on tiptoe and kissed him lightly. "Thank you."

A little surprised—and a lot chagrined—that she'd done that, she stepped back and clasped her hands together. She didn't need him to remind her to keep her distance.

"Sorry," she blurted out. "I'm just—I'm grateful, that's all." *That's all,* she repeated silently.

Colt stared at her, then said gruffly, "This is the way you should always look."

If he was going to keep looking at her like that, she was going to have a hard time convincing herself they were nothing more than friends. But she sure was going to try. She pasted on a smile and swung her arm in what she hoped was a carefree gesture.

"And how is that? Flabbergasted?"

"No, happy. With your eyes shining and your cheeks all..." He waved a hand carelessly in the air. "All pink like that."

Uncomfortable with the intensity of his gaze, Becca found herself looking instead at the front of Colt's perspiration-soaked shirt. She backed a few steps away, tucked a strand of hair behind her ear and tried to change the subject. "Yes, well, that's probably panic. Does this agent represent children's books?"

"Sure he does. Here—" He pulled a folded piece of paper from his back pocket. "This is his name and address, and how he wants you to send your stuff. He also gave me the names of some of the writers and artists he represents. I hope I got the names right."

Becca unfolded the paper and studied it, then sank to the porch. "Colt, these are real writers. We have most of their books in the school library. This guy won a Texas Bluebonnet Award.''

"Good. Maybe this agent can do the same thing for your career."

"He can't if he doesn't have that kind of book to work with. Colt, I'm nowhere close to the same league as these people."

"Says who?"

"Says *me*. And excuse me, but I know a little more about it than you do. These people are professional writers and trained artists. Not math teachers with a hobby."

Colt squatted before her and put a finger to her mouth. "Are you going to sit here and talk yourself out of even trying? Even *trying*, Becca?"

"I don't know…"

"Stop saying 'I don't know.' You've got a shot here. If you don't take it, you're going to regret it. All you have to do is give it your best shot."

"And if I'm not good enough?"

"Then, you tried. And hopefully you'll keep trying. Because that's all it takes to succeed, Becca. To keep trying until you make it." He lifted one shoulder. "And even if you don't, you haven't lost anything by trying. You're still here, you still have your day job—which you swear is enough for you, anyway—and you still have your life. You don't even have to tell anyone if you don't want to. It's up to you."

"I know this isn't the same thing, but…did you get nervous when you first started riding bulls?"

"Hell, yes. Tossed my lunch a couple of times. And it didn't get a lot better, even after years of experience. But you don't get anywhere by not trying, so I just pushed it aside and climbed on, anyway. You just have to do it, whether it scares you to death or not."

"I guess I do, don't I." The very thought terrified her, and thrilled her at the same time.

"Unless you think you can live the rest of your life knowing you had a good shot and didn't take it."

He looked so smug, she couldn't help but laugh. "I could hit you, you know."

"I doubt that. But I'd rather you did that than give back the computer."

Becca swallowed hard. "And you really think I can do it?" It was silly to need to hear it again. But she did.

He nodded. "Sure I do. I talked you up to the agent. Told him he'd be a fool if he didn't at least take a look. But then, like you said, I don't know that much about it. You could be horrible, for all I know."

Because she felt so close to tears, it felt doubly good to laugh instead. "And then won't you look like the fool."

Colt shrugged and stood, taking her hand to help her up. "Naw, he'll just assume I'm blind in love and trying to impress you."

Becca lifted her eyes to Colt's, and she thought that even under his tan she could see his face turning red. She realized after a moment that her hand was still in his, and drew it away clumsily.

"I believe this is what is referred to as an 'awkward pause'." She smiled up at him.

"Mmm." He rubbed his jaw and cleared his throat.

Becca dusted off her skirt, then clasped her hands in front of her. "Well, it appears that I have a good deal of work to do. And there's no time like the present. School let out today, so I have plenty of free time." And nothing to fill it. Never had the summer stretched so endlessly before her.

Maybe it was her overactive imagination, maybe it was because a part of her wanted it so much, but she could have sworn Colt was holding himself back from coming any closer.

Because she knew she couldn't handle it if he did, she

moved away. ''Thank you, Colt. I'll pay you back, some-day.''

And she left before either of them had a chance to say more.

Chapter 7

Becca stared at the blinking cursor and rubbed her hands together, then rubbed her palms on her legs. She shifted in her seat and tapped her foot. All she had to do was put one word on the screen, just one word, and she'd be started. It was silly to be nervous.

She had all the time in the world, she told herself. She didn't have to create a literary masterpiece before lunchtime. She could work on refining and revising until she was comfortable with sending her story to the agent. There was no pressure.

Just one word. The cursor blinked. Just to get started, she tapped her fingers lightly against the keys. Then she backspaced over the gibberish.

Okay, so she was off to a slow start. That probably happened to everyone at some point. Even if it was their fifth book. The thing to do was just get the words up there and then worry later about making them perfect. Colt said she should write the stories she used to tell him. Those stories always centered on two young children, a boy and a girl, and the adventures they got into. Becca wasn't sure those stories would really work, but it was a place to start.

She thought she remembered how all the stories had started. She typed a few lines, then a few more. After half an hour, she looked up and was pleasantly surprised to see she'd written almost a page and a half. Much of it would have to be cut, of course, but she was on her way.

She went to the kitchen for a glass of iced tea and came back to read over what she'd written. As she read, her stomach fell a little. It wasn't as good as she'd hoped.

"You're a little fool, and you have no business doing this."

The words themselves shocked her, as did the fact that she'd said them out loud. But what chilled her to the bone was that, though the words had come from her mouth, it was Mama's voice she heard.

In the span of a heartbeat, the memory was back—a memory she thought she'd banished long ago. She clamped her hands over her ears, suddenly, irrationally terrified. But the voice was inside her head, of course, and there was no blocking it out.

It was eerily clear, the memory, especially considering it had been silent for over twenty years. She'd been lying across her bed, a spiral notebook in front of her, writing in pencil the adventures of her heart. Mama was in one of her "moods," and Becca had stayed in her room all morning for fear of being spotted and becoming the target. As she wrote, she stopped occasionally to daydream about somehow selling the book, becoming rich and famous, and finding a place to live on her own. Not a big place, just a little one-room place where she could be alone to write stories and draw pictures and maybe have friends over for tea. She would have friends, if she were alone. And she would be happy.

Mama walked in, and her long shadow fell over the notebook. She wanted to know what Becca was doing writing in the middle of summer. Becca tried to think of something to tell her, something ordinary and boring so that she'd go away. But she couldn't think with Mama looking at her like that, couldn't do anything except dread what was going to happen next. Something in Becca's face must have given her away, because Mama held out her hand.

"Let me see it." She leaned down and made a grab for the notebook. Becca actually snatched it back, though she hadn't intended to do that, and was horrified that she'd acted so defiantly. She braced for the blow, but as usual Mama didn't lift a hand. Her tongue stung far worse than any slap.

Mama snatched the book out of Becca's hand and took a look at it. "Oh, you're writing a *novel*."

"It's just a story," Becca mumbled.

"Well, let's read it," Mama said with exaggerated enthusiasm, and with great drama began to read aloud the words Becca had written.

It sounded stupid, and Mama's mocking tone made it even worse. Becca sat on the bed, staring at her hands, and did her best to ignore Mama's jeering laughter.

She realized the voice had stopped when she looked down to see Mama poking her in the leg with her big toe. "Big shot, I'm talking to you. You're just a regular Hemingway, aren't you." She threw her head back and laughed. "Who would have thought that here, under my humble roof, from a nobody like me, we have the world's next literary genius. Hey, big shot." She poked Becca again, harder this time. "You too big to even look at me now?"

Becca dragged her eyes up to face Mama. Sometimes Mama would get so wrapped up in her own moods that she didn't even notice whether Becca was listening. Becca could retreat into her own mind, live in the fantasy world she'd created for her and Colt. That was where the stories came from; when she needed a place to go, that place waited for her, safe in her own mind. A place where kids were free to follow their own adventures, where they battled and triumphed over evil dragons and malicious trolls. A place where adults didn't exist.

But most times Mama wanted to look into Becca's eyes and see that she was making her point.

"This is the stupidest story I've ever heard of. What are you doing it for?"

Becca shrugged. But she should have known that wouldn't be enough.

"I *said,* what are you doing it for?"

"I just...I thought it would be fun."

"Fun? You think it's fun to make a fool of yourself? You *are* a little fool, and you have no business doing this. Who do you think you are, anyway? You think you're better than everybody else?"

Becca shook her head and swallowed hard. The worst possible thing she could do at this point would be to cry. The tirade would only go on longer.

"Sure you do. You always have. You think you're better than me. Well, okay, Hemingway, continue with your novel." She tossed the book back at Becca.

Becca took it and clutched it in her hands, keeping her eyes focused on the floor.

"Come on. Let's see you write your literary masterpiece. Come *on.*"

Becca, choking back a hot ball of tears in her throat, had stared at the lines on the page and been unable to write another word.

She had not written since.

Becca was somewhat surprised to feel that hot ball in her throat again, hard and bitter. She didn't let the tears fall, though. She didn't even remember how to cry. How long had it been since she'd actually let herself, given in to that indignity? Long before that early summer day, so many years ago. Such a silly thing to get upset about now.

But even as she told herself that, her mind returned to that moment when she'd looked up into her mother's eyes and seen contempt and hatefulness. Only now she saw it not as the child she had been, but as the adult she was now.

Had her mother really been like that?

You know the answer to that, a voice inside her said. *You've always known, you just hide it away.*

Not well enough, Becca decided as she sipped numbly on her iced tea. She could have gone the rest of her life without remembering that ugly scene.

But Mama wasn't really like that. Not really. Maybe once in a while she had a bad day, she lost her temper and said things she didn't mean. Everyone had bad days. But that woman, the woman in her memory…she wasn't just having a bad day. She had hate in her heart. What kind of person would hate her own child?

What kind of child would foster that kind of hate?

She was not in the mood to deal with this right now, Becca decided. She fled the room, not taking the time to shut down the computer, and grabbed her gardening gloves and tools off the bench by the back door. Outside, the sun shone and the air was still cool enough to be comfortable this early in the day. She let the breeze blow against her hot skin as she attacked weeds mercilessly.

But even as she worked her body in an effort to still her mind, she realized a door inside her had opened, and the memories marched out like dutiful soldiers, launching a barrage of hateful scenes that left her dazed and reeling.

There was plenty of fodder for the cannons. It wasn't just that one summer morning with the notebook. If her mother had looked at her like that one time, or a few times, Becca would have been able to bear it. But once they were let loose, the memories rushed at her by the score. There was the time she'd accidentally broken the red salad plate while she was doing the dishes. Her mother had unleashed a tirade that went on for hours, berating every aspect of her until Becca no longer remembered what had started it, until she was reduced to begging for forgiveness. The time she'd laughed at a silly joke on television, and her mother had belittled her intelligence until Becca agreed with her that she must be the dumbest person on the planet. The time she'd stayed after school to help decorate for the eighth-grade banquet, and mother had been waiting by the door with horrible accusations that Becca scarcely understood.

In a mixture of horror and morbid fascination, Becca let the memories come, let them dwell in her mind while she turned them this way and that, studied them, unable— or finally unwilling—to hide them away again.

And in each one, it wasn't the words Mama spoke, or the things she did that chilled Becca's blood as she sat in her garden under the warm summer sun. It was her eyes. Those eyes, so full of rage, turning their full bitter blast on her only child.

Colt stood on the roof and used the heel of his boot to test the new patch of shingles he and Pete had just laid. He looked over at Becca's house—something that had become more of a habit than he would like to admit— just in time to see her clutch both fists to her head and rock back on her heels.

His hammer clattered to the roof and he moved to the edge. "Becca!" he shouted.

When she didn't answer and instead began to sway back and forth slowly, his heart took up a triple-beat.

He damn near broke his neck getting down the ladder.

"What's wrong with her?" Pete asked.

"I don't know" was all Colt got out before he headed

across the field. He didn't know, and he was scared to death to find out.

Colt reached her as she staggered to her feet, looking dazed.

"Becca!" He hadn't meant to speak so sharply that he made her jump, but he was on the verge of panic. "Are you okay?"

She jerked and spun, and the eyes she turned to him were bleak. "Hello, Colt. Of course I'm okay," she said hollowly. "What are you doing here?"

Without waiting for an answer, she stumbled past him. He wondered if she really even knew he was there.

The blank look in her eyes terrified him. He closed a hand around her arm to stop her.

Slowly and definitely, in a voice he'd never heard before, she said, "Get your hand off me."

He dropped back, stunned.

She stood silent, and he saw her start to shake, saw the blank look start to crack around the edges. Desperate, he asked, "Are you okay?"

"No," she said firmly. "I'm going to be sick."

She rushed around the side of the house, and a few moments later he heard her retching. He went inside, got a washcloth from the bathroom and wet it with cool water, aware that his own hand was trembling as hers had. Good God, what had happened to shake the unshakable Becca?

He got back outside as quickly as he could. She stood with her back to him, leaning against the wall, back and chest heaving. He put the cool cloth to her face.

After a few moments, she took the cloth from him and continued what he'd started.

"Better?" he asked hopefully.

She nodded, but she still looked at the ground.

"Okay, good. Now, I'm just about to start freaking out if you don't tell me what happened."

"She wasn't like that," Becca choked out. "She

wasn't. I don't know where that came from, but she wasn't that bad."

"Who wasn't?" he asked gently.

"Mama," she said impatiently. "She had her bad days, but—but what kind of woman would hate her own child?"

He knew she wouldn't like the answer he had to that, but it didn't matter because she pushed past him and moved around to the back porch.

He wasn't sure if just sitting quietly beside her would help, but after a few minutes it started to drive him crazy. "Becca, please tell me what happened."

"It's entirely your fault, you know." She tucked her feet up on the chair with her and looked out at the yard. "Everything was going just fine until you came back."

Oh God, what had he done? "I'm sorry," he said, meaning it wholeheartedly though he didn't know what for. "I take it back, whatever I said. Or did. Or didn't do. Chri—" He broke off before he did something else to offend her. "Cripes, Becca, what happened?"

"I started remembering stuff, that's what happened. Except that—except that it can't possibly be real. Why would she be like that? That has got to be my imagination. Why would she hate me? I mean, Colt, if you had seen her eyes…she despised me."

He wanted to tell her that her mother didn't hate her, couldn't possibly have. But he was not a hypocrite, not even when he wanted so much to make her feel better. Becca was just now realizing what he'd always known: her mother and Doff were two of a kind.

Instead of saying anything, he knelt beside her chair and wrapped his arms around her. He didn't care that he had vowed to never again get close enough to touch her. Didn't care that she was blaming him now. He had to comfort her somehow, and this was the only thing he knew to do.

She must not have been as mad at him as she'd sounded, because she let him. She didn't return the gesture, just sat stiffly in her chair and stared, dazed, out at the yard.

Without looking at him, she said softly, "A few days ago you asked me how I could stand to be here and not have memories that made me crazy."

"Mmm-hmm."

"I wonder how you can have those memories at all. If this is what remembering is like, I don't want it."

"I don't want to block it out," Colt said. "I want to remember, every word and every slap. If I forgot, I might forgive. And I'm not going to do that."

"But doesn't it make you feel horrible all the time?"

"Some things you can't feel good about."

"I know, but…Mama was really just a normal woman who sometimes went through periods of—of moodiness, I guess. Sometimes difficult to be around." She plucked the arm of the chair absently. "She wasn't like that."

"Becca, I don't want to argue with you. But our houses aren't that far away. And her voice carried. I heard some of the things she said. I know—"

She shifted, and he could feel her pushing him away both physically and mentally.

"I think all your anger toward Doff is affecting me. She couldn't have been that horrible. I'm sure I'm imagining it."

"What did you remember? You said if I'd seen the look in her eyes, I would have seen that she despised you. What did she do?"

"I don't know. I'm probably making too big an issue out of a few little incidents."

"You think?"

She was silent for a long time, then finally nodded. "Yes, I'm sure that's it."

Colt took her hand and pulled her up, sat in the chair

and pulled her down to sit on his lap. He wrapped his arms around her, still holding her hand in his, and traced the delicate veins in her wrist. "You know, when you lie for her, even to yourself, it's like you're giving her permission to do what she did. To say what she did. And if you do that, you're saying that she was right. That you deserved to be treated like that."

"It wasn't really that bad, Colt. She just got in a bad mood sometimes."

"It was bad enough that the memory of it made you lose your breakfast."

"I'm emotional sometimes."

He snorted. She was the least emotional person he knew. "Listen. I want you to picture whatever it was you were remembering before. Only this time it isn't you, and it isn't your mother. It's some total stranger, with her daughter. How old were you at this time?"

"I don't...I was nine," she said softly.

He didn't want to do this to her, he really didn't, but he'd be damned if he let that old bat get away with what she'd done.

"Okay, picture a mother and her nine-year-old daughter. Tell me what you remembered. Imagine whatever happened between you and your mother, imagine it happening between two other people—"

He didn't even get the words out before she was up and out of the chair, pacing the porch. "No," she said firmly. "You're not going to do this to me. I'm sorry that you hate your father so much. I don't blame you a bit, I really don't." She hugged her elbows, fingers leaving red marks on her flesh. "But just because your father was rotten to you doesn't mean all parents are like that."

He reached a hand out to stop her, and she swiped it away, continued her nervous pacing. "I'm not going to let myself become like that, Colt. I'm not going to let the past ruin my future anymore. I've fought too long to quit feeling like a victim of my own life. I'm not going to let you come over here and talk me into hating my own dead mother.''

He told himself she wasn't really lashing out at him, she was just doing her damnedest to keep that defense up around herself. But he was getting mad, anyway. He rose and dusted off his knees. Fine, he thought. If she wanted to handle it herself, fine.

She stepped off the porch and moved back to the garden. He stood and watched her walk away, torn between going to her and shaking some sense into her, and walking away before he said something he'd regret. She had to deal with the situation in her own way.

He was ten feet past her when she said, ''Wait.''

He turned, and she looked so small and scared, standing there beside her vegetable garden holding a hand rake. She swallowed visibly and looked down at the ground.

''I'm sorry,'' she said, raising her eyes to him. ''It was kind of you to come over.''

''Kind,'' he said flatly.

''Yes,'' she said, frowning. ''Kind. You have always been kind to me. You don't deserve for me to lash out at you when all you're trying to do is help.''

He wanted to take her in his arms then, so strongly that he ached from holding back. But she stepped closer to him, her eyes so steady on his that he knew she meant it; she really thought he was kind and good. And that was enough to make him stop, make him *want* to be good enough for her.

''I was trying to write my first story.'' She closed her eyes, took a deep breath, then faced him again. ''The ones I used to make up when we were kids, like you said I should. I started remembering things about Mama, because she was the one who stopped me from writing the stories the first time. She was just…she was very angry. Very hurtful. It was an ugly scene.'' She frowned and shrugged. "And I've been afraid to write ever since. So afraid that I blocked it from my mind and refused to believe I could do it. I preferred to never acknowledge my dreams than to set myself up for that kind of humiliation again."

She squared her shoulders and gave him a crooked smile. "I'm lying to myself, aren't I. She really did hate me."

He did take her in his arms then, because there was nothing else he could do. "She hated everyone, sweetie."

"What kind of mother hates her own child? How could she do that? I was just—I was just a kid."

"You said it. She was very angry. I don't know what about. But she was definitely mad at the world."

"All this time I told myself it was okay. That she didn't mean any of the things she said. But if you could have seen her eyes, Colt…"

He held her tightly and rubbed her back, wishing he could rub away the pain she must be feeling.

"It wasn't okay. No matter what I told myself, it wasn't okay. A mother is not supposed to treat her daughter like that."

"No, sweetie, she's not."

"How could I have lied to myself all this time?"

Colt shrugged. "Because that's the person you are. You look on the bright side. To a fault, sometimes."

"I made myself blind. I must have made myself blind to what she was."

"So, now you see."

"I wish I didn't." She backed away and rubbed her hands over her face. "My own mother hated me. She really did."

He lifted her chin with one finger. "Are you going to be okay?"

She wrinkled her nose. "I will be, I guess." She sighed, then shook her head and rolled her eyes. "When did I turn into such a drama queen? Of course I'll be fine. I *am* fine."

"You're sure? Just like that?"

"Of course. I don't know why I'm making a big deal out of it. It's not as if I can do anything about it now. She's gone. Whatever I did to make her hate me, I can't make it up to her."

"You're making a big deal out of it because it *is* a big deal. The memory upset you, so much so that you got physically sick."

"I didn't eat breakfast. That's all it was. If she hated me…that was her problem, I guess."

"Are you sure? Because you still look a little pale—"

"Colt, I'm fine. Let it go."

Colt rubbed the back of his neck and bit back an argument. The thing he loved most about Becca was also the thing that made him the most nuts: she was so accepting. Too accepting. When she needed to stand up for herself, get good and damn mad, she smiled and said, "Thank you very much, that will do just fine."

"Okay," he said, dredging up patience from somewhere. "If you're fine, are you going to get back in there and finish the story?"

"Oh…" She lowered her brow and cast a quick glance at her office window. "Sure. Sure I am. But right now these weeds are out of control, and I'd rather get this done before it gets too hot. This afternoon, I'll get back to work on it. Tomorrow morning, for sure."

Colt shook his head. "She scared you away once. You're not going to let her scare you away again, are you, Becca?"

"No." Her voice was soft, lacking any conviction.

"You can't let her. If you really are okay, then you have to go back in there and fight for what you want. This is yours. Your story, your chance to realize a dream. You have to fight for that."

She stepped into his arms. "I'm afraid. I don't want to see her looking at me that way again."

He smoothed her hair back. "I know you are. But she's gone, Becca. That's all in the past, and she's gone, and you have a chance now to make everything turn out right for you. She can't hurt you anymore. Not unless you let her."

"I made a promise to myself a long time ago that I would stop letting fear control me. I've worked on the outside. I've managed to make something of myself, my looks, learned to talk to people and make friends and be a more sociable person. I thought I was doing a great job. I thought I'd conquered all my fears."

"You're doing great. You just aren't through yet. Not until you conquered the whole list, including your mother."

"No wonder you're such a successful bull rider. You just don't give up, do you."

"Nope. And neither should you. I'm not going to let you, Becca. You're too good to let another person's anger stop you."

"You're a good friend, Colt."

He smiled. He held her tightly, ignoring the warning voice that told him to walk away now, when things were back on an even keel between them. "Do you feel better?"

She nodded.

"You're not going to pass out on me or anything, are you?"

"Of course not."

Of course not. Already she was working herself back to her normal, peaceful self.

It was perfectly natural to thread his hands through her hair, to caress her back. And there was certainly nothing wrong with smelling her hair, or planting an innocent kiss on the top of her head.

If he'd stopped himself at that, everything would have been okay. But once his hands found their way up the back of her shirt and against the soft smooth skin of her back, the caress of comfort became one of pleasure. His pleasure and, judging from the soft mew in her throat and the way she leaned into him, hers as well.

She reached slim-fingered hands up and pulled his head down to hers, bringing her mouth up to kiss him.

Lord, had he ever known anything so good as sweet Becca in his arms? Tasted anything so good as her against his lips. Experienced anything so satisfying as knowing that she wanted him? That she really believed he was a kind person?

But it was a mistake. Because he wasn't the person she wanted him to be. She knew it, but was as much in denial about him as she was about her mother.

He pulled away. "Becca, no."

"You told me not to let fear control me," she said. "I'm going after what I want."

"You don't want this."

"Yes, I do. And so do you. Don't lie to me by denying it."

"Okay, I won't deny it. I want you so badly, I can't even think straight. I want you right here, right now, down in the dirt with the sun shining on my back."

Her eyes grew wide. *There,* he thought. *That ought to scare her away.*

Except, it didn't. She just kept looking at him with that light in her eyes, like he was some kind of hero. He backed away, holding her hands together between them in case she got any more ideas of tempting him with them. He wasn't sure how much more he could take.

"But you're walking away, anyway," she said flatly. "You want me, you care about me, you're one of my best friends. But you keep walking away. Why?"

"Because, Becca." He let her hands drop and moved

farther away, while he still could. "Because, I care about you. Because you're upset and vulnerable right now, and I don't want to wonder later if I took advantage of that. Because you deserve better. Because I *am* one of your best friends. How many friends do you have, Becca?"

She shrugged. "A few."

"I don't have very damn many. And I'm not going to risk losing my best one by using her while she's in a low moment."

"I'm a grown woman, Colt. I'm responsible for myself."

"Good. Then, if you still feel the same way later, we'll both know I wasn't taking advantage of you."

"But you're not—"

"And we'll both know that you're not taking advantage of me. Using this as an excuse to not think about your mother."

That stilled her, and she looked at the ground for a moment. When her eyes met his again, they were so unbearably sad that it was a struggle to keep from turning back, to keep from using his body to ease her mind, if only for a while.

But she believed he was good and kind, and he wanted to be that for her. And the right thing to do was to leave her untouched, until the time she came to him not because she needed an escape, but because she wanted to be with him.

Becca took a deep breath and wondered for the dozenth time if this was a bad idea. She looked around the clearing, half hoping for some forgotten, critical item that would serve as an excuse to back out while she still could.

She had blankets for the ground, candles for mood, a bottle of wine and two glasses, a sexy peignoir. She had protection discreetly tucked away under a pillow.

Now all she needed was the seducee, and her seduction

scene would be complete. Oh, yes, and enough nerve to actually go through with it.

She'd used their old signal, the tire leaned against the tree. She couldn't decide whether she hoped he remembered, or hoped he didn't remember. If he came, and if she was once again left standing alone—this time in an ivory silk negligee—watching him walk away, she didn't know if she could take it.

She heard footsteps in the grass behind her, and for a moment she pressed her hand to her fluttering stomach. Her mind searched wildly for an excuse for being where she was, the way she was—some legitimate reason to back out while she still could.

She took a deep breath and turned, letting the skirt of her negligee swirl softly around her legs.

"Hello," she said as she turned to face Colt.

He froze where he was, staring at her. His mouth opened and closed a few times, before he finally said, "I saw you had moved the tire."

"You did remember. I was wondering. I would have felt pretty foolish to set all this up for nothing. More foolish than I already do, I mean." She was babbling. She clenched her hands together to keep them from shaking, and found to her mortification that as soon as they stopped, her legs started.

"What are you doing, Becca?" Colt asked.

"See, I was kind of hoping that much would be obvious. I have—" She looked around her, not because she didn't remember what was there, but because she found she couldn't look at Colt anymore. "I have candles, blankets. A bottle of wine. And a sexy peignoir. And..." She toed aside the pillow so he could see the foil-wrapped condoms she'd brought. "I wanted to bring some mood music, too, but I couldn't find any batteries for the radio and the extension cord certainly wouldn't reach all the way out here—"

"Becca." Colt stepped closer and cocked his head, peering intently at her. "What are you doing?"

"I'm not letting my fear stop me from getting what I want. You told me to stop doing that, and you were right. I'm tired of fear holding me back. And before you even ask, this has nothing to do with Mama, and with how upset I was yesterday. This is just between you and me." The words came out in a rush. "You said you wanted me. You said you'd thought about it every day for the past twelve years. And constantly since you got back to Aloma. You did say that, when we talked out here last week. And yesterday you said you wanted me so much you couldn't think straight."

She folded her arms across her chest and hugged her elbows, waiting for some kind of response. He nodded, slowly, almost cautiously, and she wondered again if this had all been a very big mistake. She'd intended to be as straightforward as she could about the whole thing, to face it matter-of-factly and state her case. But she had to force the next sentence from somewhere deep inside her.

"And I want you. There. I've said it." She couldn't catch her breath. She put one hand to her breastbone and forced herself to inhale. "I want you to make love to me. I think it would be—be nice."

"Nice," he echoed.

"Yes, nice." Nerves on edge to begin with, and irritated at his lack of response, she flattened her lips and narrowed her eyes. "Am I just kidding myself to think you might be a little flattered, or intrigued, or—or at least interested?"

"Oh, I'm interested. I'm just wondering the same thing I've been wondering all along—why are you choosing me for this?"

"Why *not* you?"

He was silent for a very long time, his dark eyes boring

into her. When he did speak, his voice was steely calm.
"And I'm supposed to be flattered by that."

"I didn't mean it like that. I just meant—oh, good
grief." She raked a hand through her hair, pulling it loose
from its pins. She paced on the pallet she'd laid out, feeling every bit the fool. "I didn't mean that at all. I'm
making a mess of this. But I don't know what to think.
One minute you seem like you really—" Her tongue
tripped over the words. "Like you really want me. Then
the next, you're pushing me away. I can't figure out what
to do. I know what I want. I think I know what you want.
I just can't figure out what the problem is. You said I
deserve better. But Colt, I can't think of anyone better to
share this moment with than my best friend."

She reached down and plucked a bobby pin from where
it had lodged in the lace of her robe. She rolled it between
her fingertips, then finally looked back at Colt. He was
silent, his jaw working.

"You could do me the courtesy of answering me, at
least. I may be ignorant and naive, but I've never been
less than honest with you. You owe me the same. You
can't look me in the eye and tell me you want me, and
then reject me without at least a reason. If you don't want
to be with me, I deserve to know why not."

"I'm not exactly a guy out of a fairy tale, Becca."

"Who said I was looking for a fairy tale?" She was
practically yelling now, pacing back and forth on the quilt,
her hair blowing free in the wind. "Who said I was looking for more than—than—"

"A roll in the hay?"

"Don't say it like that!" She spun on her bare heel and
glared at him. "For heaven's sake, Colt, what is wrong
with me? Could you just tell me that? What is so wrong
with me wanting to hold someone, and *be* held by someone? What is so horrible about me that I can't have that?"

"Oh God, Becca." Colt's voice was hoarse as he

crossed the few feet between them and took her by the arms. "There's nothing wrong with you. I just—I just think it's a mistake to save yourself for this long and then blow it all on someone like me."

"I don't think it's a mistake. It's what I want."

He closed his eyes, then opened them and faced her, his face sober. "Becca, I've never been with a..."

"The word is *virgin,* Colt."

"Okay, virgin. I've never been with a virgin before. I don't know if I can be gentle enough—"

She stepped close and took his hands in hers. "You know what you do when you don't know what to do, right?"

He shook his head, and she almost felt sorry for him, he looked so confused. "What?"

"You pretend like you do know."

"Don't use my own words against me."

"It's good advice. Pretend you've already been with four virgins—"

"Oh, Lord."

"Sorry, I couldn't resist. What do you think I'm looking for, Colt? A fairy-tale hero? Pretend like you *are* that. What would you say to me right now if you were a hero from a fairy tale?"

He was silent for a very long time, and she couldn't read the expression on his face. For one horrible minute, she was sure he was about to turn around and walk away, leaving her there to feel more wretched than ever. She saw the muscles in his throat work as he swallowed, and she dropped her eyes, not wanting to watch as he wrestled with the decision.

"You're sure about this, Becca?" came his gruff question, finally.

She wanted to be flippant, to make him think this was not a big deal for her. But her voice lodged somewhere in her throat, and all she could do was look up at him and nod silently.

"Then, why are you shaking?"

"Because I'm nervous. Why are you?"

"Because." He took a deep breath and tightened his grip on her arms. "Because I'm trying to keep from ripping this damn thing off you and throwing you on the ground."

She felt her eyes widen, and she must have looked pretty silly because for the first time, he gave her the semblance of a smile. "Don't worry. I can be gentle. I can make this special for you. I want to make it special for you."

He tucked a strand of her hair behind her ear. "If I were the hero in a fairy tale, first of all I'd probably not be having the unchaste thoughts about you that I am. But I'd also tell you, I watched you out here one time, when we were kids. You came down here, stripped down to your underwear, and went swimming."

"Colt! You spied on me?"

"Yep. And I enjoyed it, too. Not very heroic of me, was it?"

"How old were we?"

"Let's see…twelve or thirteen. Thirteen, I guess. That's the year I almost flunked Texas History because I couldn't keep my mind off how you looked coming out of the water. I had all kinds of fantasies about what would have happened if I hadn't hid behind the bushes like a chicken. I came back every day until it got freezing outside, but you never did that again."

"No. Mama found out, somehow, and…well, I never came back." She forced that memory aside and focused instead on what he'd said. "Thirteen, huh? You must have been easily impressed. I was skinny and quite unattractive then."

"I thought you were the most beautiful thing I'd ever seen. You're still beautiful."

"Ah, now that's something a hero would say. Keep pretending."

"I'm not pretending, Becca. Look at me."

She lifted her gaze to his dark one, and for one dazzling moment she believed he meant what he said. When he looked at her like that, she felt beautiful. And that made it easy to step close to him, to lift her lips when he lowered his.

She was expecting that same mind-bending intensity she'd felt when he kissed her before. Instead his touch was gentle, whisper soft. His lips moved over hers tenderly.

"Keep looking at me, okay, Becca? Don't look away."

He kissed her for a long time, until she thought he would never stop, until she thought she would die if he did stop.

He moved his mouth to her neck, glided it along her throat and shoulders, as if he had all the time in the world, whispering things to her, soft, senseless things that would have tugged at her heart had she not known he was only saying them because he thought she needed to hear them, because it was part of the game. A part of her did need to hear it, she supposed, because that part of her wept with the sweetness of it.

He lifted her chin and, his eyes on hers, skimmed both hands lightly over the tips of her breasts. Tiny arrows of sensation shot through her, making her gasp. Her eyelids fluttered closed.

She wanted to remember every moment, every sensation. She wanted to be able to recall the feel of his arms around her, in the long days ahead after he was gone. She wanted to be able to close her eyes and recall the smell of him, the taste of him, the sensation of being swept away on a current of passion.

"No, look at me," he murmured, and cupped his hands around her breasts. He rubbed his thumbs over the hard nubs of her nipples, and Becca couldn't stop the moan that escaped her.

She wanted to look away, but every time she tried, he forced her eyes back to him. She felt vulnerable, more exposed when he looked in her eyes than when he looked at her body. It was terrifying, and thrilling.

"Put your hands on me." His voice was rough. Hesitantly, she slid her hands inside his shirt. With one hand, she unbuttoned his shirt, then slipped it off his shoulders, down his arms.

His eyes narrowed, and he moved to shrug the shirt to the ground. He brought his hands back to her, and she palmed his chest.

"I can feel your heart," she said, amazed and gratified that her touch could make it beat so rapidly.

"I'm surprised it's not making the ground shake. Kiss me, Becca."

She moved her lips over his, growing bolder with each tortured groan he let out, each sharp intake of his breath. His grip tightened on her shoulders. He moved his lips to her throat, and with a moan her head fell back. He lowered his arms, wrapping her in iron bands that comforted rather than imprisoned. She could feel the hard muscles of his biceps, bunched tightly against her arms.

Gradually, her inhibitions faded and her need increased. Slowly she let out the reins, and discovered a charging, runaway beast waiting at the other end. She couldn't get enough, wanted to return every touch, every taste in kind, immensely pleased that each caress she gave him was met with equal urgency.

His fingers played over her skin, rough calluses that swept over her, sending her blood racing close under her skin.

He took her hand and drew her down to the pallet, then

knelt before her. He streaked hot kisses along the lace neckline of the gown, making her frantic for a closer touch. She threaded her fingers through his hair, holding him close. Bringing his lips back to hers, he smoothed the straps down her arms.

Despite everything, despite how good it felt and how much she wanted it, she flinched a little when the gown slid down. She hoped he didn't notice, but he did.

"It's okay, Becca," he murmured against her hair. "It's okay. We have all night. Just relax and enjoy it."

She took a deep breath and tried to do as he said. No matter what happened after this, it was enough. It was heaven, feeling his lips on hers, on her body. It was thrilling, that thunderous jump in her heart when his hot mouth closed over the pulse beat at her throat. And it was pure bliss—a bliss she'd never known—when with a sweet, almost painfully sweet, tug he drew her into his mouth, and she felt he was drawing her out, the heart of her that had been hidden in the dark all her life.

If she never had anything else, she would have this night. The memory of this night would keep her warm for the rest of her nights.

She let herself relax, let her cheek fall on his hair and breathed in the scent of him, his hair, his skin, felt the ripple of muscles as she skimmed fingers over his back, down his arms. He drew back and slipped the gown up her legs, over her hips and finally over her head. His eyes burned black in his face, his jaw clenched, and her heart leapt at the strange sense of power she felt, lying before him.

She reached for the buckle of his belt, but he covered her hands with his and stopped her. She drew her hand back, doubtful for the first time.

He lifted her hands and brought them to his mouth, kissing her knuckles. "Wait just a minute, okay?" He gave her a crooked smile.

He put her hands on his shoulders, then wrapped his arms around her waist. He brought his mouth back to her breast, flicking her taut nipple with his tongue. She moaned and sagged back against the blanket. Gently, he lowered to the ground beside her.

He raised himself over her, kissing a heated trail between her breasts, slowly, deliberately, until her head swam and colors flickered behind her closed eyelids. The ache was sharp and sweet now, so fierce that it frightened her.

"I've dreamed of this," he said gruffly. "Of seeing you like this, touching you like this. I haven't slept in two weeks, Becca, for thinking of this."

She roamed her hands over his back, thinking to drag him with her. But when he drew her breast into his mouth again, her only thought was to hold on to him like a buoy in a storm.

It didn't matter anymore if this was the first time or the last time. She was caught in a torrent of sensation that hummed in her ears and thrummed in her veins. She clung to him as he drove her body tighter and tighter.

He stroked her skin, lighting fires everywhere he touched. Slowly, but deliberately, his hands skimmed up her leg to cup her moist softness.

She gasped, both in surprise and in pleasure. His head came up to watch her reaction as he softly ran his fingers down her, lighting new dark fires.

She had known he would touch her. She hadn't expected it to feel so good, so primal and raw and alien from anything she'd felt before. She hadn't expected to settle into the sensation so comfortably, with a sense of rightness, with a sense of millions of years of instinct coming together.

She moaned, low and guttural, in her throat, and clutched at Colt's shoulders. He said something, but for the life of her she couldn't make sense of it. Her head was spinning and every part of her felt wrapped up in this moment, with no past or future.

"Becca," he growled. He edged down her, kissing her flat stomach. He gripped her waist, his heart tripping out of control. His blood raged in him, threatening the tenuous hold on his control. But it was worth it. It was worth ten times as much torture, to see her squirming against him, her cheeks flushed and her eyes hooded with need. It was worth it, to hear her gasp and moan his name. To know that he—no one else, just he—had been the one to show her this side of herself.

Besides, in about five more seconds his heart was going to burst and he wouldn't be alive to wonder if he was going to make it or not.

He held her tightly, covering her mouth with his. She felt incredible, soft and slick and hot, and a red haze of need enveloped him. She groaned in pleasure, and he nearly lost it.

He kept kissing her, until the moment he sensed her last shred of inhibition slip away, and she was with him again, in the moment, lost to every other thought. He moved his hand against her, as excited by her reaction to his touch as he was by her touch. He pulled his head back and watched with fascination and intense hunger as she looked at him, dazed, not seeing him. She turned inside herself, experiencing that headlong rush that had been a mystery to her until now.

Her eyes flew open, her head whipped side to side on the pillow, and she raised her hips off the ground, pressing against his hand. Her breath came in shallow gasps, as did his. He held her tightly as she cried out his name and shook in his arms. He thought not even his own completion could be as satisfying as watching her.

He knelt above her, undressed hurriedly, and eased

himself between her legs. She clung to him, murmuring something over and over in a strangled voice.

He told himself he wouldn't push too hard. He would take it slow, give her time to adjust to him. But…she was hot. And tight. Fresh drops of perspiration broke out on his upper lip. He gripped her waist. Slowly, torturously, he pushed himself into her, while hunger clawed at him, raw and ruthless, screamed at him to finish it.

He could do this. He could. He was not an animal.

But when she convulsed and raised her hips, he was lost.

She locked her ankles behind his back and drew him in. With an oath, he felt her tear beneath him, and couldn't have stopped himself if his life depended on it. He plunged.

He lay against her, torn between worry that he'd hurt her and the pure, sweet agony of being sheathed in tight molten heaven. For a moment he was too mindless to move. Then she moved her silky legs against his, urging him on.

Despite himself, in an instinct old as time, he moved within her. He heard her bite back a gasp, and froze. "Am I hurting you?" he asked gruffly.

"Yes," she said, her voice a hell of a lot clearer than his. "Don't stop."

To emphasize, she locked her legs tighter and rocked under him. He tightened and flexed, his body ruthlessly tossing aside caution and consideration. He grew dizzy with the effort to hold back. With a few thrusts, he let out a groan, feeling as if his heart were also pouring through him, into her. With a violent shudder, he called out her name as she had called out his, and followed her over the crest.

It was some minutes before any of his blood made it back to his brain. He lay sprawled on her, a dead weight that must be uncomfortable for her.

"Unnnhhh," he moaned, moving to roll away. She tightened her arms and legs around him.

"Stay," she whispered in his ear. "For just a minute."

He would have been happy to stay for the rest of his life. Though he was more than a little nervous about facing her, he pulled his head up so he could see her.

He kissed her, softly, hoping the tenderness now would make up for any he may have lacked earlier. "Are you okay?"

To his utter amazement, her lips curled upward in an unabashed smile. She nodded.

He noticed then the tears in the corners of her eyes, the faint path they'd traced down the side of her face to her ear. Moved, he rubbed his thumb lightly over them. "I'm sorry," he mumbled, knowing the words wouldn't help.

"Why are you sorry?" she asked, from her expression honestly baffled. "I asked you to do it."

"I know," he said, scowling. As if he wouldn't have jumped at the chance. As if it were all a big favor he was doing for her. "Did it hurt much?"

She smiled again, sweetly. "Not much." Idly, she ran her fingers through the hair that dripped over his forehead. "It was a good hurt. I suppose that makes no sense, though, does it?"

He grunted and shifted his weight to his arms. It made a lot of sense, actually.

He took one corner of the blanket in his hand, locked the other around her shoulders, and rolled, reversing their positions. He tucked it around them, warm against the night breeze, and caressed the satiny skin of her back, the line of her shoulder blade, the thin curve of her spine. She relaxed against him, and his worries eased a bit.

She tucked her head against his shoulder, and he looked up at the stars, feeling a strange sense of wholeness and completion that he'd never felt before, anywhere. He stroked her hair, loving the feel of the soft, silky strands against his rough, callused fingers.

She shifted and murmured something, sleepily, into the skin of his shoulder. Colt felt himself stir to life once again. *No,* he said firmly to his nether region. She seemed happy. He wasn't going to push his luck.

"Tell me why," she whispered. "Why did you change your mind? What made you say yes?"

"Besides the fact that a beautiful woman was standing before me asking me to make love to her?"

She toyed with the hairs on his chest and smiled. "Besides that, yes."

He thought about it, knowing he couldn't speak the truth; not all of it, anyway. But he could tell her part of it. "You remember how you said I made you feel like you were back in high school?"

"Yes."

"You make me feel like that, too. You always made me feel good, Becca. Like I was all the things I wanted to be. Like I really was some kind of Prince Charming. And...and I wanted to be that for you. If you really wanted to share this time with me, then I wanted to prove you were right to trust me."

He lifted his head to meet her eyes. "I'm not the man you want, Becca. I'm not the man you think I am. But you make me want to try to be."

Chapter 8

Colt found it difficult to concentrate on his work during the next week. Though he worked hard refinishing cabinets and replacing the worn linoleum floor, he caught himself daydreaming and finding excuses to quit early every day. It didn't take Jas and Pete long to catch on to the reason why. And as the code of conduct for manhood indicated, they needled him about it at every opportunity.

Colt had never been the type to take teasing with any humor, but for some reason he found himself laughing with them, not bothering to deny that his interest lay across the field. He joked back, enjoying both the humor and the work they did.

Actually, he and Pete did most of the work. Jas stood around, most of the time directly in the way. Colt figured out finally that he was there to jump in whenever he thought Colt was straining his back. On more than one occasion, their eyes met in a silent war of wills over an object Jas thought was too heavy for Colt to lift.

Despite the coddling and ribbing, Colt found he was

enjoying himself. When they hung the new mirror over the pedestal sink, he was somewhat surprised to see his own face, smiling in the reflection. He hadn't given it any thought before, but the reflection that faced him was generally closed and brooding, or at the very best, solemn. For a second the open, affable face in the mirror caught him off guard.

He was back in the house that to him had symbolized all that was wrong in the world for so long, but he found his mind dwelled on that less and less. He was surprised to realize he got a sense of satisfaction from restoring the house, taking something old and worn and making it new and livable again. Seeing the progress of his labor, even as he nursed a constantly aching back. It felt good, working at something real, tangible. For the first time, he was putting his energy into something and making a difference with it, instead of merely hanging on until the horn blew. Pete felt it, too, he knew.

But then, Colt thought, maybe the smile on his own face had more to do with what he did at night, rather than during the day. He'd always known Becca was pretty, under those frumpy clothes and clunky glasses. And after that night twelve years ago, he'd known she could be passionate, too. But his blood sang just thinking about how she melted against him with the lightest of touches, the simplest of caresses. It was a surprise that suited him.

He'd thought he was hungry for her, for her sweetness so innocently mixed with passion. But she was just as hungry, and it made something in him feel powerful and alive for the first time in a long time. It made everything else seem too distant to worry about—Doff, and the house and his back. Leaving.

And after a few days, he began to have some hope that maybe he hadn't inherited all of Doff's bad traits, after all. Most. But not all.

Now he wiped sweat off his forehead and rocked back

on his heels, examining the ceramic tile he and Pete had just replaced. The bathroom was coming along pretty quick. Pete was a hard worker, and so was Jas, when he wasn't smarting off. The house was well on its way to becoming livable again. The roof was replaced, new windows installed and caulked. He could walk around the front porch now without fear of falling through. Pretty soon his work here would be done.

"I guess we'll shut it down for today." He rose, grimacing as his knees popped and his back protested.

"You all right?" Jas asked, pulling away from the wall.

Colt nodded and moved past him into the hallway, walking off the stiffness. He was in too good a mood to talk about his back. The doctor had given him some exercises to do, and he did them. Other than that, he didn't like to dwell on the condition of his back or how his future depended on it. Whether it would allow him to return to the circuit or not.

"You guys want to see something great?" Pete asked, digging his wallet from his back pocket. He pulled out a piece of newspaper, carefully folded into a square, and handed it to Colt.

Local Junior Places Second In National Competition, the headline read.

"This is your son?" Colt asked, reading that Jeremy Huckaby had placed second in a national writing competition for college students.

"Yep, that's my oldest. He's there on a full scholarship, too. Books, tuition, the whole nine yards. That's not some cheap state school, either. Only thing he has to pay for is his housing." Pete's creased face beamed with pride.

"That's cool, Pete," Jas said. "Really cool."

Pete took the paper back and folded it neatly, nodding to himself. "Yeah, I don't know where he got his brains from. God knows, it wasn't from me. But I sure am proud of him."

While giving Pete a ride home a few minutes later, they stopped at the Circle D convenience store so Pete could buy up all the remaining copies of the *Aloma Sentinel,* and send copies of the article to relatives. Colt had a hard time seeing Doff going through the trouble of reading an article about him, much less cutting one out and wasting a stamp to mail it.

When they pulled up in front of the Huckaby house, Pete reached for the door handle and then froze. A young man stood in the open doorway, looking back over his shoulder and laughing at something inside the house. He carried a book bag in one hand. He said something and laughed again, nodding.

Colt cast Pete a quick glance. Pete's face was lit with hope. The boy faced front then, and saw Pete. The boy's smile vanished, and his face dropped into a sullen, resentful look.

Pete took a deep breath, jerked on the handle and pushed the door open. "Hey, Jeremy," he said, his smile bright. Colt had worked with him enough to see the tension behind the smile. "I didn't know you were going to be here today."

"Because I didn't want you to know. You're home early," the boy said, his tone an accusation. He hitched the book bag over his shoulder. "Get fired already?"

"We knocked off a little early today. Congratulations on the essay contest. Your mom and me are real proud."

Jeremy stared at him, stone-faced. He looked off down the road, toward town.

Colt didn't know why he got out of the truck. This was a family problem. It wasn't his business. And Pete certainly didn't need his support.

He stuck out his hand out for Jeremy to shake. "Colt Bonner," he said. "You must be Jeremy. You look a lot like your dad."

Judging by the expression on his face, Jeremy didn't

take that as a compliment. "Yeah," he said, "I've heard that before." He hitched the bag higher on his shoulder. "I'm outta here," he said, turning to look over his shoulder at JoAnn. "I'll catch my ride in town."

Pete watched him walk away, his face grim. He looked at JoAnn, who gave him a halfhearted smile and a shrug.

"That was rude, boss," Pete said. "I'm sorry."

Colt shrugged it off. "No harm done. I'll see you in the morning."

He climbed into the pickup and caught up with Jeremy a few seconds later. "Want a ride?"

Jeremy cut his glance to the side and kept walking.

"I'm heading through town. Could drop you off at the Circle D."

Jeremy eyed him cautiously, then stopped and grabbed the door handle. He tossed the book bag on the floorboard and hopped in. "Thanks," he said, staring straight ahead.

Colt drove, his eyes on the road. "Pete showed me the article about the essay contest. Congratulations."

"He's *showing* people?" Jeremy groaned.

Colt couldn't help but laugh at Jeremy's dismay. "Yeah, he's proud of you."

Jeremy snorted. "I'll bet he is. You know he's an ex-con, right?

"Yep."

"And you trust him enough to give him a job, anyway?"

"Looks that way."

Jeremy scowled at Colt. "Your choice, I guess."

"Yep."

They rode along in silence for a moment, then Jeremy narrowed his eyes at him. "He didn't ask you to give me a ride so you could have a talk with me, did he? Try and convince me of what a great guy he is and how I should just forgive and forget the whole mess ever happened?"

"Um, no."

"Because that seems to be the common theme right now. 'Forgive your dad, Jeremy.' 'It's time to move on, Jeremy.'"

"I'd have to say it hasn't come up."

"Oh." Jeremy fiddled with his book bag and looked out the window. "Well, good. Because it's not going to happen."

Colt pulled into the Circle D parking lot. "Your choice."

Jeremy eyed him for a moment, then opened the door. "Yeah. My choice." He climbed out and grabbed his book bag. "Thanks for the ride. Keep an eye on my dad."

Colt nodded and watched him walk away. Bratty little snot, he thought as he drove away. He wanted to shake the little fool by the scruff of the neck for treating Pete the way he had. Couldn't he see the guy was trying to make good? Didn't he realize that everyone made mistakes?

Colt stared at himself in the rearview mirror. Good Lord, he sounded like Becca.

The whole ordeal put him in a foul mood. He decided to see if Jas was up for a card game, but his friend was gone by the time Colt got home. He considered calling Tanner and Haskell, but the thought had little appeal.

Finally, he gave in and did what he knew he'd wanted to do all along. He set off across the field to Becca's house.

Becca slipped past the office door and refused to look at the new computer. She had other things to do. Just because school was out didn't mean she had nothing but time on her hands.

That excuse had carried her through almost an entire week. She'd managed to get the spring cleaning done, her assignment in to Dunleavy's a few days early for a change, and shampooed the floor mats in her car. And after all, during the past week…other things had diverted her attention. She felt her cheeks grow warm, knew it was silly to be embarrassed by her own thoughts in her own house, but she was.

Oh, she'd spent plenty of time at the computer, too, of course. Playing. Learning the new program, exploring. Telling herself that she had all the time in the world to write.

The truth was, though, she was running out of things to do. And in the back of her mind, moving ever closer to the front, was the niggling knowledge that she was avoiding the real purpose of the computer. It wasn't that she didn't want to write. It wasn't that she didn't have ideas. The fact was, she was afraid. But she'd vowed not to let fear stop her, ever again.

She didn't think she'd regret the personal challenge quite so soon. She sighed, dragged her feet into the room and jabbed a finger at the start button on the computer.

She had confessed to Colt that she was still a little nervous about writing, despite her resolve not to let Mama's bitterness stop her. He suggested she use the writing in the same way she had when they were kids. When she started feeling sad or depressed, he thought, she should turn her attention away from the memories and pour it all into the story. And maybe he had a point. Maybe she could eventually use her own imagination to wash all the bad memories away and replace them with better—if imaginary—ones.

She sat at the desk and tapped her foot. Surely that couldn't be too hard. After all, she'd lived in a fantasy world most of her life, pretending her home was happy, pretending *she* was happy. It should be easy enough to get that entire pretense onto the screen.

Except, her fingers wouldn't move. She rubbed her palms on her jeans and flexed her fingers, telling herself to just start, anywhere, if for no other reason than that Colt would give her a hard time if she didn't.

It didn't feel right, though, this continual escapism. Her entire life she'd been content with make-believe, with the notion that reality was subjective and that she could make of her life and her world whatever she wanted to. But it wasn't working anymore.

She didn't have to look far to know why it wasn't working, either. Through the past week, through the thrill and bliss of discovering herself in Colt's arms, the knowledge had waited in the back of her mind that no matter what else, her own mother had hated her. She couldn't just tell herself that Mama was dead now and it didn't matter. Or that the reason for that hatred was for Mama to know, and Becca didn't need to worry about it.

She had to know why. And was at the same time terrified of knowing.

She knew—she figured she'd always known—how to go about finding out. It had been in the back of her mind for almost four years.

When she'd finally faced the task of cleaning out Mama's things several years ago, she'd found a box under her bed. A hatbox, covered in blue satin faded to a dusty color, worn through at the edges. A wide, gray ribbon was tied around it, and the satin was still shiny and dark beneath the ribbon.

Becca had pulled the box up onto the bed and stared at it, wondering what it contained. The chances of it being an actual hat, she knew, were pretty slim. A cautious shake confirmed that, and she heard papers slide and tap against the inside.

Mama had wanted it to stay hidden, she knew, or else Becca would have seen this box before. What kind of secrets did it hide?

Thoughts had raced through Becca's head, each more ridiculous than the last, as she sat on Mama's chenille bedspread and swung one foot. Love letters from Becca's father? She thought that highly unlikely. On the few occasions Mama had mentioned her father, she'd done so with such seething hatred that Becca doubted she would have left any memento of him unshredded or unburned. Keepsakes from Becca's own childhood—her first tooth, baby pictures, maybe a christening gown? She almost laughed at that idea, and would have if the lump in her throat had permitted.

That left nothing but the truly outlandish: fake passports, identification and top-secret plans from Mama's secret life as a Russian double agent? Not likely, either, since as far as Becca could remember, Mama left the house on Wednesdays to do the shopping, on the third of the month to pick up the welfare check, and never in between.

A recipe for a still, perhaps? Becca did laugh then, hysterically so, and recognized by the strange tightening in her chest that the day was taking its toll on her. She could face this another day. She did not need another confrontation with her mother's ghost.

Finally, she'd tucked the box away in the attic. At that time, school had just been starting and Becca had told herself that she didn't have the time to go through all the things right then. It would have to wait until the next long holiday, or maybe Christmas break. But she'd known even then that she wasn't going to face that box. Not at Christmas break, and probably not ever. If she'd been completely honest with herself, she would have known that she was afraid. Afraid of finding out what Mama had wanted to keep secret. And, irrational as it was—Mama had been dead for six months at that point—afraid of what Mama would think if she went rummaging through her private things. It had taken three solid months of coaching herself to even throw out Mama's bath powder.

Of course, Becca didn't *know* for sure that the hatbox

in the attic held all the answers she was looking for. But it was probably a good place to start.

She pulled the attic stairs down into the hallway and stood staring up into the dark hole. She was thirsty, she realized. This could wait until after she had a glass of iced tea.

Three glasses of tea and a few trips to the bathroom later, she stood staring up at the stairs again. This was ridiculous, she decided. She should either get up there and dig through the box, or forget the whole thing and quit letting it eat at her. Either way would work.

Make a decision, Becca, she told herself.

Her feet stayed planted.

Okay, so talking to herself wasn't working. What was she so afraid of? She knew her mother hated her. What difference could that box possibly make? Maybe she'd find out exactly what her mother really hated. Maybe she'd understand, finally, and feel better about the whole thing.

Maybe she would see why, and know that her mother had a right. Had a legitimate reason. Maybe she would finally know what was so terrible about herself, and she'd no longer be able to lie to herself and run from that knowledge. Maybe she would hate herself, too.

Then everything she had worked for would be for nothing, but at least the struggle would be over. She could give up, resign herself to being the undesirable she always knew she was, and learn to live with it. As tired as the thought made her, it also set her free.

She climbed the steps slowly, one at a time. She moved to the attic window and shoved it open. Dust tickled her nose and had her sneezing within minutes, but she didn't consider going back down. She knew right where the box was; she brought it over to the light in the open window and tugged off the ribbon.

Whatever she had been expecting to find, a man's handkerchief wasn't it. It rested on top of a jumble of cards and papers, thin white cotton faded almost to yellow. Becca lifted it and shook it out. It smelled musty. On one corner was a thin blue monogram, the initials RHL. This was the only decoration on the handkerchief.

She laid it aside and reached for the next item on the top of the stack. A newspaper clipping, folded crookedly. When Becca unfolded it, the brittle paper tore a little in her hands. She was able to read, though, about a car accident in North Carolina. Robert Henry Linsey, his wife Eleanor and their two-year-old son Michael all died in the crash.

She studied the picture of the family at a happier time, dark and grainy and faded with age. For all that, though, it was remarkably easy to see the resemblance between her and the man in the picture. He was tall, but thin for a man, with light red hair and freckled skin. The nose was the same, straight and somewhat narrow. The shape of the eyes was the same as hers, too, though she couldn't tell the color from the picture. The mouth was different, wider than Becca's own, in a smile now frozen for all time, a smile so wide and so obviously content that it hurt Becca's throat to see it.

She didn't know how they were related; Mama never mentioned cousins or aunts or uncles, and eventually Becca had learned not to ask about them.

They were all happy, the little boy with a cheesy little grin holding a toy truck to his chest, the mother with a lipsticked smile and a hairstyle that said she visited the beauty shop faithfully for her weekly appointment. It was Christmas, the caption said, just a few weeks before the tragedy.

Becca gingerly unfolded a crease in the top edge of the paper and read the date. She had been almost three at the time of the crash. Of course, she could not remember that Christmas, but she remembered many more as a child. She would be willing to bet she'd never once smiled for the camera like that, that Mama had never dressed up and put a proud hand on her shoulder and leaned over her like the woman in the picture did the little boy.

She wanted to stare at that picture for hours, but laid it beside the handkerchief and pulled out another piece of paper—a receipt or invoice; she couldn't really tell what it was for. A dry cleaning receipt. A small calendar with dates sporadically circled in blue ink.

She kept digging, sure she would find something more, something clear.

She had to get to the bottom of the box before she found it: a small stack of letters and notes folded together. They weren't tied or secured in any way, but their placement spoke of the fact that whoever put them there saw them as a group.

They weren't in any order, she realized as she unfolded the dry papers one by one, straightening the creases and reading every word. The one that said, "You must not come over here like that. I'm running out of excuses," was farther up the stack than the one that said, "Last night was everything I dreamed of, and more. I can't wait for the moment we can be together again."

Becca pulled a box over beside her and straightened all the papers, laying them out flat to study them and put them in order. It was easy enough to guess the beginning note. It sounded almost stilted in its forced casualness. It suggested they meet after work—in an out-of-the-way place across town, of course. There was no sense in starting rumors when all they were going to do was talk.

The notes weren't dated, so Becca had no way of knowing how many times the two met before talk became more than talk. Judging from the number of notes, it wasn't long. Becca had to give Mama credit—the guy was a charmer. And maybe a part of him actually meant it when he wrote of how being with her—he called her his darling, precious Charlotte—was like all the moments of his life converged together to build that one perfect moment, that being with her made the rest of the world fade away and seem insignificant. No wonder Mama had fallen for him.

And fallen for him she must have done, because after three such dramatic professions of devotion, the tone in Rob's (he signed them all that way—Rob) letters became progressively more reserved. He still professed to be devoted to her, but gently reminded her that they must be careful. He was not a free man, and she must be more guarded with what she said and how she acted around other people.

There was not one note from Mama, but her desperation was easy to read in his answers to her. "You must not beg like that, Charlotte. It is shameful. I don't want to do it, but I may be forced to spend some time apart from you, just so you can get back some sense of balance."

One letter out of all the others chilled her. She read it, then read it again, to make sure she knew what she was reading. "I'm very sorry that you're in the position you're in, sweet Charlotte. I did warn you to be careful, though I suppose recriminations are out of place now. But you know that there are options. You don't have to carry this stigma around with you for the rest of your life. You don't have to let this ruin everything. And it will ruin everything, Charlotte, make no mistake about that. I can arrange for it to be taken care of. Just give me the word, and I will take care of everything."

Becca let her hand drop to her knee and stared at the dust motes floating in the shaft of light from the open window. It was growing warm in the attic. It must be getting close to noon, she thought dully.

Taken care of. He could have it all arranged.

That smiling, red-haired man who so obviously adored his son wanted Mama to have Becca "taken care of." It spoke volumes of what he felt—or didn't feel—for Mama. For her.

Mama must have known it, too, and known she was losing him. Several following notes urged her to "be reasonable" and "think of their future." To be fair, he never once spoke of love, and he didn't write one word about commitment. That probably made it easier for him when the time finally came to break it off.

Because Mama refused to "be reasonable," he found it necessary to end their friendship. *Their friendship.* That was the first of the notes, Becca guessed, written in that distant, cold tone. He refused to be blackmailed in that way. If she insisted on pursuing this, he would be forced to seek legal action. It wasn't good for his wife to be subjected to this, especially in her condition. And the last note—or what Becca guessed to be the last—wondering how she could be so stupid as to wag her little brat around for all the world to see. Had she no pride?

Becca stacked the notes back together and thought that no, Mama probably didn't have any pride left by then. Becca knew nothing of Mama's family, her background before they'd come to Aloma, what her grandparents had been like or even where they lived. But she thought a person must not have much pride to get involved with a married man to begin with. And a smooth tongue like Rob's was probably hard to resist.

By the time he was through with her, well, she must have hated herself. Becca closed her eyes and ran her fingers over and over the edge of the stack of papers, letting that thought form and become solid. Mama must have hated *herself.*

Becca jumped when she heard a footstep on the landing. She looked up to see Colt, his head bent under the low ceiling.

And in that moment she realized he was the one person on earth who had the power to have her begging, as Mama had begged. He wouldn't even have to try, she thought. As she looked into Colt's dark, brooding eyes and felt the urge to throw herself into his arms, she thought she truly knew what Mama must have felt—that desperate, impossible love that blinded a person to everything and everyone else, that took priority over everything. Including herself.

Becca felt her throat close and tears burn behind her eyes for the girl her mother had once been, at how her heart must have shattered. Surely only a heart that had been burned beyond repair would have been as bitter and hurtful as Mama's had been.

As she looked up at Colt and fought the urge to run sobbing to him, she knew without a doubt that, if she let things go as they had been, she was headed down that same lonely road Mama had gone. He would not mean to break her heart, of course. But he would break it nonetheless. If she let him.

"No," she said.

"No, what? What are you doing here?"

Becca shook her head to clear it. "I'm...I'm going through some of Mama's things."

"Oh." He rubbed his chin and shifted his feet. "I saw you through the window. I called you, but I guess you didn't hear me."

He sat on the box she'd had the notes spread out on. "You okay?"

She nodded. This was what love was like, Becca thought. It made you desperate, it made you sad. And in the end, it made you bitter.

She looked up at him and wondered how she would ever look at him the same way again. "I'm fine," she said. She might be fine, she might not be. She couldn't tell. She didn't really know anything at that moment.

"You sure?"

She stood and dusted off her jeans. "Of course I'm

sure.'' She dropped the stack of notes back in the box.
As she did, her gaze fell on an envelope with familiar,
almost childish handwriting. She stared at it, feeling the
world shift underneath her almost imperceptibly.

Her mind shied away from it; she piled the rest of the
stuff on top and put the lid back on. ''It was just some
old papers and stuff. How about a glass of iced tea?''

''No, I came over...'' His voice trailed off, as she
brushed past him and moved down the stairs. ''Okay, tea
it is.''

He made another attempt as they stood in the kitchen.
She handed him a large glass of tea and drained half of
one herself, staring at something that wasn't there.

''You're sure you're okay?''

''I'm fine,'' she murmured.

''I have to go to Abilene this afternoon to pick up some
supplies. I was going to see if you wanted to come
along.''

She shook her head immediately.

''I thought we could grab some dinner while we're
there. Maybe catch a movie.''

She looked at him then, really looked at him for the
first time. ''I'm sorry,'' she said. ''My mind is on something else.''

''So I gathered.'' He leaned against the counter and set
down his glass, then took hers and put it beside. He rested
his hands on her shoulders and ran his thumb along the
band that held her hair back. ''Want to talk about it?''

She shook her head again, but this time met his eyes.
''No. I'm going to take your advice and write about it.''

He nodded and looked out the window behind her, told
himself he was relieved. He wasn't good with long talks,
anyway. ''Okay. Want to write about it tomorrow? Come
with me tonight?''

She was already off, though, leaving him standing alone
in the kitchen. He followed her into her studio, where she

flipped through the stack of canvases against the wall and mumbled to herself.

"I know it's here. Of course it's here, where else could it be?" She roamed the room, finally emerging from behind a large cabinet. "I knew it was here." She looked at the painting in her hand, smaller than the ones against the wall.

Colt felt as if he might as well have been somewhere else, as much as she was aware of him. It bothered him more than was comfortable. He stepped up and looked at the painting over her shoulder.

Whatever he was expecting, this wasn't it. Her other paintings had been of real places—places he even recognized if he looked close enough. This painting wasn't really of anything. It was much more abstract, all dark blues and thin jagged blacks that faded—or grew, actually—into golds and vibrant reds.

"This is it," she said to herself as she brushed past him. "This is what I'm going to write."

He hung around for a few more minutes, trying to get her to talk to him. He wondered if he'd done something or said something to make her mad, but she didn't really seem angry. Just, like she didn't have time for him. And he decided he had other things to do aside from sit around and wait for her to toss him a scrap.

"I'll catch you later, Becca," he said over his shoulder as he left.

Becca watched him walk back across the field, his hands stuffed in his pockets, his back stiff.

"I'm not going to do it, Colt," she whispered. "I'm not going to let myself become like her."

Chapter 9

Becca found that once she knew where she was going with the story, the ideas came fast and furiously. A little slower came her skill at working with words. She attacked the project with all the energy she had. Every time her mind turned to the picture in the attic of the happy family, she blocked it out and refocused on the story before her. Every time the unfamiliar burn of anger and resentment started to well up inside her, she pushed it aside and covered it over with her story.

Colt came over every day, but she thought of the box in the attic and the pain in her mother's heart, and made excuses to spend as little time with him as possible. Every time she felt the urge to turn to him, to let him comfort her, to even talk to him about the emotional highs and lows she was going through, she determinedly shoved the urge aside and refocused on her work.

Lord, she missed him, even though he was so near she could look out her window and see him anytime she wanted. She missed talking to him. She missed having someone.

You must not beg like that.

She was strong enough to do this on her own. She'd been on her own for as long as she could remember, even before Mama died, and she could certainly manage to be so again. She wasn't going to fall into the trap of needing Colt to make her happy.

She got little sleep, lived on what she could find in the pantry and refrigerator, and let the laundry pile up. Her roses and petunias withered under the hot Texas sun without the vigilant care she normally gave them. She wrote, rewrote, discarded and wrote again. She kept the abstract oil painting by her desk, to remind her of the feeling she wanted to capture.

Recalling the emotions she'd experienced when she'd done that painting was not easy. She forced herself to step back and remember that time as clearly and clinically as she could—a time not long after Mama died, when something in her wanted to break free and start living her own life. Looking back, she supposed that painting had represented an unconscious goal to her—a coming out of her own darkness into light, into life. She'd let herself believe she would accomplish that goal.

Now, she wasn't so sure. She pushed that question away with all the others.

The final book resembled her beginning efforts very little. She was surprised to find that as the words came, the story took on a life of its own. She realized that the theme she'd been trying to capture—that every person has worth, that every child needs to see the brightness and goodness in themselves—was still present. But the characters were different.

Less like her, a voice inside her said. *Not so close to home.*

She pushed away that voice, too. It didn't matter if

she'd removed herself from the story a little. It was a good story. And what if no one could tell she was writing out of her own experiences? All that mattered was that the story spoke to someone.

She saved the story one more time onto disk and printed up a hard copy to go with it. She took one last look at the artwork. She had mixed emotions about sending it, too. She liked it, but she wasn't quite sure a children's book editor would. Most of the books targeted at the age group her book was aimed at had elaborate paintings with lots of detail. Her drawings were more simple and spare. Though she liked them and thought they complemented the story, she wondered if an editor would feel the same.

Maybe she should redo the artwork, she thought as she rubbed the back of her neck. In fact, maybe she should throw it all out and start over. Everyone had a few practice books in them before they got published. She was sure she could do a better job on the next book, on the next drawing. She could do better, given more time.

But that would be chickening out, and she swore she'd never do that again.

Before she could give herself time to think about it, she took the disk and hard copies and slid them into an envelope. She wrote a quick cover letter, quashing the tremendous urge to apologize for what was inside. Almost as an afterthought, she wrapped the oil painting she'd used for inspiration, dashed off a quick note explaining that she had more experience working in that medium and could furnish artwork in that form if it was preferred.

She picked up both packages, but found her feet rooted to the floor. *She was really going to do this.* She was really going to send her book to an agent.

She felt a little queasy.

She sat on the sofa and stared at the door. The urge to call Colt, to let him know what she was doing and let him encourage her, was almost overwhelming. He would tell her he believed in her, that he had faith in her. He would make her believe this wasn't a foolish dream she was pursuing.

Where was her faith in herself? Before he'd come back to Aloma, she wouldn't have dreamed of leaning on someone else for encouragement, because there had never been anyone else to lean on.

She looked at her watch, stood and marched out the front door, not giving herself time to think, to reconsider. Like everything else, she blocked the doubts from her mind. In less than half an hour the post office would be closing, but it would only take a few minutes to get into town and get this mailed off. Then it would be out of her hands.

Her determination carried her down the front steps and to her car.

Which had a flat tire.

Colt closed his toolbox and straightened to see Becca standing before him, holding an armful of packages. He smiled at her, experiencing a rare moment—the satisfaction of hard work, the warm summer sunshine, and the pretty girl standing in front of him all came together to make him glad he was there.

It chafed to acknowledge how glad he was to see her, how relieved that she'd come to him after a week of brushing him off. But it had been a good day. This morning when he did his back exercises, he noticed an improvement from the weeks before. And the work on the house was progressing, giving him a sense of satisfaction he hadn't often known. And now Becca was before him, looking pretty enough to kiss. So he pushed the thoughts aside and smiled again.

Becca cocked a brow at him and offered a puzzled smile, when he tweaked the end of her nose and gave her a quick kiss, in front of Pete and Jas. Apparently she hadn't seen him like this often. Probably because he hadn't *felt* like this often. He told himself it was because Pete, Jas and he were making quick time of the renovations, his back felt good, and he could get back on the road sooner than expected.

The thought of being back on the road dragged at his good mood, though, so he stepped up and gave Becca another, more thorough kiss. Several things, including his mood, lifted immediately.

"Hello," he said, pulling a worn rag out of his back pocket and wiping his hands. He nodded at the envelope. "What's that?"

"Just my work this week for Dunleavy's." She held the envelope tight to her chest. "I was going into town to mail it, but my car has a flat. Can you give me a ride?"

"Sure. Or I can take it and mail it for you." He reached out to take the package, but she stepped back.

"No, that's okay. I—I have to talk to Willa at the post office, anyway."

"No problem. Hey Pete," he turned and called. Pete walked around the back of the house, carrying a shovel. "You ready to knock off for the day? I'm going to give Becca a ride into town."

"Sure, boss. Hey, Becca, how's it going? I need to stop at the hardware store, too, if we have time."

Colt drove them back to Becca's house first, where the two men took the flat off and Colt threw it in the back of the pickup. Becca watched, fidgeting and checking her watch. Colt glanced up and grinned. "In a hurry?"

"Well, the post office is going to close in fifteen minutes."

"Then, we'd better get going. I'll just leave the car jacked up and put the spare on when we get back, okay? We'll drop this one off with Johnny—he's still fixing flats, isn't he?"

* * *

When they got to town, Colt dropped Becca at the post office and the tire at Johnny's service station, then went with Pete to the hardware store. When Becca finished at the post office, she walked over to the hardware store and waited in Colt's pickup.

She clasped her hands around her knees, fluctuating on a moment-by-moment basis between being thrilled she'd mailed her manuscript, and horrified and sure she'd made a mistake. The agent would never agree to represent it. Worse, he would take one look, and laugh at the very idea behind her book and the obviously untalented and uneducated writing. He would cringe at the artwork. He would send it back on the next post and tell her never to submit to them again.

Or, he could love it, pound the pavement until he had an offer for a twelve-book contract and a fat advance check.

She groaned and dropped her head back on the seat. The door opened beside her, and Pete climbed in.

"You okay?"

"Yeah, just…a headache."

"Mmm." Pete rummaged through the small brown paper sack he'd brought out. "Colt is ordering a bay window for that dining room. He'll just be a few more minutes." He held up a small chrome piece and turned it in the light.

Becca looked inside and watched Colt talk to Terry, the owner of the hardware store. Colt said something, then both men laughed. Becca smiled, not realizing until that moment just how rarely Colt smiled; seeing him actually laugh was even rarer. She had to admit that for the past week she'd avoided him, had been afraid that being around him made her more vulnerable to him. Seeing him like that affected her more than was comfortable.

But she was strong, wasn't she? The fact that she'd just

taken a giant leap—without Colt's help—and could still manage to breathe was proof of that.

She wasn't like Mama. She wasn't going to lose control, lose herself in being with Colt. She'd learned long ago to hold a part of herself back, to keep it locked away and safe. She would need that part of herself when Colt left again.

He laughed again and said something that had Terry laughing, too. As much as Colt disliked the idea of being back in Aloma, something here agreed with him.

The thought drifted through her mind that maybe it was her, and she let it sit there for a few minutes before she realized how good it made her feel. She decided to get her mind on something else. Someone else.

She turned to Pete. "Is Bradley enjoying his summer vacation?"

"Oh, yeah. His sixteenth birthday is next week, and he's driving us crazy with everything he wants. JoAnn's planning a party. You ought to come out."

"I doubt he'd be thrilled to have a schoolteacher at his birthday party. Especially during the summer when most students feel like they've been freed from jail—" She realized her error as soon as it was out, and brought her knuckle to her mouth.

He just laughed, though, still looking at whatever it was he held in his hand. "I know how he feels. I felt the same way when I was a kid. I guess all kids do."

"I suppose so," Becca said, relieved she hadn't offended him. When she was younger, Becca had hated to see summer vacation come. She'd always wished Aloma would switch to year-round classes.

"Do you think Jeremy will come to the party?" She hesitated to ask the question, but Becca knew the boy well, and both JoAnn and Pete had been open and honest about the problems they'd had with their older son.

Pete dropped the part back in the bag and shook his

head. "I hope so. He's crazy about his little brother, and he wouldn't hurt him for anything. Unless it meant hurting me, too."

Colt climbed into the cab. "Who's hurting you?"

Becca cast a quick glance at Pete. Colt knew about Pete's situation, but she wasn't sure Pete was comfortable discussing it. It certainly wasn't her place to enlighten him.

But Pete leaned up and looked Colt squarely in the eye. "We're talking about Jeremy. You met him out at the house, remember? Bradley's birthday is next week, and we're hoping Jeremy's grudge against me isn't going to keep him away from the party."

He maintained the eye contact after he'd stopped talking, and Becca looked from one man to the other. Neither said anything, and neither did anything. But the sudden tension between them was as palpable as the vinyl seat at her back.

"Hmm," Colt said. Without another word he started the pickup and drove out of the parking lot.

"Is he still terribly angry with you?" Becca asked Pete.

"I assume he is. He won't speak to me. He only comes out to the house when he knows I won't be there. It's tearing JoAnn apart." The anguish he tried to keep from his voice proved JoAnn wasn't the only one being torn apart. "We're all so ready to put this whole mess behind us. But he won't let it go."

"Give him time. He'll come around. A person needs his family."

Colt made a noise beside her, and Becca turned. "What?"

"Nothing." His knuckles stood out white on the hand that gripped the steering wheel, and the corner of his jaw twitched. His eyes remained firmly on the road before them, and he didn't make another sound until they pulled up in the Huckaby's driveway.

Pete grinned when he saw JoAnn on the porch. She came out to the pickup, kissed her husband, and greeted Becca and Colt.

"Did you get the parts?"

Pete held up the paper bag. "I hope this fixes it." He turned back to Colt and Becca. "I did some work for an old boy over in Merkel a few weeks ago. When the job was over he told me he didn't have any money, so he paid me with an old broken-down dirt bike. If I can get it running, it's going to make a good birthday present for Bradley."

"You've got a few hours to work on it. Mark Peterson got a new computer game this afternoon, and Bradley's over at their house checking it out. I wouldn't be surprised if he called later and asked to spend the night at the Peterson's."

Pete waggled his brows. "Good. I can use all the time I can get. Thanks for the ride, boss. I'll see you tomorrow."

"Yeah," Colt said gruffly, and moved his fingers in a slight wave.

They pulled back onto the road. Rolling the window down, Colt kept his eyes straight ahead and his mouth shut. Becca scooted over by the passenger door and wondered why she'd gotten herself involved with such a moody person.

He turned in to her driveway, got out and began putting the small spare tire on her car. Becca went inside, and came back a few minutes later with two glasses of iced tea.

"Want to talk about what's bothering you?"

He spun a nut onto a bolt. "Nothing's bothering me." He put the lug wrench on and tightened the nut. From the bulge of his forearm muscles, Becca could see that nut wasn't coming off for a long time.

"You were in a good mood until you heard Pete and me talking about Jeremy. Why does that bother you?"

"Why should it bother me? Why should I care?"

"That's what I was wondering."

"It's his problem, not mine."

"Yes, it is."

"If he's stupid enough to think the kid ought to just forgive and forget everything his own father put him through, he's the one who's going to be disappointed, not me."

"You don't think Jeremy will come around?"

"Why should he? I mean, Pete's a good worker, and I'm glad I hired him. But he screwed up the kid's life."

"Everybody makes mistakes, Colt."

"He didn't just forget to pick the kid up from football practice, Becca. This was more than a mistake. He knew what he was doing, he knew it was wrong, and he knew what could happen. And he chose to do it, anyway. That's more than just a mistake. I can't act like it never happened."

Becca cocked her head and watched, as Colt jacked the car back down to the ground. "Forgiveness isn't easy, Colt. But it's necessary."

"Necessary for what?" he asked with a sneer. "What is it that's so great about pretending something never happened? When you *know* it happened, when you can still *feel* it happening even if it's twenty years later? How is that necessary?"

"It gets rid of the hate in your heart," Becca said quietly, as Colt tossed the tools back in the trunk.

"No, it doesn't. It pushes it back down and it sits there like a big lie. Is that what you want, Becca? Have you gotten rid of the hate in your heart, or have you just painted a new scene over it and pretended like it was the truth, like your fake window and fake tree in there on the wall?"

Becca glanced down at her fingers twined together in front of her, at the way one finger pulled on the other, then looked back at Colt. "I told you it wasn't easy, Colt. And it's not. But I truly believe forgiveness is necessary. And so I'm trying to forgive Mama."

"How? How can you? God, Becca, when I think how you looked the other day in your garden, and then again in your attic, how upset you were—I've never seen you so torn apart. She did that to you. Just the memory of her did that to you."

"I know that."

"Maybe you can forgive her, but I'm not going to."

"What?"

"I said, maybe you can forgive your mother, but not me. You were *crushed,* Becca. And a week later, you're acting like everything's fine and dandy."

"That's not how I'm acting. I know very well what Mama was like, Colt. I remember more than I care to. I wish I could forget again. But I can't make myself. I think I will always be sad for what I didn't have, just as you will be."

He snorted at that and turned his head. Becca stepped closer, urgent that she answer his question. They both needed to hear it.

"It's a tragedy, really, Colt, that we can't turn back the clock and make it all come out differently. Oh, Colt, when I think of all the ways life could have been different between Mama and me...when I think of all the good, special times we could have had, *should* have had, and remember how she ruined them all with her bitterness and hatred. Of course I resent it. It makes me want to cry to think about all the special memories I should have, all the things she denied both of us. She was wrong. It's just that simple.

"But, Colt, I think she hurt me because *she* hurt. All that anger and hatred was directed at me, but she meant it for someone else. When she looked at me, she saw someone else.''

"Who?'' Colt asked.

"Someone who hurt her. Someone who hurt her badly enough to leave her bitter to everyone. There's nothing I can do now to change that, just as there was nothing I could do then to change it. The only thing I can change is what is in my heart, and make sure I don't take the hatred she gave me and carry it on. I won't do that. I won't foster it and let it grow. It's stopping with me. Someday, I'm going to have a family of my own. And if I don't forgive her, all I'll do is pass on the same mistakes she made.''

Because the urge was so strong to put her arms around him, to let his presence comfort her the way she wanted to comfort him, she folded her arms across her chest and leaned back against the trunk. "I won't be like you, Colt. I won't nurse those memories and let the hurt build a wall around me. I won't use it as an excuse to keep from getting close to anyone, to trust anyone or even myself. I won't live that way. I'm not going to make the same mistakes she made.''

She expected him to turn away, half wanted him to turn away. But he stood and stared at her, with something she couldn't read in his eyes.

"Yeah, well, a fat lot of good it's doing me, isn't it? I'm here, aren't I? I follow you around like a stupid mutt, don't I? I look up, and you're standing there, and before I know it I'm thinking you're the best damn thing I've seen all day. And that's on a good day. On a bad day, I take one look at you and feel like you're the only good thing left in my life.''

He pulled himself away from the car and dug his keys out of his pocket. "And all you do is push me away. For all your talk about open hearts, you haven't had any trouble at all putting up a wall against me over the past week.'' He swallowed and tilted his head. "But I guess you're saving that forgiving heart for the real Prince Charming. Someday.''

As he walked away, Becca leaned against the car and kept her arms wrapped tightly around her waist to keep from calling him back.

He was right. Of course he was right. She had put up a wall against him. It shamed her to know she was taking the coward's way out.

But she also knew she had to survive. Maybe she hadn't been ecstatically happy with her life before Colt came, but she had been content. She couldn't give that up, too, when he left.

She was afraid of the pain that would burn her until her eyes were as full of bitterness and pain as Mama's had been.

So she had to keep up a wall, until the man came she could give her heart to, on her own terms. And Colt Bonner was not that man.

The sharp knock at the door startled Becca out of her reverie. She stuck her finger in the paperback she was pretending to read, and lifted the curtain.

Colt stood on her doorstep. And he didn't look happy.

Fighting the urge to launch herself into his arms when she opened door, she flipped on the porch light but left the screen closed. "Hi.''

"I was in town so I picked up your tire at Johnny's. I already put it on, and the spare's back in the trunk.''

"You did? I didn't even hear you." Her heart ached at how good it was to see him. She'd been despondent all afternoon, knowing she'd hurt him, amazed that she could.

"Yeah, well…'' He rubbed his chin and looked off, then shoved his hands in his pockets. "You busy?''

"Very. I'm reading the same paragraph over and

over.'' She leaned her head against the doorjamb. ''Do you want to come in?''

''I was going to see if you'd like to come out. Maybe go for a drive.''

''It's after ten o'clock.''

''You have a curfew?'' He grinned at her, such a lopsided, unsure grin that she would have gone anywhere with him.

''Let me get my shoes.''

She slipped into loafers and met him on the porch. When they got to his pickup she started to move around to the passenger door, but he took her hand and held the driver's door open for her. She slid onto the bench seat and sat in the middle, a little amused at herself for being so thrilled to feel the outside of his thigh warm and solid against hers, to marvel at the muscle play when he shifted gears as he drove.

It was okay, she told herself as she watched the blinking dotted line of the highway being gobbled up by the headlights. He was right; she'd built a wall. So she could allow her head to be turned by him, allow him to bring out in her all those feelings most women experienced at sixteen. It was a physical thing, a chemical reaction. And it was okay, because she knew what she was getting into.

If this afternoon had done anything, it had confirmed in her mind just where her boundaries lay. She and Colt had a shared history, a similar difficult background, and a very real and touching connection now.

I see you and feel like you're the only good thing left in my life.

Declarations like that—if she believed them—had the power to make her want more. Had the ability to make her start expecting more. Had the power to have her begging for more. *If* she believed them, which she would never, ever be stupid enough to do.

She had known going into this, of course, that she must

be very careful. She'd learned throughout her life that wanting more than life gave only brought disappointment. She had learned to accept and be satisfied with what life brought. All her brave vows to take control of her life and go after what she wanted had taken her a long way. But her trip to the attic, her final confrontation with Mama's ghosts, had proved that this trip was a short one, and one she'd better enjoy while it lasted.

And she could handle that. Because she deserved what she was experiencing now, the warm glow and feeling of…possession as she rode beside Colt through the dark. She knew where the danger lay. Danger lay in ignoring the fact that this was a temporary fling. In pretending for even a second that it could ever be more. She was sowing some wild oats, finally. And Colt was…

She didn't know what all this meant to Colt. Mama had always said men wanted one thing and that was all. That Colt cared for her as a friend, she had no doubt. But she also knew just as surely that the physical relationship between them meant nothing more permanent to him than it did to her.

And that was okay, she told herself, yet again, as the telephone poles flashed by in the night.

Yes, she knew where the danger lay. She knew the line that she would not cross, the line that divided a beautiful moment in time that she could cherish for the rest of her life, and the other side. Begging for more than was offered. Becoming bitter and filled with hate when the ''more'' didn't come.

You must not beg like that.

And as long as she kept that in the front of her mind, she was safe. They were both safe. What she'd experienced with Colt was special, and beautiful, and she would not ruin it for them both.

She didn't ask where they were going, content to let Colt show her when he was ready. They drove past the town, past the cotton gin and the turnoff to the lake. He turned the pickup onto a dirt road that wound up a hill. As they bounced along, Becca looked sideways at him. His jaw was firm, his face solemn, but he wasn't vibrating with anger the way he had been that afternoon.

They reached the top of the hill, and he stopped, killing the lights. The darkness engulfed them immediately, until her eyes grew accustomed. The moon was bright enough to cast shadows from the rocks, squatty mesquites and yucca plants that dotted the hill.

Colt opened the door and took her hand, leading her easily into the dark. He moved around the back of the pickup and opened the tailgate, leading her up to sit on it. Still he said nothing.

She told herself she enjoyed the quiet and the time with him, until the thought occurred to her that he'd brought her here to break up with her. She was prepared for that, she told herself, even as her stomach slid and her heart started a sickening thud. She'd lived with disappointment before, she reminded herself, and could get through this, too, given time. Several decades.

She couldn't take the not knowing anymore. "What are we doing here?" she whispered.

"Shh."

Okay. She couldn't take it anymore. "Listen, about this afternoon—"

"Shh," he said again. He turned to her and took her hands in his, his eyes dark and brooding as they looked into hers.

He was silent for a while. Her dread built. He had something he didn't want to tell her. Which could only mean one thing.

But finally he spoke. "I just wanted to be with you. Just for a little while. Just you, without your mother, or Doff, or Pete and his problems, or anyone else. I thought it might be easier if we were up here, away."

He turned to face her, his voice soft in the still night, the moonlight silvering one side of his face, casting the rest in shadow. "I just wanted to be with you for a while."

The tortured look in his eyes had her stroking his eyebrow. "Shh," she whispered, though he didn't say anything else. "We are. It's just you and me, right now."

She leaned up and kissed the lines her fingers had tried to smooth away, then his cheekbone, then his mouth. Up here, away from town, away from everyone else, it was easy to believe they were the only people in the world. It was easy to believe all the problems in their past were *in* the past, and couldn't touch them here. It was easy to believe everything was good and solid and easy between them.

It was dangerously easy to believe it would always be this way.

He lay back and pulled her gently down with him, until she rested against his chest, her chin on her folded hands. They lay like that for a time, her staring into his eyes, the moon casting every plane of his face in sharp relief. He threaded his fingers through her hair again and again, his eyes solemn and unwavering on her.

"That's the most beautiful thing I've ever seen," he said, in a voice so unlike his own that she wondered if she was imagining it. "The moonlight through your hair is like something out of one of your fairy stories. It takes my breath away."

He rolled over then, tucking her up close to him and kissing her.

She closed her eyes and prayed for the strength she knew she would need, not to beg when it was all over.

Chapter 10

As epiphanies went, Becca thought the next morning, this one wasn't up there with the theory of gravity, or even the invention of the waffle iron. It was a simple statement, after all, and one she'd repeated to herself many times over the years.

It's not your fault.

She shouldn't have been blindsided by the realization, not so much so that she actually gasped and felt the world tilt. She'd told Colt that she knew Mama's anger had been directed at her but meant for someone else. And a part of her had understood that, and meant it.

But somewhere in all her supposedly enlightened talk and civilized declarations of understanding, a part of her still believed she had done something wrong, or that something had been fundamentally wrong with her. That it had, in fact, been her fault.

Telling herself she wasn't to blame, even telling Colt that, was a universe away from believing it herself.

When the realization finally struck her, it did so with

the force of a blow. Not being to blame meant there was no real reason for her ever to have been different.

All those years of wondering what she'd done to make everything wrong for Mama, wondering what she could do to make it right, and finally, the last years of accepting the knowledge that it wasn't anything she'd done at all, simply that she'd *been*, that had made everything all wrong—all those years, and all along none of Mama's unhappiness had been her fault.

Of course, this revelation came through the eyes of an adult, a logical, sympathetic adult. A part of her wondered, even now—especially now!—what would have happened to Mama if she hadn't become pregnant. Would she and Rob have stayed together? Would he have left his wife for Mama? What had Mama been like, back then? The letters referred to the passion they shared, the way she made him laugh, the way she brought joy to him, remembering the silly things they'd shared, private jokes that brought a smile to his face in the middle of the day. It was impossible to imagine Mama being silly, even as a young girl. She must have been a different person then.

Since Becca had found the letters, she hadn't stopped wondering about what love had done to Mama. Losing her love, or bearing Becca, or both, had made Mama lose everything that made her joyful, everything that was carefree and innocent and good. Becca had taken from her Mama everything that made her lover want to be with her, and left her only the bitterness and rage that made him leave.

It's not your fault.

Becca rubbed her forehead, tired to her core of letting these thoughts spin through her head. Between trying not to think about Colt, her determination to write another book as quickly as possible, and dodging thoughts of Mama—not to mention the man in the picture—her mind had been spinning so she wondered if she wasn't going crazy. She certainly wasn't getting anything done.

She'd once been good at escaping. Mama had belittled her so many times for daydreaming. But whenever she had the chance, Becca remembered with a sad smile, she had escaped into that private world of her own. A world that Mama couldn't even begin to touch, and could not ruin with her hatred.

Close your mouth, you tryin' to catch flies? You look like a retard.

In that moment of deep, soul-searing pity for that lost child, Becca felt, truly *felt* for the first time that there was no reason for her life to have been that way at all. There was nothing preordained that meant she couldn't be happy. From the very first moment of her life, she had been nothing more than a helpless victim between two people who, even now, she barely knew.

She'd told Colt that she understood his anger toward his father, that she felt it just as he did but intended to put the anger and resentment behind her. And all along the truth was, she'd run from that anger, too cowardly to look it in the eye.

Until now. Now, with the realization that it really *wasn't* her fault, her mind cracked open so suddenly and clearly that it actually hurt, and she saw for the first time how she'd been cheated. She saw not only how she'd been robbed of her childhood back then, but how that still affected her now.

Like a torrent, images swept into her mind of all the ways her shyness and awkwardness had robbed her of what she could have been. What might her life have been like, if she'd been given just a little encouragement, just a kind word once in a while? Would her voice still quake every time she had to stand up in a group of adults and speak? Would she have to work up her nerve just to say hello to someone she passed in the grocery store, someone she'd known all her life? Would she still have to give herself pep talks before dealing with a wayward student?

Would she be stuck here, in this house, telling herself she was content and had everything she needed? Would she, at thirty years old, still be trying to convince herself that she was content with life's leftovers?

An emotion filled her that was so foreign and so frightening, and yet so right, that she couldn't contain it. Anger. Rage. Righteous, indignant fury. It ate at her. Clawed at her. Made her very skin itch. It thrummed through her veins, making her muscles twitch, her mind race, her nails bite into her palms.

What had Mama done to her? What had that hateful, spiteful, bitter old woman and her self-centered, cold-blooded lover made her? A frightened little rabbit, afraid to live, afraid to do anything, afraid even to try. Even now, presented with the prospect of a lifelong dream made possible, she was paralyzed with fear. And that was nobody's fault but Mama's.

She paced the room, rubbing her bare arms furiously, letting the rage build, giving it free rein to feed on itself. Finally, she was angry. At last, she let glorious, powerful fury flow through her, carry her, lift her up and above the fear. She actually felt taller, bigger, stronger.

For the first time in her life, she made no excuses for Mama. She didn't blame her attitude on poor health or tight finances. She refused to say it was okay, refused to think even for a second that what Mama had done was normal or right.

For the first time in her life, she refused to believe that she'd ever deserved to be treated the way Mama had treated her. Yesterday she'd told Colt that it made her sad to think of all the things she'd missed out on. She'd gone on and on like a simpering idiot about how she refused to carry hate in her heart.

Well, she had hate in her heart now. She spun on her

heel and slammed a fist into her palm. Throbbing, white-hot hate. For the first time in almost four years, she wished Mama was here again. Here, standing before her so Becca could scream at her, shake her until her teeth rattled. Make her pay.

The fury clawed inside her until she saw nothing but red, felt nothing but the electric current of it. She was moving, mumbling, scene after scene of Mama's hateful eyes, hateful voice, hateful words flowing through her mind. But now, instead of blocking the memories out, she let them come, welcomed them. And with every word she heard in her head, she fought back. Fought with her fists, fought with her voice, fought with her mind. She picked up a book, hurled it at the wall, hurled it at Mama.

She fought back, avenged that innocent child who had done nothing except be brought into the world through someone else's choosing. She fought the memories with her fists, with her own thoughts. Again and again she heard the satisfying *thud* of books, the knock of brushes, the crash of jars as they slammed against the wall and landed on the floor. Every blow was a blow for that child, the child who had had no one else to fight for her.

Colt walked in just in time to see her throw a jar of royal-blue paint at the wall. For a moment he felt disoriented, as if he'd stepped into another dimension, one where Becca looked like Becca but was in fact someone entirely different.

Frozen, he stood in the doorway and watched as she picked up another book and threw it. It slid and landed in a puddle of blue and yellow paint. She had her back to him, her sides heaving, her fists clenching and unclenching. She stared at the mess she'd made, and a low, pitiful sound emerged from her throat.

''Oh, baby.'' He hadn't meant to say it out loud, hadn't

meant for her to hear the sympathy in his voice. But she heard, he knew from the way her whole body jerked.

She turned slowly, and when he saw her face he was struck once again with the bizarre thought that the person before him wasn't really Becca. His Becca's face would never contort in rage like that. Her smile would not thin to this slash of a mouth. Her eyes would not glitter with fury the way this woman's eyes did.

He knew, of course, that such a notion was ridiculous. Knew it because, strange as it seemed on Becca, he recognized the emotion he saw there. Knew what it was, and felt unbearably sad and somehow responsible to finally see it mirrored there on her face.

So when she came at him, he half expected her to turn that rage on him. Expected it, and didn't turn away. Instead, he held his arms out, and she threw herself into them.

He meant to comfort her, to let her pour herself out to him and release all that energy he could see was still strumming through her.

He wasn't prepared when she latched on to him and pulled his head down so she could crush her lips to his. Her hands roamed over him—anxious, fretful hands that tugged at his clothes while her lips cruised over his lips, his face, his throat. She backed him against the wall, pulled his shirt loose from his jeans, and began sliding it up his ribs, her hands hot and her eyes blazing with an intensity that had his blood going full throttle.

"Becca, what's—?"

Before he could get any further, her mouth was over his, blocking the question. "Shh," she hissed between her teeth as she leaned in to him.

He cupped her jaw between both hands and forced her to look him in the eye. In unison, their breath came ragged and loud in the silent room.

He recognized that wild look in her eyes. Raw determination, defiance, anger. The same things he'd felt before climbing on the back of a bull. And he understood immediately his place in this drama.

"You don't want—"

"Please stop telling me what I want."

He couldn't catch his breath or regain his balance. His senses were full of her. "Okay, then I'll tell you what *I* want." He took her hands between his and held them still between them. "I want you to tell me what happened. I want to know what's going on. And I *don't* want you to use this—" he looked down, at the place where their bodies touched "—as an escape from whatever's going on in your head."

"All right, I'll tell you what's going on. I'm mad."

"I see that."

"I don't think I've ever been mad before. Not really. And I don't know how to handle it."

He looked around at the mess she'd created. "This is one way, I guess."

"And I'll tell you something else. I'm tired of you treating me like a china doll. I want to be treated like a woman. Like a real woman." She tugged her hands free of his and slipped them around his neck. "I don't want to be treated like a precious ornament that needs to be packed away in cotton and protected from everything. I want you to treat me like a woman who has something you need, an adult who can give as well as take. That is what is going on, Colt."

She stepped back, gave him a look that shot straight through him. "Now. Are you sorry you asked?"

He cradled her face in his hands, his heart full with the knowledge that finally she trusted him enough to drop her guard. He kissed her, fully, finally without holding back. He kissed her the way he'd wanted to kiss her for longer than he could remember.

"No," he said against her lips. "I am definitely not sorry I asked."

Her hands were everywhere at once, quick, nimble slender hands that slid over him and touched off bonfires. He led her down the hall to her bedroom, allowing her to undress him as they went. She had him lost, fighting through a fog of need so intense it burned him from the inside out.

It terrified him, how darkly thrilling it was. He feasted on her neck, tasting her the way he'd wanted to from the very beginning, explored every inch and evoked every moan he'd needed to hear.

And in return, she moved over him with equal fever, taking as he took, giving as he gave. They rolled over the bed, hands tearing at clothes, skin against skin, matching breath for breath, sigh for sigh, heartbeat for heartbeat, until she rose above him and joined him.

He cupped her neck in one hand and urged her to look at him, needing to see the echo of his desire.

"Look at me."

Her eyes squeezed tighter, and the sight shot a hot bolt through him. "You look at me, Becca. This is me with you. I want you to know it's me."

He gentled his hand on her face, stroking his thumb against her lips, over and over. Her eyes froze to his, and what began as a wild storm ended tenderly, with them rocking slowly together, unable to look away.

Afterward, she collapsed against him, and he tucked her head into his shoulder, her hair falling into his face, and breathed in the scent of her.

She rose up on her elbow, her face solemn, and looked him in the eye. With her thumb she smoothed the skin above and between his eyes.

"I was completely out of control," he said.

"I know." Her voice was soft. Her gaze traveled his face, her thumbs and fingers moving softly over his skin.

"I didn't mean to be rough."

"I know that, too."

He waited for her to become angry. He knew now that she was capable of intense rage, had witnessed it himself just moments before.

"Thank you."

He lay silently for a moment, then blinked. "Thank you?"

"Yes, thank you. For trusting me enough to lose control."

He started to tell her that trust had nothing to do with it, that she'd had him on fire and he had been unable to contain it. But that was blaming her, and he'd been the one at fault. She hadn't had any idea what she was getting into.

He consoled himself with the knowledge that at least now she knew the real him, knew what he was capable of. She would no longer romanticize what he was, no longer think she could see past the bad in him.

"Look at you," she said softly, stroking his hair. "Lying there, beating yourself up."

"I'm not going to pretend that I didn't just treat you like—"

"And I thank you for that. Even if you didn't mean to do it, it was exactly what I needed." She moved her hand down and tugged at his chin.

"You needed me. I made you need me, Colt Bonner, and don't you try to deny it."

"Okay," he said weakly. It was, after all, the truth, even if it did feel like he was shirking his responsibility.

"Do you have any idea how that made me feel? Me, the helpless, powerless Becca Danvers, skimming along the surface of life, nothing too bad, nothing too good ever touching me? All my life, Colt, someone else has made decisions for me. I've always accepted them, too, and not once complained. God,'' she said with a disgusted sigh, ''I've been such a weak fool.''

''No,'' he said firmly. He took her chin in his hand and forced her to look at him. ''Don't ever say that. You're one of the strongest people I know. If things are changing for you right now, it's because you're ready for the change.''

The corner of her mouth tipped up, but there was only irony in her eyes, not humor. ''You sound like me. 'Everything happens for a reason.'''

''Maybe it does, I don't know. But I'm not going to lie here and let you call yourself weak. You're stronger than you'll ever know.''

Her face grew solemn again, and he knew that for all her talk, whatever had set her off was still eating at her. He wanted to believe that he could help her with whatever was haunting her. But there was something he had to know first.

''You say that was what you needed. But I saw your face, Becca, and that wasn't a satisfied look.'' He had to know, had to be the one to say it, no matter what she thought her part in all this was. ''It was more than you'd bargained for, wasn't it?''

The cords of her throat moved as she swallowed, but she didn't look away. ''Yes. It was.'' She looked down and traced the tan line at his neck. ''I wanted to make you need me. I wanted to feel powerful and competent and able to take charge. And I did. But I didn't expect to feel such a need, too. I didn't know I could feel like that, could be like that. I did make you need me, but I needed you just as much. It scared me.''

She lay against him and tucked her head up under his chin. Colt stroked her back, long, languid strokes that reached down to her hip, and realized that the line he had been afraid of crossing from the very beginning was behind him now, had been crossed in the space of a heart-beat. And he had no idea how he was going to get back.

They showered together, and afterward Colt stood behind Becca as she dragged a comb through her damp curls. Her lower lip was caught between her teeth, and her eyes had a faraway look. He placed his hands on her shoulders, still wet from their shower, and kissed the top of her head. If she noticed, she didn't react.

She wasn't as comfortable being around him as she'd pretended to be. That was okay, he told himself. No more than he'd expected, no more than was right.

"You want me to leave now?" He was ready for her answer, ready to accept the fact that everything was different now and that she realized she could no longer trust him. She wasn't the type to come right out and say anything, so he'd make it easier for her.

"No." She lay the comb down and turned to him. "I want you to go up in the attic with me."

"The attic?" Nothing about the past hour had made sense.

"You don't have to, of course. I just—there's something up there I need to look at. Something I've been trying not to think about." She curled her upper lip. "I used to be good at not thinking about things. Since you came back, I haven't been able to ignore much of anything."

Now he was the one who wanted to thank her for trusting him. He couldn't get the image of her studio out of his mind, of how lost she'd looked when he'd walked in on her. If whatever was in the attic had something to do with that, he wanted to personally be the one to destroy it for her.

He squeezed her arms and kissed her shoulder. "Let's go."

They dressed, and she pulled down the attic stairs. Her back stiff, she marched up the steps before him. She didn't hesitate as she moved silently through the attic and picked up a round box. She sat on a trunk and held the box in her lap.

Colt opened the window beside them, allowing the evening breeze to freshen the room. He tested a box opposite her with his hand, then sat.

She stared at the box for a long time, and he wasn't sure what he should do. He could feel the dread in her, could feel it build in himself. He wanted to tell her to leave whatever was in the box alone, and that shocked him. If anyone believed in facing up and conquering what was bothering them, he did. It was an entirely different matter, though, when it was Becca sitting there, her thin shoulders braced.

He reached over and took her hand, rubbing his thumb over the back of it. "If you want to wait a while…"

"No." She took a deep breath and cast a quick glance at him. "I already know what's in here. I saw it the other day, when you came up here and found me. But I wasn't ready to look at it yet. I didn't want to admit what it was."

She lifted the lid on the box and sifted through the envelopes and clippings inside. She pulled out a newspaper clipping and handed it over, not looking at him. "I think—no, I know this is my father."

He took it from her and studied the picture. "I never heard you talk about your father."

"Because I never did. I never met him. One time I worked up the nerve to ask Mama who he was. The look she gave me…" She shivered in the warm room. "I never asked again."

She returned her attention to the box and set aside a stack of papers. "These are their notes to each other. Well, his notes to her. There isn't anything in here written by her. Notes and coffee shop receipts and ticket stubs. A bunch of mementos, I suppose."

Her voice was flat and dull, as if this were all removed

from her. She kept digging, and her fingers closed around the envelope at the bottom of the box. She stared at it for a long time, then finally drew it out.

''More letters?''

She shook her head. ''This is my application to art school in New York. The one I thought I'd mailed my senior year in high school. I have no idea how she got ahold of it. But this is it.''

''They never got it?''

She shook her head slowly, and he ached at how old and tired she suddenly looked. ''Never got it. I never had a chance, did I, Colt?''

In a flash, he was on his knees before her, his arm around her waist.

She didn't resist, but she didn't acknowledge him, either. She stared at the envelope, and her eyes hardened. ''I heard somebody say one time that it doesn't matter where you come from, it only matters where you're going. And boy, I latched on to that and believed every word of it.'' She gave a short, bitter laugh. ''But I wasn't going anywhere, was I? I was a fool ever to think I could.''

''Becca, don't do this.'' His hand rubbed up and down the curve of her waist, wanting so badly to take her in his arms and make her forget all of it.

She looked at him, contempt in her eyes. ''How can you even say that to me? You, who carries your bitterness around like a suit of armor, tell me not to admit that she ruined everything for me? She didn't just take my childhood, Colt. She took it all. My entire life. My future. She hated me so much, she couldn't stand to see me have even the chance of a normal life. She had to keep me here, make sure I knew every day of my life what a mistake I was. I'm through pretending it doesn't matter. It does matter, Colt. It matters to me very much.''

His chest hurt for her, he wanted so badly to take all

the hurt and bad feelings from her, gladly would have taken them all inside himself to protect her from them.

"But you've got another chance, Becca. That agent said he'd look—"

Her eyes narrowed. "When did you become so naive, Colt? It is so far past too late for me. Even if that stupid agent did buy anything of mine, it's not the same. It's too late for me to just leave everything and start over. At eighteen, New York and Paris would have been exciting and adventurous. At this age, it would reek of desperation. It would be foolish. I'm too old to be foolish."

He took the box from her and set it aside, pulled her close. She sat stiffly against him, and he could feel that her mind was somewhere else, lost in her own bitterness.

Since he'd walked into the house, he'd felt as if he'd stepped into an alternate universe. Even now, it felt as though their roles had been reversed. He was the one trying to reach out to her. She was the one with the wall of bitterness, holding her away from him even as he held her close.

"What could I have been, if she'd just left me alone? What could my life have been like?"

He wanted to tell her that if the old woman hadn't interfered, she wouldn't have been there for him when he needed her most. That she wouldn't be the woman he couldn't seem to get out of his mind now, couldn't seem to go one hour without thinking about, without wanting to go to.

But that was selfish, and certainly not the dream she had for her life. So he remained silent and held her close. Guilt ate at him, because she'd told the truth when she said he was the one who got her started down this road. If he hadn't come back, hadn't pushed her into pursuing her dream, she would still be content with her life.

He didn't know if she could forgive him for that, and

was sure he wouldn't forgive himself. And even worse was knowing that when she eventually got past this point and was ready to move on with her life, he wouldn't be around to see it.

Chapter 11

Colt sat on the examining table and buttoned his shirt. He drummed his fingers on his knee, bounced his leg impatiently, and checked the door for the fifth time in a minute-and-a-half. Drawing in a big breath of air, he blew it out in a disgusted gust.

He'd had enough of hospitals, doctors' offices and everything medical to last a lifetime. The too-bright lights, the smell. The air that stank of desperate hope and fear and relief and grief blended together, of life ripped of its distractions and pared down to the bare essence. Sitting, waiting—he *hated* waiting—for someone else to decide if he had a future.

He tugged on his boots and hopped down from the table, studying an artist's rendering of the four chambers of the heart.

The door opened, and Dr. Prichart breezed in and flipped the switch for the X-ray light. He clipped two black X-ray sheets to it.

"I still don't believe it," he said, shaking his head.

Colt's stomach dropped. "Believe what?"

"This is incredible." Dr. Prichart stood, transfixed, in front of the X ray. "Who did you say did your surgery?"

Mumbling the name of the doctor in Portland, Colt edged up behind Dr. Prichart and studied the view of his backlit spine.

"Well, the man is a genius. Either that, or you have amazing recuperative powers."

Dr. Prichart shook his head again and clicked his tongue, then began to point out to Colt the details of the X ray. Colt let the words drift by him as he realized the gist of what the doctor was saying.

"I can ride again?" Colt interrupted.

Dr. Prichart turned and scowled at him. "You realize that if that bull's horn had struck you half an inch further to the left, you wouldn't be walking? Or standing, or doing anything but sitting in a wheelchair and breathing through a tube?"

"I realize that. Can I ride again?"

Dr. Prichart sighed. "Sure. Give it another month, please. During which time, you *will* go to physical therapy." He lowered his brow threateningly at Colt.

Since Colt outweighed the guy by at least thirty pounds of solid muscle, it was an idle threat, but Colt nodded, anyway.

"I know you haven't been going. Are you doing your exercises at home?"

"Yeah," Colt said. *Most of the time.*

Dr. Prichart gave him a look but didn't comment.

"Continue the exercises at home. I heard you're renovating your father's house."

Colt grunted. He'd never seen this guy until a few weeks ago. But of course, everyone in the county knew his business.

"Be careful. Don't lift anything heavy."

Colt cast his gaze to the side, and the doctor shook his head.

"I know I'm wasting my breath. But as your doctor, I feel compelled to warn you, even if I know it's going unheeded. Come back in a month and we'll x-ray again. Do you want another Loratab prescription?" He clicked the ballpoint pen in his hand and pulled a prescription pad out of the pocket of his white smock.

Colt shook his head, and the doctor nodded. "I figured a tough guy like you wouldn't need any painkillers." He pocketed the pad, but continued to click the pen restlessly.

He turned again to look at the X rays. "If the X rays still look okay next month, and if you still want to get yourself killed on the back of a bull, I don't see any reason to stop you. Besides common sense, I mean."

Colt cleared his throat, feeling a little dazed. This wasn't what he'd expected, not at all.

"I thought my career was over."

Dr. Prichart unclipped the X rays from the light and shrugged. "By all rights, it should have been. Someone upstairs was watching out for you. You can thank God and your surgeon.

"Of course, proper gratitude would be to take the gift you've been given and protect it. But, as my wife is always telling me, I'm just a doctor. I'm not God, and it's not my decision. It's your body, your life. Do whatever you want with it."

His career wasn't over. Colt sagged into a chair and rubbed his chin. Doff, in his dying moment, had not taken his career from him. For over three months, he'd harbored the bitter knowledge that Doff had finally gotten the last laugh. But he'd been wrong. For three months, he'd burned with a hatred that was unnecessary, that was just plain wrong. And for some stupid, insane reason, now that he knew it wasn't true, now that he should have felt relieved, elated, avenged, he only felt...drained.

Whatever he wanted. That's what the doctor said. He could do whatever he wanted.

The bitch of it was, he no longer had any idea what that was.

Possibly the last person Becca expected to hear when she answered the phone was someone claiming to be the owner of the Kline Agency.

She thought at first it must be a joke. But it definitely wasn't Colt's voice, and he was the only one who knew about her book. She hadn't even told him yet that she'd sent it in.

As she stood in the front hallway wondering how to respond, the voice asked again, "Hello? Are you there?"

"Yes, yes, I'm sorry. I'm here."

"I wanted to let you know I looked at your submission. How long have you been writing children's books?"

Too shocked to lie, she blurted out the truth. "About two weeks."

He mumbled something that sounded suspiciously like "I should have known."

Even as her heart sank, Becca asked herself what she had expected. She hadn't really thought he would take one look at her book and fall in love with it, had she? "I suppose I made a lot of beginner mistakes."

"Mmm, a few. We can correct them. What I meant is that people tend to get bogged down with what they've heard are the do's and don'ts. Which, unfortunately, means they give up a lot of freshness and originality. You don't have that problem. Quite a few others, but freshness and originality aren't any of them."

"Oh." Not having a clue as to whether this was a good phone call or a bad one, she didn't have any idea what to say, either.

"You have others, don't you?"

"Others?"

"Other books. I tell you, I'm not sure what I expected—something about cowboys and bull riders, I suppose. I'm a big fan of your boyfriend's, and my grandson is an even bigger fan. He's going to get a big kick out of that rigging, I guarantee you. And to tell the truth, I figured I'd take a quick look at your proposal, hate it and send it back. Bonner said Evan could keep the rigging no matter what. But this book… I really think I might be able to sell this book."

Her breath caught somewhere in her chest, Becca finally managed to squeeze out a "Really?"

"I'm not guaranteeing it. And it's going to need some work. How long did it take you to write this?"

Thirty years, she wanted to say. "A week."

"Well, it shows. But I think you've got a good skeleton here, and if you're willing to do some work on it, I think I might be able to take it somewhere. Generally, if I see a lot of work is going to need to be done, I send out a thanks-but-no-thanks letter and see if you've got the stamina to revise and resubmit. I don't have a lot of time to baby young writers along."

"No, sir." She felt as if she was in one of the high school football coach's preseason pep talks.

"But I really think we can pull something out of this. And it doesn't hurt anything that you've got ties to Colt Bonner. I told you I'm a big fan."

"Yes, sir."

"When's he coming back to the circuit? He could have taken that ride in Denver without breaking a sweat. Those clowns couldn't make a good show of riding the mechanical horses outside the grocery store."

Becca opened her mouth to say she didn't know when Colt would be back, but it soon became apparent Mr. Kline wasn't waiting for an answer.

"Working on anything else?"

She expected him to interrupt her again, so she hesitated before she answered. "I've been kicking around a few ideas." Of its own free will, it seemed, her knee started to bounce, the idea finally sinking in that she might actually sell her first book. Her first book! "Nothing finished yet, but some...ideas." She dug her fingers into her knee to stop the shaking. "I'm working on something right now. It's called *It's Not Your Fault.*"

"Good. Why don't you put together a proposal. You know what that is?"

"Yes." She'd find out.

"Good. Put together a proposal for, say, three more ideas. I don't want to go banging on doors and sticking my neck out for one book. I want a client I know can produce consistently. You did the writing and artwork yourself, right?"

Her knee bounced harder, and she ground her fist into it. "That's correct."

"Sometimes that's harder to sell. Houses have artists they like working with. Looks they know their readers will buy. But I'll do what I can in that direction."

Her knee bounced so hard that her heel started to knock against the floor. She stood, but sat again when she felt as if she might pass out.

Kline didn't seem to notice that she wasn't talking. "Okay, here's what I'm going to do. I'm going to look back over your package and make a few suggestions. I'll have it in the mail to you in a few days. You look it over, see if you can make the changes. Keep in mind, you're not held to anything. You don't have to do anything you don't want to do. Of course, I won't represent it as it is. And you'd be free to pursue another agent. But I don't think you should worry too much about the changes. I won't ask you to change anything that will affect what you're trying to say. Just clean it up a little."

"Of course." She grabbed a handful of flannel shorts

leg and wadded it up, wondering if this was actually happening. "I'm sure it will be fine."

"Good. Look for it in a few days. In the meantime, get those other ideas down and we'll see if we can sell a few books."

Becca stared at the phone for a full five minutes after she hung up. She saw that her shorts were still wadded in her hand, and she stood and smoothed out the wrinkled mess. Someone—someone who didn't even know her!—thought her story held promise. Thought there was a possibility.

She couldn't wait to tell Colt, and to thank him for getting her started.

Becca grimaced. She'd vowed she wasn't going to go running to Colt at every opportunity. She wasn't going to get into the trap of needing him.

Too late, a voice inside said.

She ignored that voice. Colt deserved to know. If he hadn't pushed her, she never would have written the book.

She looked out the kitchen window to see if his pickup was at his house. He'd said he had a doctor's appointment that afternoon, but he was back now, sitting on the back porch with Jas. She felt her face break into a grin. He was going to be so proud of her!

Jas sat on the back porch and blew smoke rings. Colt watched the rings drift up, slowly, stretching bigger and bigger until they shredded gently apart.

"The house looks pretty good," Jasbo said absently. "I guess we're finished, except for the trim. Are you going to do any landscaping before you put it up for sale?"

Colt nodded, only half listening. *Whatever he wanted.* He couldn't seem to get that concept out of his head.

Jas sat on the step below Colt and rested his elbows on his knees. "It was bad, huh?"

Colt rubbed his chin and nodded, before he realized he had no idea what Jas had just said. "What?"

"At the doctor's office this afternoon. Bad news."

Colt dragged his mind back to reality. "No, actually, it was good news."

"What did he say?" Jas turned and looked at Colt intently.

"That I have to go back to physical therapy, and I shouldn't lift anything heavy. But in about a month, everything ought to be back to normal."

"And you can ride again?"

"Yeah. I can ride again."

Jas stared at him for a moment, then turned and looked down at his hands clasped between his knees. He heaved a great sigh. "What a relief." His voice sounded a little strangled.

Colt drew his head back. Jas acted as if it was his own career that was at stake. And in that instant, it became perfectly clear. Why Jas was here, why he jumped in and took over every time Colt tried to lift anything. It was more than just concern. Jas felt responsible.

When Jas spoke again, his voice was tight. "I thought I'd ended your career, Bonner. I really did."

Colt felt like an ass for keeping Jas hanging. He should have known how he would feel. The guy considered himself as infallible as a bullfighter. Probably because he was damn close to it.

But this time, it didn't matter how good Jas was. When Rascal tossed him, Colt had no one to blame but himself. And he would have told Jas that, months ago, if he'd been able to admit it to himself.

"You didn't end anything, Jas. You saved my life."

"I let that one get away, Bonner. And you paid for it."

"Just because you saved my butt from getting trampled a few dozen times, you think you can do anything."

"I should have been quicker. He had you pinned up

against that wall, and I honestly thought he was going to run you through. I should have gotten there quicker.''

"It was my fault." Colt couldn't stand it anymore, seeing Jas beat himself up for something that had nothing to do with him. He stood and walked over to lean his back against the support post of the porch. "It was my own fault. I wasn't focused. I shouldn't have even gotten tossed on that ride."

"But—"

"I said it was my fault." Colt swallowed against the irritation in his voice. It wasn't directed at Jas, but at himself. *Just spit it out, Bonner,* he told himself.

He stuck his thumbs in his pockets, studying the toe of his scuffed boot. "Right before that ride, this girl came up, from the front office of the coliseum. She had a message for me. She said she'd been trying to track me down all day. My father had died that morning, she said. My father was dead."

It was the first time in twelve years that Colt had called Doff that. Not by his name. Not by some derogatory term like "the old drunk" or "the sorry bastard." He called him "my father."

Colt cleared his throat and refused to look at Jas. "Anyway, that was about ten minutes before I rode. And I kept thinking about this stupid, sappy song I heard when I was a kid. It was about this high school football player whose father was blind, and the old man died one night before a game. The kid played his heart out and won the game, because it was the first time his father had seen him play. I kept thinking that it was the first time Doff had seen me ride." His face twisted in a grimace of a smile. "Except it rattled me. I couldn't focus. And I got tossed."

"You should have scratched the ride, Bonner," Jas said.

"Yeah, I should have. But I had too much pride to let Doff spook me. I wasn't going to let him beat me. And when Rascal pinned me up against the fence, I thought, 'Well, this is it. Doff won. He had the last word.'"

Jas was silent for a moment, studying the ground, then he lifted his head again. "Except, he didn't. You can ride again. And you can beat his record."

Colt nodded. "Yeah. I've thought about that."

"I don't think you've thought of anything else *except* beating that record. Not as long as I've known you, anyway." Jas grinned and stood. "I gotta tell you, Bonner. This is a load off my mind. I thought you had lost your dream and it was all my fault. But you can do it. Hell, you'll be back in the running in no time. There's still the better part of the year to compete. You can do it! You've got a chance to beat the world record. You don't have to spend the rest of your life stuck out here in the middle of nowhere, playing house with the pretty schoolteacher."

Colt scowled and stood upright. He saw a slightly shocked look on Jas's face at the same time he heard a rustle behind him. He turned to see the pretty school-teacher standing there.

"Becca!" He shot a look at Jasbo, who looked like he wanted to sink through the porch. "What are you doing here?"

"Just being the pretty schoolteacher," she said, giving him what might have passed for a smile. She looked a little dazed, and the muscles of her throat worked as she swallowed. "You don't have to stop your conversation on my account. Go ahead, really."

Jas lit another cigarette and looked uncomfortable. "I didn't mean any offense, Becca."

"None taken." She smiled at Jas like she couldn't be happier. "Who would be offended at being called pretty?"

Colt moved off the porch and kissed Becca. "I didn't know you were coming over."

"I—um—" She glanced toward the house. "Curtains.

I noticed you didn't have any curtains in the kitchen, and I thought it might help sell the house, you know, make it a little homier, if you did. So…''

"So, you brought curtains?"

"No-o-o." She scratched her head. "I wasn't sure what size. I'll need to measure. That's why I'm here."

She moved past him and into the house. After mouthing, *Shut up,* to Jas, Colt followed her.

Becca stood in the living room looking around. She turned to Colt when she heard his boots on the floor. "It doesn't look like the same place."

"Amazing what a few coats of paint will do." He'd patched up the hole he'd made when he shoved Doff into the wall a dozen years ago. It was as if the Bonner family—such as it was—had never been there.

"It's more than that. You used just the right colors, for this room and for the lighting and everything. It seems…I don't know. New again. Clean. Like a clean slate."

He nodded, walking around the living room, his boots echoing off the wood floors. He'd taken down the dark paneling and resurfaced the walls, painting them a creamy shade of ecru. It made the room look bigger, airier. He'd done the window and door trim in a pale yellow, and cleared the heavy bush away from windows. The result was a sunny room. A room where a small family could spend Sunday morning over a late breakfast, reading the paper.

He knew what she meant. Looking at the room now, it was easy to believe no harsh words had ever been spoken here. No drunken rages had ever been fought. No fists had flown. No tears had been shed.

Becca took a deep breath and smoothed her hair back. "It looks great, Colt. You shouldn't have any trouble getting out of here in time."

"In time for what?"

"To go back on the road with Jas. If you need any help

finishing up, let me know. I have a lot of free time now that school is out."

Colt rubbed his jaw, hard. "You heard Jas?"

"Yes. Colt, it's okay. You can talk about that in front of me."

She turned away and skimmed one finger along the window trim. "I knew," she began. "I knew that you would be leaving. I knew when I started this whole…this whole thing between us, that you would be leaving soon. There's no reason to hedge around the subject in front of me."

"Is that right?" He watched her as she moved slowly around the room, looking at everything but him.

"Yes, that's right. I told you from the first, Colt, I don't expect anything from you but what we agreed on."

"Yeah, part of our *arrangement*." It was okay, he told himself. He certainly didn't need any emotional entanglements or messy goodbyes, either.

She moved to the kitchen, picked up his retractable tape measure from the counter and measured the width of the window.

Letting the tape snap back into place, she turned. Looked at him. Smiled. "I don't want you to be uncomfortable. I know you have a life away from here. I don't blame you for being anxious to get back to it."

He nodded and reached out to take the tape measure from her. He didn't intend to snatch it out of her hands, didn't intend to toss it into a drawer. But he did. And when he was met with her wide-eyed stare, his anger leapt even more.

"Well, that's just great, Becca." He bit the words out. The drawer had popped back open a little with the force of his slam, and he shoved it back in again with a *bang*. She jumped.

"Scaring you?"

She stared at him, then shook her head. "You startled me. But I'm not afraid of you."

"Maybe you should be. Matter of fact, maybe you shouldn't have gotten messed up with me in the first place. You know what kind of background I come from." He slammed the drawer again, looking around and wishing for something else to slam.

"Are you *trying* to scare me?"

He didn't answer.

"You can make me jump, Colt. But you can't make me run. I'm not afraid of you."

"Then, you don't have the sense God gave a rock, because you ought to be. You know as well as I do what I'm capable of."

"I know better than you do."

"What the hell's that supposed to mean?"

"It means I know you're not Doff. I know you're ten times the man he was. I know that, even if you don't." She looked down and toyed with her rings. "I understand that you're anxious to get back to your life, Colt, that this is just a temporary thing between us. You don't have to pick a fight with me, get me mad at you, so you can leave."

It seemed to him he wasn't the one being anxious. "So you don't care if I go?"

"Of course I care. The past few weeks have been great for me, emotional though they've been. But I understand why you have to."

Great for her. Like good therapy, or getting a massage. But she understood. Oh, yeah. That theory of hers that you took what life offered and didn't complain. Nothing was worth fighting for. No matter what it was. No matter what had happened between them.

She was so cool and composed. *Come here, Colt. Go away, Colt. It's all the same to me.*

He rubbed his jaw again, then turned to the back door.

He fished his keys out of his pocket and tossed them to Jas. "Get lost."

He turned back to her, saw her standing in the middle of the kitchen with that cool, serene look that had him itching to rattle her. "The doctor said I can do whatever I want."

Her chest heaved a little, and she smiled. Maybe it was his imagination, maybe he just wanted to see a slight tremble in her smile.

"I'm glad. I'm glad you're okay." She tapped her fingers together. "So...what do you want?"

He stepped close, his blood pumping hot and fast, telling himself it was physical need, only physical, that was pushing him to the edge.

"Right now—" His throat was closed, he was choking on the need to be inside her, the need to prove to her that what was between them mattered. "Right now, I just want you."

Chapter 12

He just wanted her. Even though she had cautioned herself not to grow to need Colt, Becca found herself drawing on the knowledge that he *did* want her the next day as she set out to confront yet another old ghost. She stood at the counter of the tiny post office and watched Willa Barrows sort mail. Willa hadn't heard her come in, and while Becca knew she should alert the older woman, she dreaded doing so.

Confrontation had never been—and undoubtedly never would be—her strong suit.

Willa turned and spotted Becca from the corner of her eye. She gasped and dropped the stack of letters she held. ''Becca Danvers, you scared the life out of me! Don't sneak up on an old lady like that.''

She slid her purple-tinted glasses back up the bridge of her nose and gave an ineffective push at her fluffy white curls. ''What can I do for you? Mailing your assignment for Dunleavy's?''

Becca shook her head. Now that the moment was here,

she wasn't sure she wanted to go through with it. Why was she here? she wondered suddenly, desperately. She was going to be a writer, a published artist and author. She didn't have to go through with this.

But she needed to know. Deserved to know.

She pulled the envelope from her satchel and laid it on the counter. "I need to talk to you about this."

The envelope was surprisingly white, for being over twelve years old. Becca figured it hadn't seen the sun since that day she'd mailed it.

"Is there a problem?" Willa picked up the envelope and studied it. "What's—?"

She froze, and the envelope in her hand began to shake a little. After a moment she looked up and asked Becca, "What's this?"

Becca wasn't sure if it was the rise in Willa's voice, or her wide-eyed look of innocence that gave her away. But Becca was sure Willa was lying.

The spurt of anger that was becoming increasingly familiar leapt within her. Even Willa had betrayed her. Willa, who had no reason to do so.

Becca clenched her jaw and snatched the envelope back. "You know what it is." Training won out over temper, though. Even now, even as the anger bit at her, even knowing she had every right to feel that anger, Becca hesitated to say what she really wanted to say. But she wasn't about to step out of this room without a word.

"You know what it is, Willa Barrows. It's written all over your face. You know what it is, and you know what you did."

She decided to leave it at that. Let the woman deal with her own guilt.

But she got as far as the door before she stopped and turned. "I just—" She faced the older woman and twisted the strap of her satchel. The haunted look in Willa's eye made her own voice catch with emotion she hadn't ex-

pected to feel. "I want to know why." Her voice came
out a strained whisper.

Willa stood silent for a time, then raised the hinged
counter and motioned with her head for Becca to come to
the back. "I suppose you have a right to."

Becca followed her into the back room, where Willa
poured two cups of coffee without asking if Becca wanted
any. Becca sat on an old folding stool and, because her
hands shook, clasped them in her lap.

Willa sat across from her, one foot on the rung of her
chair, one elbow on the metal utility table beside them,
and put her hand to her mouth. Her face was ashen, and
she suddenly looked like such a tired, beaten old woman,
Becca felt guilt mingling with her anger. Telling herself
that she wasn't actually the one who started it did nothing
to relieve her guilt.

"I wasn't going to do it," Willa said. She flattened her
lips together. "I wasn't. Your mama came in and told me
what she wanted me to do, and I just flat refused. That's
a crime, you know. Because it's wrong. It was wrong of
her to ask that."

"But you did it."

Willa nodded almost imperceptibly. "Yes. I did it."

For the first time, Becca began to feel there was a story
behind this whole mess. She leaned back and told herself
to be patient. She needed to hear it, and maybe it would
do Willa some good to tell it.

"Like I said, I refused at first. I never did like your
mother that much. I'm sorry if that's disrespectful, her
being in her grave and all, but she always acted like she
was so much better than everybody else, never would
have anything to do with anybody. But then, I wouldn't
have done what she asked, not for my best friend. After
a solid fifteen minutes of arguing about it, she could see
I wasn't budging, so she told me what was in that envelope. She said at first she didn't want to see you get hurt

by being rejected by that art school. Said you had no talent and didn't have a chance, and she was doing it to protect you.''

Willa rubbed her upper lip and frowned. ''As you can imagine, that didn't exactly sway me. Then she said how, in case you did get accepted, there was no way she was going to let you move all the way to a sin haven like New York City. Said it wasn't a safe place for a young girl to be alone, and how would I like it if something happened to you and it was on my head. That didn't change my mind, either. Finally she turned up that nose of hers and walked stiff as a stick to the door. I couldn't believe the nerve of her, asking me to tamper with the mail like that.''

She cleared her throat and rubbed her lip again. Becca leaned forward on her stool.

''She got to the door, though, and it was like all the starch just went out of her. She stood there, one hand on the door, and just sagged. I could have sworn she got six inches shorter, right before my eyes. She turned around, and her face was as pale as my shirt. She had big tears in her eyes, and that just floored me. Charlotte Danvers, with tears in her eyes. She just stood there, and looked as pitiful as anything I've ever seen, and she said, 'Don't make me beg. Please don't make me beg.' But she was begging. She was begging with her eyes and with her soul. Becca, I could see it. It was killing her.''

Willa shook her head and raised her coffee cup to her mouth with a shaky hand. ''I just—well, I'll never forget it. Never, as long as I live. Like I said, I never liked that woman, but I've never felt sorrier for anyone in my life. Everyone has to let go of their kids at some point, and I know that as well as the next person. It 'bout killed me to see my Paul go off to college. But, Becca, you were all she had. All she had in this world. And both of us standing there that afternoon, we both knew she couldn't make it without you. I felt in that moment that I could either help her, or help plan her funeral a few months down the road.''

Becca had come to the post office expecting confrontation, hoping for an explanation and perhaps vindication. She hadn't, even for a second, expected to feel such an overpowering urge to see her mother again, to throw her arms around her neck and do whatever she could to break through that icy wall. A renewed, raw sense of loss struck her, and she resented it. She'd been through enough. After everything else, it wasn't fair for Mama to come out looking like a martyr.

''I was wrong to do what I did,'' Willa said. ''And if you want to press charges, I won't deny it. It's a crime, like I said. If I don't go to jail, I'll at least lose my job and my pension. But I suppose somebody has to pay for what we did to you, and I'm as guilty as she was. But I'll tell you what, Becca. If I had it to do over again, I'd do the same thing.'' She shook her head again. ''I never saw anything as pathetic as your mama that day, standing there shaking and crying. It shook me up. It really did. And I knew I couldn't live with myself if I didn't help her, wrong as it was.''

Willa was still shaken up, Becca saw. It shook Becca up as well, and she didn't like it. She'd become comfortable in the past week, seeing Mama as a one-dimensional, self-centered, embittered woman. Seeing her that way took all the blame and responsibility from her own shoulders. She wasn't ready to take the load back on again.

She rose on unsteady legs and picked up her satchel. She wasn't sure what to say, didn't trust herself to speak. She didn't even know what to think. But she knew she didn't like this new feeling. The anger had been a defense, a way of making sense of it all.

This pity for her own mother, for the woman who had taken her life and manipulated it beyond all reason...there was no defense for that.

"Thank you for telling me," she finally said. She couldn't bring herself to look at Willa, couldn't stand to see the mixed fear and pity in her eyes. "It won't go past this room."

She moved to leave, but Willa grabbed her hand. "It was wrong, I know. But it wasn't a mistake, was it? I mean, you're happy here, aren't you? I've told myself that for the past twelve years, that everything worked out for the best. It did work out for the best, didn't it?"

Becca thought of four years of high school, promising herself on practically a moment-by-moment basis that her life would begin when she could get out of Aloma and into the world. She thought of four years of college, still hanging in the shadows, crushed by the knowledge that her one chance for escape hadn't materialized, convincing herself that it didn't matter, that she didn't want it that badly, anyway.

She thought of that night, twelve years ago in Colt Bonner's pickup, when despair led her to rashly beg him to take her away from Aloma, convinced that her life would turn out to be...well, exactly what it had, in fact turned out to be.

She finally turned and looked Willa in the eyes. But she didn't know how to answer the question. She didn't know what anything meant anymore. So she pulled her hand away and left the building.

It was just her luck, Becca thought, that one of the two people in the world who would be able to take one look at her face and know something was wrong was right outside the post office door. She didn't even get a chance to collect herself before Corinne Haskell pulled up to the drive-up mailbox.

"What's wrong?" Corinne asked as she dropped her letters through the slot.

Becca shook her head and tried to make it to her car. Corinne pulled closer. "Becca, what happened?"

Becca closed her eyes. "Nothing."

"Don't give me that. You look like you're going to pass out. What happened?"

Becca whirled and shouted at Corinne, "Nothing happened!" She was shocked. Shocked that she would do such a thing to her best friend, and right in the middle of town no less. But she did it, anyway. "Nothing happened, nothing's wrong, there's nothing going on! Okay?"

"Like hell," Corinne said calmly. "Get in." She reached over and opened the passenger door.

And because Becca didn't know what else to do, only knew that she didn't want to be alone, she got in.

"Okay, we've got some options. We can go back to my house and get some ice cream and you can talk over a big bowl of mint-chocolate chip. Or we can drive around and you can talk until I run out of gas. Which is it?"

"Take me out to Tumbleweeds," Becca said. "I need a beer."

Corinne raised an eyebrow but didn't argue. "Tumbleweeds it is."

Once they got there and she stood before the bar, Becca realized one minor flaw in her plan.

"I don't know what kind," she said in answer to the bartender's question. "Can't I just have a beer?"

He raised a shoulder. "You want me to decide?"

"Please do."

She sank down on a bar stool and let her satchel fall to the floor beside her.

"Just a soda for me, Rodney," Corinne said as she straddled the seat beside Becca.

"You're going to let me drink alone?" Becca asked irritably. "What kind of friend are you?"

"The best one you've got. Is this about Colt?"

Becca gave a short, humorless laugh. "For once, no. This is about Mama."

"My second guess. It's always either men or parents,

isn't it? Or bad haircuts.'' At Becca's look, Corinne shrugged. ''Sorry. An inappropriate attempt at humor. Okay, what did Mama do?''

Becca took a tentative sip of her beer. It was as horrible as she remembered from twelve years earlier. She briefly considered hedging Corinne's question, but realized she didn't really want to. Corinne really was the best friend she had, the best friend she had ever had. And for once in her life, pity seemed like something she could use.

She picked up the satchel and took out the envelope. ''I applied for this art school in New York City.''

''You're leaving Aloma?''

''No, I applied in our senior year in high school. It was my futile attempt to leave Aloma a dozen years ago. This is the application.''

''Honey, I'm sorry. You didn't get in?''

''I didn't get in because the application never made it. I mean, I might not have gotten in, anyway—but now I'll never know, will I?'' She slapped the envelope down on the bar and took another drink of her beer. It didn't taste so bad this time. She groaned. ''For at least five years before graduation, I told myself to be patient, that I had gifts to offer the world, I had special talent. And that if I could just make it out of Aloma, I'd prove it. I'd show the world. And then for the next twelve years, I told myself to accept the fact that I had no talent. That it was all just a schoolgirl's dream of fame and fortune. That if I'd had any talent, they would have seen it in this application.''

''But it never made it?'' Corinne asked quietly.

Becca shook her head. ''Mama went to the post office and convinced Willa Barrows to dig out the application for her. She hid it in a box under her bed.''

Corinne took a deep breath. ''Okay, we'll skip the entire issue of Willa Barrows doing something so ridiculously stupid for now.''

"I promised her I wouldn't tell anyone. Look at me. Two sips of beer and I'm already singing like a canary. This stuff is awful. Rodney, get me a soda, too." She pushed the beer away and made a face.

"Why would she do that—?"

"Because she was a crazy old bat." A hand reached over Becca's shoulder and picked up the envelope.

"Hello, guys," Corinne said, looking up at Toby and Colt. "What are you doing here?"

Toby nodded in the direction of the door where Luke was coming through. "Luke has been pouting that we haven't had any male bonding since Colt came back. So he drug us out here for some quality time."

Becca closed her eyes. She wasn't ready to see Colt right now. She didn't have any of the defenses in place that she needed to be around him. She took a deep breath, snagged the beer back for another bracing gulp and turned to give him what she hoped passed for a smile.

He took her hand in his and studied her face. "Hey," he said softly.

"Hey." Because the urge was so strong to throw herself into his arms and cry like a baby, she let herself indulge in a loose hug. And if she stayed there, her arm wrapped around his waist, her senses honing in on the solid feel of his arm around her shoulder, she told herself it was because she didn't want to rebuff him and cause an awkward scene.

"Well, she may not have been crazy, but it was a horrible thing for her to do." Corinne spun her glass on the bar. "Good grief, where are the mothers from the books? The ones who baked cookies and hugged their kids."

"Don't look this direction," Colt said. "I haven't seen my mother in twenty-eight years."

"Well, my mom was great and still is. And she bakes awesome cookies." Toby wrapped his arms around Corinne.

"Thank goodness for mothers-in-law. So, we have four people, and one good mother out of the bunch. How sad is that?"

"How great is it that we all have a chance to start over with our own kids, and do it the way we think is right?"

Becca tried, she really tried, not to look at Colt when Toby mentioned family. There was absolutely no chance she and Colt would start over with their own kids.

She faced front and took a drink of her soda. "Let's talk about something else."

"We just started talking about this."

Becca cast a quick glance at Colt. "Let's talk about something else."

Corinne leaned over and gave Becca a quick hug. "Okay, but when you do get ready, I'm a willing listener. You're not alone in the rotten parent department, Becca, and I know how much it hurts."

Luke had struck up a conversation with a woman by the jukebox. She laughed at something he said, swinging her long blond hair and flashing dazzling white teeth. It suddenly seemed so unfair to Becca that she'd been born who she was, when the odds were just as good that she could have been born the girl who now hung on Luke's arm and graciously accepted what Becca was sure were flowery compliments any woman would love to hear.

After Luke fed quarters into the jukebox and started to dance with the girl, Colt squeezed Becca's hand. "Dance with me."

"I don't know how." The last thing she needed right now was to be close enough to compare herself even less favorably to the golden girl. It wasn't even the girl's looks, Becca realized, that made her so envious. It was the way she seemed to have absolutely no inhibition at all, to not even be thinking about how she looked, wondering if she was making a fool of herself, wondering if she belonged there.

"I'll show you."

"I'm really not in the mood to make a fool of myself in front of all these people."

"All what people? Corinne and Toby can't see past each other. Tanner doesn't know there's anybody else in the place except for the girl in his arms. Jas will still be focused on the pool table at nightfall. And Rodney's watching wrestling. That just leaves you and me." He took her hand and tugged gently.

"Colt, really. Maybe some other time."

"We may not get another time."

She remained seated.

Colt frowned at her, looked out the open door to the bright afternoon outside, then back at her. "I've never asked you for one thing, Becca. I'm asking you, just once, to dance with me."

Becca swallowed, feeling ashamed because he was right. He'd never asked her for anything. "I'm sorry. Of course, I'll dance with you."

He led her onto the floor and quietly instructed her. She felt clumsy and stupid at first, but in a surprisingly short time she fell into the rhythm. It was easy with Colt leading, the gentle pressure of his hand guiding, the soft bump of his thigh against hers. She concentrated on the feel of it, the steady pulse of the music and the way her body blended to it, and blocked out the rest of the afternoon.

Blocked out the image of Mama, crying, trying not to beg.

"You went to the post office?" Colt asked after a while.

"Mmm-hmm." She pressed her cheek against his chest and hoped he wouldn't ask more.

"What did Willa say? Was she the one who gave the envelope to your mother?"

"Colt, I really don't want to talk about it."

After a pause, he said, "No, you don't want to talk

about it with *me*. You were talking just fine until I showed up.''

Becca leaned her head back to look at him. "This is the kind of thing you want to talk over with a friend, Colt, not..." She didn't really know what to call what he was to her now. "Boyfriend" sounded juvenile, "lover" crass.

Colt's eyes narrowed and a muscle in his jaw twitched. In that moment, Becca realized what she'd forgotten in the past weeks. "I mean, you are my friend, Colt, it's just that—"

"I've got it, Becca." He kept dancing, but the relaxed, fluid grace was gone from his movements. His whole body had bristled against hers.

"Colt, don't be mad—"

"I said I got it, Becca. Don't sweat it."

Jas walked up and tapped Colt on the shoulder. "You gonna hog the lady all to yourself?"

Without looking at her, Colt handed her over to Jas and walked away, his neck stiff.

She fell into step with Jas, but her mind was on Colt, standing beside the pool table while Toby lined up for a shot. She realized Jas had said something to her, and she dragged her eyes away from Colt.

"I'm sorry, I wasn't—what did you say?"

Jas was a faster dancer than Colt, and she stepped on his foot when he led her into a spin. He grinned good-naturedly. "Good thing you don't weigh a lot. I said, don't look so crushed. Bonner stays mad at least eighty percent of the time. Heck, he's even been mad at me a time or two, if you can imagine that."

He smiled down at her, sympathy in his eyes, and the sight made her throat close and her nose burn.

"Whatever you did or didn't do, he'll get over it."

She nodded, but wondered. Wondered if either of them would ever get over it.

"I don't really feel like dancing anymore," she told Jas, who seemed to understand. She went back to the bar and picked up her soda. Corinne joined her a few moments later.

"So, do you want to talk about it now?"

"I never noticed before how stubborn you are."

"Guilty. It's because I've never seen you look like this."

"I'm fine."

"You don't look fine. You look trapped, as a matter of fact." She gave Becca a gentle squeeze on the elbow. "Tell me the truth. How much of this has to do with your mother, and how much of it has to do with Colt?"

Becca looked over at where Colt stood beside the pool table, staring into space. Luke nudged him, and he hunkered down for a shot.

"I don't even know anymore. It's all tangled up together. He's the one who got me started down this road." She told Corinne about the tales she used to make up for Colt, the new computer, and his insistence that she send the stories in to the agent.

"It's like a dream come true that I'd forgotten I even had, Corinne. That I made myself forget I had. I told myself for so long that it didn't matter, that I had no talent. I told myself that I didn't want it for twelve years. I told myself that until I believed it."

"But you were basing that on the fact that this art school hadn't accepted you. Now you know it's not true. Maybe this agent will want to take you on as a client."

Becca gave a jittery laugh. "He already does."

Corinne grabbed her hand. "No! Really?"

"Really. He called yesterday and said he thinks he might be able to sell the story, if I make some changes to it."

"Are you going to make the changes?"

"Are you kidding?"

"Becca, that's great. Congratulations. Why didn't you say anything? Aren't you excited?"

"Sure, I'm…" What was she? She *had* been excited. She had been so excited that she thought it would be enough for her. She had thought that when Colt was gone, she would have the comfort of a promising new career to keep her busy, keep her company. Keep her happy.

She looked over at him again. Now the book seemed flat. A lonely woman's substitute for a real life.

Corinne put her chin in her hand. "You remember what you told me about two-and-a-half years ago?"

"You're not going to throw something I said in my face, are you?"

"I needed to hear it then, and you need to hear it now. You said everything happens for a reason. What you have to do is decide the reason for your mother keeping you from going to art school."

"Because she wanted to keep me here with her."

"And what does staying here mean for you?"

"It means I might really have had a chance to go to New York. And Paris. Instead of telling myself for twelve years that I was happy to be a math teacher."

"But you're not happy being a math teacher, so—"

"Oh," Becca said with a wave of her hand. "Of course I'm happy. Who wouldn't be happy, teaching such an important—"

"Oh, stop. Don't repeat your brainwashing nonsense to me. Teaching is not for everyone, Becca, not by a long shot. There's no reason for you to feel guilty if it isn't for you. You're not answering the question, though. What *positive* thing have you gotten from staying in Aloma? From putting your dreams on hold? What have you learned from it all?"

"No wonder you got mad at me when I gave you this lecture. It's very irritating."

"Think."

Becca tapped her fingernails on the bar. "Well, I suppose I have learned to stand on my own two feet. If I had gone to New York when I was eighteen, I probably would have been too scared to get off the bus."

"Okay, so you're more self-reliant and prepared now than you were then. What else?"

Becca shrugged. "I have been forced to learn how to overcome my shyness, to a certain degree. If it had ever been possible for me to lock myself away in my studio and write and paint all day, I would have. But teaching and being a part of the community instead of an outsider, I've really learned how to deal with people. Sometimes it's still hard, though. Sometimes I have to *make* myself go up to someone at the grocery store just to say hi. I couldn't lock myself away from the world, from what scared me, which is probably what I was trying to do by running away to New York."

"You have a lot of friends in Aloma now, Becca. People like you."

"Sometimes that really surprises me, too. I never expected to have friends. I felt so unpopular the whole time I grew up here."

"These are things you would never have known if you had left."

"That's all well and good, but it doesn't seem like a lesson that should take anyone twelve years of their life to learn."

Corinne glanced over her shoulder, in the direction of the pool table. "You're overlooking the obvious."

"No, I'm avoiding thinking about the obvious."

"Is it Colt, do you think? Maybe you stayed so you could be here for him when he needed you."

"If I did, somebody made a big mistake. Because he doesn't need me." The past few weeks were among the best in her life, and the worst. She had told herself that she was ready to experience life for once, ready to quit protecting herself and to take the good with the bad. She'd gotten both.

"Then, turn it around," Corinne said gently. "Maybe you stayed here so he could come to you."

"To put my entire life on hold for twelve years, to hide from myself and my own dreams, so I could have two weeks with a man I have no future with? What kind of divine purpose is that?"

"Ask yourself this. If you *could* do it again, go back in time and make everything work out the way you'd originally planned, from high school graduation on, if you could have at this point become a well-known artist and writer, would you do it now? If it meant giving up what you've had the past few weeks with Colt?"

Becca let the images from the past two weeks flow through her mind. The funny thing was, she expected all the passionate moments they'd shared to be what she would miss most. Passion and excitement were what she'd been looking for, when she asked Colt to be her lover.

But the small things were what came to her now. Colt lifting her hair in the moonlight. Sitting on her back porch with him wrapped in a quilt... Colt laughing with her, teasing her. Having someone to share her day with. Having someone she felt connected to.

No, she wouldn't go back and change that—not for anything in the world.

"I guess you're right. Colt is the reason I'm here. And now he's leaving." She rubbed her forehead. "Can we just... Just take me home, okay?"

Chapter 13

Becca stood on Colt's front porch, wondering why she didn't just raise her hand to knock.

But she knew why. This was it. The first step in the entire "goodbye" ordeal. Telling herself she was ready for it did nothing to get her hand to the door.

As it turned out, she didn't need to knock. He walked around the side of the house.

"Hi." Her voice burst out on pent-up nervousness. She held up the package of curtains she'd bought as an excuse to come over. "Curtains."

His eyes narrowed when he saw her, and without a word he moved past her and into the house.

Well, that answered her first question. He was still mad after her slip-up at Tumbleweeds. She sighed and followed him inside.

In the kitchen she tore the rod from the package, pretending everything was normal. She did have a mission, after all. Colt watched her work, leaning against the counter with his arms crossed over his chest.

His brooding silence unnerved her, and the curtain slipped off the rod. "I kept the receipt, if you don't like these. They had some others with little strawberries around the edge, and I started to get them. But I thought that might seem too feminine. I mean, if a single man wanted to buy the house—" The rod slipped from her hand again. With a gusty sigh, she turned to him. "Why are you glaring at me like that?"

"Haskell told me about the agent," he said flatly. "Congratulations." The word was like a curse.

"Oh." Her mind raced to catch up. She had assumed he was still mad about what she'd said while they were dancing at Tumbleweeds. "Mr. Kline himself called the other day. How about that? He said you'd given his grandson a rigging. He seemed very proud of it. What is a rigging, anyway? Is it very expensive?"

His face perfectly blank, his eyes continued to bore a hole through her composure. "It was the rigging I used when I won my last two titles. Were you planning on telling me? Or just your friends?"

"Colt, you are my friend. I just..." How could she explain it?

"Don't worry about it, Becca. Like I said yesterday, I get it. That's the kind of news you share with your closest friends, not the human equivalent of a fake tree in a fake window."

She set the curtain rod on the counter. "What are you talking about?"

"I'm talking about you, and this whole charade we're playing out. You can't have what you really want, so you settled for me. You plugged me in to your little pretend scene, just like the painting on your studio wall."

"How do you know what I want?"

"Because I can see it all over you, dammit, every time you look at Toby and Corrine. It's all over your face, Becca, so don't try to deny it. You want the perfect sto-

rybook marriage like they have. Well, I'm not Haskell.
I'm not anything like him, and I won't ever be. We both
know that.''

"You're being unfair. I never compared you to Toby,
and I never felt like I was settling when I was with you.''

"I'm sure you didn't. You were only in it for the sex,
and that was great, if I do say so myself. I guess you got
your little problem taken care of, so when the *right* guy
comes along, you won't have any awkward explaining to
do. I filled my purpose pretty well. Got you nice and
broken in for Mr. Right.''

Becca gasped and jerked back. She knew she should
fight back, knew she didn't deserve this, but the hot anger
in his eyes had her mind locked on one thought: *Get out.
Get out, run away.*

"Don't act so shocked.'' His lip curled. "That's what
this has been about from the beginning. A little pretend
for a while, so you can see what it feels like to have a
lover. Sowing a few wild oats with someone you knew
wouldn't stick around and mess things up later on. Is that
why you're here now? One more for the road?''

Becca couldn't breathe, couldn't think. She'd known
parting from Colt would be hard, but it was so much
worse than she ever could have imagined, so much
blacker and bleaker. In the midst of a storm of panic and
pain, her mind latched, ridiculously, on the real reason
she was here, as if by turning the conversation back to
normal, they could actually *be* normal again. "I was supposed to invite you over for dinner tomorrow night. Toby
and Luke are planning a surprise party for you, a going-
away party. I wasn't—I didn't think we would—'' She
clamped her mouth shut before she said anything else stupid, and tried to muster up some shred of composure. She
lifted her chin. "I suppose I should tell them not to bother.
Or to have it somewhere else.''

He rubbed his chin and looked out the window. "Tell

them I'll be there." He didn't look at her, but she didn't think he saw whatever was outside either. "Anything specific you'd like me to wear? I don't want to mess up my last night in the role."

Becca backed away, feeling queasy and dizzy with the hurt. "I never knew you could be so cruel."

He was silent for a moment, then said quietly, still without looking at her, "Yeah, I forgot for a while, too. Good thing we both remembered in time."

I can't go through with it, Becca thought as she lay awake that night. She couldn't go through with throwing a party for Colt after he'd deliberately hurt her as he did.

"Is that why you're here? One more for the road?" The words echoed through her mind all night, searing into her each time, until she was surprised they could still hurt her. But they did.

In the morning, as she cleaned house and made ice cream and sprayed mud off the patio set, she told herself she simply could not bear to go through with this party. There was no possible way she could face everyone, and Colt, and not cry and make a miserable fool of herself. She reached for the phone five times to call it all off. She could not imagine having the strength to see him again.

But each time she reached for the phone, she drew back her hand and continued with the plans.

Because as impossible as it was to see him again, *not* seeing him again, letting it all end this way, was even worse.

He'd said he would come. She would have to trust that he would, trust that she wouldn't be left trying to explain to the others how she'd botched everything. If that happened…well, if that happened she was out of luck. Because she didn't understand it herself.

Summer thunderstorms had fallen earlier in the day, but the skies cleared off enough for Becca to stick with the plan for an outdoor party. She hung Japanese lanterns from the porch. She put the stereo on the front porch and connected three extension cords together so she could plug it in inside.

She bought food, made iced tea and enough potato salad to fill the fridge. The package came from the Kline Agency, and she studied the revisions and made plans on how she would implement the agent's suggestions.

She did everything she could think of to keep from thinking about Colt.

She showered and pulled on khaki shorts and a denim shirt, then checked herself in the mirror. Vanity and pride had her reaching for the powder and concealer. She didn't want Colt's last glimpse of her to be of a pale face with dark circles under her eyes from lack of sleep.

Toby and Corinne arrived first, looking nauseatingly in love with each other. Corinne brought paper plates and napkins, and Toby brought what he called his "world famous barbecue ribs." Pete and JoAnn came next, and Luke not long after.

"Everyone's here except the guest of honor," Corinne said, pulling plastic wrap from a bowl of fresh strawberries.

Becca resisted the urge to look once again in the direction of the Bonner house. *Not the Bonner house much longer,* a voice inside spitefully reminded her.

If she focused on making sure that everything was set up, that everything was going smoothly, he would come. If she kept her head down and thought about everything else except him, the night would pass without her making a fool of herself. If she kept busy, the next week would go by. If she kept her mind off him, the next month would be past her. And she would go on with her life.

She poured lemonade and traded recipes with JoAnn. She celebrated with Pete and JoAnn the victory of Bradley's birthday party, because Pete had gotten the minibike running, which Bradley loved, and Jeremy had swallowed his anger at Pete long enough to come, which the whole family loved.

She swatted Luke's hand out of the rolls, and talked teaching with Corinne.

And finally he came.

She wanted to smile with relief when she saw him, so she went into the house on the pretext of getting a spoon for the potato salad. He wore jeans and a white shirt, and his hair was still damp from the shower, curling dark tendrils at his collar. Through the open window, she heard him apologize for his tardiness and Jas's absence.

"He met a girl at the ice cream shop and decided he preferred her company." He sank into a lawn chair with a groan. "I didn't know how much crap you have to sign to get rid of a house," he said. "I was there all afternoon, and have to go back tomorrow."

Tomorrow, before he and Jas left.

She made it through the dinner. She ate, though she tasted nothing. She talked, though she couldn't remember five minutes later what she or anyone else had said. But she made it through.

She did not look at Colt. He did not look at her.

She was in the kitchen wrapping leftovers when Corinne came in to help. Corinne didn't beat around the bush.

"Have you told him how you feel?"

If she looked at Corinne, she would cry. So instead she looked at the dishes. "What's to tell?"

"I don't know. 'I'm crazy about you'? How about, 'I want you to stay'?"

"I'm not going to beg him, Corinne. I won't do that."

She did look up then, with a careless shrug and a philosophical smile. "I wanted to know what it felt like. All of it, the good and the bad. So now I don't have to wonder anymore."

Corinne shook her head and wiped off the ketchup bottle. "You know, I'm glad Toby didn't have your attitude. Who knows how long it would have taken me to make up my mind, if he hadn't pushed? He knew what he wanted, and he went after it. He went after me. And he didn't let up until I admitted I wanted him, too. I can't tell you how that made me feel, Becca. At that point in my life, it was really, really nice to be wanted. To be needed."

Becca leaned against the refrigerator door and folded her arms across her chest, hugging herself. "I'm not the pushing type, Corinne. I never have been. I'm not the type to go after what I want, no holds barred." She cleared her throat and went on. "Colt is. He told me he is. He decides what he wants and he goes after it." She intently studied the pattern of the spoon in her hands. "And he's not going after me. That much is pretty clear."

Despite her resolve to stay calm, her voice quivered and she had to close her eyes for a second. "It was nice while it lasted, Corinne. It was a lot of fun. And I wouldn't trade the past few weeks for anything in the world. But it's time to get back to reality. He doesn't belong here. It's time for him to go on with his life. It's time for me to go on with mine."

Corinne looked up at the doorway behind Becca. Becca turned her head. Colt was standing there, his face blank. He didn't look at Becca.

"Toby and Tanner got to telling stories of their skinny-dipping days down at the quarry." He rolled his eyes and gave a tolerant half-smile. "Pete wanted to look at the place, so they went down there."

Corinne put down the dish towel she was holding. "I'll go help JoAnn fold down the tables."

Tension filled the small kitchen as Becca put away the dishes. Colt picked up a bowl, his brow lifted in question. Becca motioned with her head toward a top cupboard. Silently, nice and civilized, they put the room back to rights. When they were finished, Colt leaned lazily against the counter, and Becca wiped the stovetop that was already spotless.

She folded the cloth carefully into a neat square, laid it across the sink and lifted her head to look at Colt. He was watching her, his face closed, his hands in his pockets. He blinked slowly, his jaw set.

"Despite the impression you seem to be under, I'll miss you," she said, then cringed that the words had actually come out.

"You'll get over it," he said flatly.

So much for parting on a good note. She forced her face to convey peace. "So, you have to go back to the Realtor's tomorrow, and then you're leaving?"

He nodded, his face a stone-cold blank.

"I have to tell you something," she said, taking another fortifying breath.

He came away from the counter, his hands rising slightly. If he touched her now, she'd come undone. She moved past him, toward her office.

After a moment, he joined her. She bent and tugged a cardboard box from her shelf of books. The box was old, and had once held ten pounds of frozen hamburger patties. Now it held a blue scrapbook.

"I found this when I...when I found Doff. After the funeral, I went back and got it, because I didn't know how long the house would be empty and I didn't want anything to happen to it." She fingered the ragged edge of the album, where the cloth was wearing off the cardboard cover. "I didn't tell you about it at first, because...well, because you seemed so mad at Doff and like you didn't want to talk about it."

She looked up at him, finally. He stared at the book, his jaw tight, a vertical line between his brows. She rose and pulled her chair out from the desk. She put a hand to his shoulder and gently pushed him back into it. He sat without a word, his eyes still on the scrapbook.

"I was wrong not to show you at first, and I'm sorry. I felt like you had enough to deal with at that time, and maybe you needed some time back before you saw it. And then later, I just forgot about it. I had other things on my mind." She felt a little sick when she smiled. He didn't seem to notice.

She sighed and handed him the notebook. "It's you. It's all you—pictures and articles and ads. He kept everything."

Becca had pored over the scrapbook the first weeks she had it. Doff never once mentioned Colt to her, in all the years she'd looked in on him. He pretended he had no son. But the evidence that he'd never forgotten was in Colt's lap right now.

Slowly, as if in a daze, Colt turned the pages of the scrapbook. His face remained carefully blank. Becca looked away, not wanting to intrude on a private moment.

She couldn't stop herself from touching him, though. She put her palm on his head, much as she would a small child. He reached up and held her wrist, distracted, still looking at the book.

He blinked a few times, rapidly, when he got to the pictures of himself as a child. There were only two—one of him as a fat, diaper-clad baby, held in the arms of a pretty, dainty woman standing beside a bush. The bush that Colt had cut away from the living room window.

In the other, he was about five. He sat straddling on a bale of hay, tiny boots on his feet and a straw cowboy hat on his head. His face was grim, and his dark eyes stared solemnly into the camera, giving lie to the orchestrated setup. His mother had left by that time.

The scrapbook was so clumsily put together, it was almost laughable. Some of the articles were held to the pages with gray duct tape. There were older articles where

Colt's name was one buried amidst many, and Doff had underlined it in shaky blue ink. Most of them, though, featured Colt. There were programs from rodeos, ads that Colt had done for hats and boots. On the last page was a mysterious scrap of paper that meant nothing to Becca, and a crumpled-up cigarette wrapper. Colt fingered it and swallowed.

Becca knelt in front of him. This was a curve she knew he hadn't expected. He thought of Doff as completely bad, and he was very nearly right. Doff had been a hateful old man, rude and mean and bigoted. He'd been abusive to Colt, had treated his young wife so badly she'd chosen to give up her child rather than stay with him. He was a drunk who'd run off everyone close to him.

But he'd been proud of his son.

Colt finally raised his head, his expression confused. "*He* kept this? He kept all this?"

Becca nodded, her heart in her throat. Instead of Colt the man, she saw Colt the boy.

He looked back at the scrapbook and shook his head. "He couldn't have...are you sure it wasn't you, Becca? You didn't put this together, to try and get me to—"

"Colt," Becca said sadly.

He shook his head. "No. Okay. Okay." He looked around the room, trying to get his bearings. He stood and paced the room, stopped in front of Becca's desk, head bent, rubbing his forehead. He took a deep breath and blew it out. "I never thought he would..." He shook his head again. "Thanks, Becca. For keeping it. It doesn't really change anything, but—"

There was a commotion outside. She stood and looked out the window. Jeremy Huckaby stood in the yard, talking to Corinne and JoAnn.

Becca raised the window. "What's going on?"

"Bradley had an accident!" JoAnn said.

"It's not that bad, Mom," Jeremy protested. He turned

to Becca in the window. "He was riding his minibike and wiped out in a mud puddle."

"He's not supposed to ride it without his father or me there."

"Well, he did. He just needs a couple of stitches, okay? Don't panic. I took him to the hospital, but they can't do anything until you sign the papers."

JoAnn looked frantically around. "Pete has the keys."

"I'll take you," Corinne said, reaching for her purse.

"I have to tell Pete." JoAnn started toward the mesquite trees that sheltered the quarry.

"I'll tell him."

Becca looked up to see Colt standing behind her, once again composed.

"I'll bring him to the hospital. You guys go ahead."

Colt looked over at Pete, who fidgeted in his seat like an impatient child.

"Did he say where he was hurt?"

"I told you, Pete. He tore his knee a little. Needed a couple stitches. It's no big deal."

Pete nodded. "I'll just be glad to see it myself. Kids are a constant worry, you know that? Constant."

Colt saw Becca's hand give Pete's knee a comforting squeeze.

"I know," Colt said, just to shut him up.

Unbidden, an ancient memory surfaced in Colt's mind. He'd been about twelve. He was already accustomed to living in constant fear of Doff by that time. If the man was drunk, he was in a rage. If he was sober, he was merely impossible to be around.

Colt had been swimming with Toby and Luke all day, in the quarry. He woke with a fierce earache, a sharp pain that pierced his inner ear. He sat on the edge of the bed for an hour, afraid to stir and wake Doff. Finally, the pain got bad enough to make him desperate.

He tiptoed into Doff's room. Maybe he was dying. Maybe it was a brain tumor, stuck in his ear. He nudged Doff's shoulder.

Doff came awake with a snuffle and snort. "Wha—?"

"My ear hurts," Colt said.

Doff groaned and mumbled and reached for the lamp. "Well, what do I look like, a doctor?" He stared at Colt, and at the tracks of tears on his cheeks.

He sighed heavily and hauled himself from the bed. "C'mere."

Doff rummaged through the medicine cabinet in the bathroom and pulled out an ancient bottle of oil. He twisted off the cap and smelled it, then moved to the kitchen. He poured a bit of the oil in a spoon, struck a match under it.

"C'mere," he said again. Colt stood before him, wondering if Doff was about to feed him boiling oil. "Tilt yer head. Like this." Doff tilted his head until it was almost horizontal.

He wasn't going to feed him boiling oil, he was going to pour it into his ear. Colt didn't know which he was more afraid of—disobeying Doff, or frying his brains with boiling oil.

He tilted his head. The warm oil slid into his ear and soothed it. Colt closed his eyes, so relieved from the pain that he slumped. Doff's fingers, rough with calluses, massaged the base of his ear for a few moments. It was unexpectedly tender, to feel the contact of Doff's hand, but without the pain Colt had always associated with it. A lump had swelled in his throat.

The fingers moved away, and Colt opened his eyes to see Doff twisting off the cap of a whiskey bottle. He poured a quarter of an inch into a dirty glass. "Drink this." At Colt's hesitation, he growled. "Drink it. Little bit like this ain't going to make you act like me. It's the same thing they make cough medicine with. It'll help you sleep.''

Colt didn't point out that he had an earache, not a cough. He took the glass and put it to his mouth, his lips tight around the glass. The whiskey dammed against his lips, and he let a tiny drop through. It was sharp and warm on his tongue. He opened his mouth and swallowed the lot. Colt gasped as it turned into fire in his throat.

Doff laughed, a hacking, choked laugh, as he shuffled in his underwear back through the kitchen and to his room. It was a good five minutes before Colt stopped coughing and went back to bed.

Now, driving Pete to the hospital, Colt realized that moment, with Doff tenderly rubbing his ear, was the only fond memory he possessed of the man. One moment, when he wasn't berating him or beating him. If anyone had asked him, he would have said there hadn't been one. But there had. One.

"Pete, when you got out of jail, what did you tell your kids?"

Pete looked across the dark cab at him. Colt knew he was out of line but he didn't take the question back.

Pete shrugged. "That I was sorry for what I'd done. That I wasn't going to do it again."

"And what did they say?"

"Bradley said it was okay. Jeremy stood up and left before I got the first word out."

Colt nodded. "Did you try to tell him again? That you were sorry?"

Pete shrugged. "I tried to talk to him lots of times. Explain, kind of, why I did it. He won't talk to me."

They drove in silence for a few minutes.

"You should try again."

"He won't listen to me. He's stubborn as a damn rock, that one."

"Try again."

"I told him I was sorry. A dozen times. Or tried to, at any rate. He won't listen."

"So make him listen. Wrestle him to the ground and hog-tie him, if you have to. *Make* him know. And keep making him listen until he finally gets it."

Pete hesitated, then asked, "You think that would help? I don't want to push him further away."

Colt sighed, feeling suddenly drained and tired. "I don't know." He shook his head. They pulled up in front of the emergency department. He felt again the scratchy blue material of the scrapbook under his fingers. "I don't know if it would help or not. But it would be a hell of a start."

As Pete reached for the door handle, Becca put out a hand to stop him. "Colt is right. He might be mad for a while, but you can't give up. It will mean more to him than you can know to find out you care enough to keep trying."

Colt drove to the small cemetery the next morning and killed the motor. He groaned and rubbed his hand over his face, thumbing the lid off the foam coffee cup and closing his eyes as the scalding liquid ran down his throat. It was early; he was usually still working the kinks out of his back with his exercises and nursing his first cup of coffee at this time.

But he had a lot to do today, and he'd be damned if he'd start letting Doff scare him off now.

He found the grave with little trouble. The grass was just starting to come in, pale green patches in a pallet of dark brown. He stood at the bottom of it and stared at the simple tombstone.

DOUGLAS JAMES BONNER

He wondered briefly how Becca had known Doff's middle name, but didn't dwell on it. She would have made it a point to find out. She hadn't thought it necessary to put anything else—nothing sentimental like Beloved Father or He Will Be Missed—and Colt was glad of that.

He rubbed his lower lip and took another sip of coffee, his eyes steady on the tombstone. He realized suddenly why it was so important for people to have funerals and graveyards and markers. Getting the news that Doff was dead had not made it real in Colt's mind. Coming back and finding him gone had not made it real. But standing in front of a gray slab with his father's name and two dates carved on it made it real.

Doff was dead.

He took a breath and puffed his cheeks, blowing it out. "Okay, Doff. I'm here. I came. I came out here to tell you…well, to tell you a lot of things. I came out here, actually, to tell you that you are—you were—a bastard, and I hope you're frying in hell right now. But I get out here and…and I guess I don't really hope you're in hell. I don't know what I hope about you."

He stopped and shook his head. He never could think straight when he was around Doff. "I came out here to put this—put you—behind me. I've hated you for so long, I don't really know how I'm going to live without that hate driving me on. But I'm going to do it somehow. Because I'm tired of you still having control over my life. You were a terrible father. You really were. You…" Colt's brows drew deeply down. He didn't like saying this, didn't like even thinking it. But he'd come out here to be honest, and he was by damn going to do it right. "You hurt me, so many times, and you're not going to hurt me anymore. You were wrong. You hit me when I was a kid and didn't know how to fight back. You humiliated me and ridiculed me when I thought you knew everything, and I thought you were right. You told me I was stupid and clumsy and screwed up everything I touched, and I believed you. You took advantage of your power over me, and you were wrong.

"You took my childhood and made it one long series of miseries. I was either afraid of you, or wishing I could do something about you, knowing I couldn't, hating myself for being afraid. The good memories I have of growing up all center around other people—Haskell's family, my friends. You told me—" His throat closed up and his voice grew hoarse, and he had to fight to get the words out. "You told me that my mother left because I cried all the time and she couldn't stand to be around me anymore. I looked her up, you know. I found her. Because I always wanted to know—I had to know—if it was true. I wanted to hear from her how bad a baby I really was. And when I found her, you know what I realized? That it didn't matter if I was the worst baby in the world. I was a baby. A *baby*. I didn't have any control over myself or anything else. It didn't matter at all that she really left because of you, that you drove her away. You should never have told me something like that, even if it was the truth."

He took another deep breath. He was surprised to feel a sense of calm descending over him. So this is what it felt like to let go.

"You took my childhood and made it a nightmare. And since then I've given you too much of my adulthood, being afraid that I'm like you. And I'm not going to let you do it anymore. I came back to Aloma because I just couldn't let everything end without a word. I stayed in your house and worked myself until I was exhausted, because I was looking for something in there, something of you, something of us that would give me some clue as to what...I don't know. What I did wrong. What I could have done differently. Because I couldn't handle the thought of everything just *ending* like that. I couldn't let you have the last word."

He rubbed his temples. "But you're gone, and I'm having the last word, to your tombstone. So I guess it's time I finally came to grips with it. The past is the past. It's time it stayed there. I have a chance now, a chance at a happy life, with a good woman. And I'm going to take it. I'm going to have what I always wished I had—a normal life, a life with people I love, people I laugh with and enjoy being around.''

He looked at the ground. "To do that, I have to put you and everything else behind me. So…I forgive you for everything you did. I'm letting it go. I'm going to do my level best never to think of you again, and if I do, I'm going to try to think of only the good things.''

Peace and acceptance. Yeah, Becca was right. Not fighting the way it had been. Accepting simply that it had been, and that he did have the strength to move on. Not hating, not resenting. Peace and acceptance. He could do this.

"I'm thankful that you didn't send me to a foster home, though God knows why you didn't and God knows how much better my life could have been if you had. But it could have been worse, and I might always have wished to be with you, so at least I don't have that to deal with. And I'm thankful that you put me on the back of a baby bull when I was a kid. I know you only did it to see me get knocked on my butt, and to get a laugh out of your drinking buddies. But when you made me ride that baby bull, I found out I was good at something. I've made a lot of money on the back of a bull, and that money is going to help me get started on a new life. Riding bulls has taught me discipline and determination, and taught me that I don't screw up everything I touch.''

He rubbed his jaw and stepped up closer to the tombstone. "So, I'm taking those two things, and I'm leaving the rest of it here with you. I'm going to go and live my life now—*my* life—and I'm going to keep you out of it.''

He looked hard at the tombstone, his eyes narrowed.

He could feel a chunk of the granite in his throat. He kissed the tips of his fingers, then ran them slowly across the name carved in stone. "Goodbye, Doff," he said quietly.

He turned and walked away.

Becca opened the door to the post office, hoping she would see Mavis behind the counter and not Willa. No such luck.

She gave Willa a neutral smile and laid her package on the counter. "Good afternoon."

Willa returned the weak smile. Her hand shook as she placed the package on the scale, and she cleared her throat three times while she waited. Becca tapped the counter restlessly.

Willa tossed the package on the counter and reached for her stamp. "Oh," she said. "I thought this was your Dunleavy's assignment. But this isn't going to Abilene."

The urge to tell the old lady to mind her own business, she'd done enough, was strong, even though Becca knew she wouldn't actually have had the nerve to say that. But she looked into Willa's face, and realized the woman was only trying to reestablish a connection, to make things okay between them again.

What the heck, Becca thought, more out of tiredness than any urge to mend fences. She'd been up all night, making the revisions she'd just received yesterday. Anything to keep from thinking about Colt. "No, this is actually a children's book I wrote. A literary agent is interested in representing it. Is it too late for it to go out today?"

Ignoring the question, Willa's face broke into a wide grin that threw the mass of wrinkles on her face into relief. "Oh, that's wonderful! A children's book. That's wonderful news. I'm sure it's a beautiful book. When can I read it?"

"It has to be bought and published first."

"It will be. Of course it will be, and it'll be a huge hit. You know it will."

Becca realized that she didn't really care at this point if it was or not. She would, she promised herself. She would care, as soon as she got the feeling back in her body, as soon as her heart and head came out of this aching limbo. Everything would be okay again, someday.

Someday. She would celebrate and breathe and be happy again, someday real soon.

She let Willa prattle on, and found it almost amusing that just a few days ago she'd thought what this woman and Mama had done was the end of the world. She'd thought she hurt then. Now she knew what hurt really was.

Willa reached across the counter and squeezed Becca's hand. "I'm glad, Becca. I'm glad you're going to be all right."

Becca nodded. "I'm all right," she said, as if saying so would make it so. "I'm fine."

She walked back to her car, dropped down into the seat and repeated the words to herself. "I'm fine. I'm fine. I'm going to be fine. I didn't lose it, I didn't lose control, I didn't beg, and eventually I'm going to be even better. I'm fine."

The car was hot, and she felt the perspiration start to break out on the back of her neck and forehead. She tilted the rearview mirror to look at her reflection. "I'm fine," she said aloud.

Her face was pale, with red splotches from the heat. He was leaving today. Maybe already gone.

"Like hell I am," she said, loudly and definitely. She was not fine, and at this point it felt as if she never would be again.

She started the car and drove to Corinne's house. Thankfully, Corinne answered instead of Toby.

"You okay? No, don't answer that, I can see that you're not. Come in."

"I don't know what to do." Becca launched into a nervous pace as soon as she cleared the door. "I can't just let him go, but I don't know how to stop him."

Corinne leaned on the arm of the sofa. "Why don't you try telling him how you feel?"

"Because he won't believe me, not now. He'll think it's just part of a role I'm playing."

Corinne frowned. "Why in the world would he think that?"

Becca waved the question aside. "Long, very messed-up story. I have to do something drastic. Something that will get his attention."

"I have this sexy little red dress that would look great on you. It always gets Toby's attention."

Becca shook her head. "Wouldn't work. He thinks I'm only interested in him for sex. That would just confirm his suspicions."

"Only interested—" Corinne hooted with laughter. "You? That's the most ridiculous think I've ever heard."

"I told you it was a messed-up story."

"Is he blind? Does he not see the way you look at him?"

"He looks at everything through that colossal chip on his shoulder. I have to let him know I want him in my life. That I—I need him. I wish I could make him see himself the way I see him." She stopped pacing. "I have an idea."

"Great. What do we do?"

"It's not a very good idea."

"Then, let's get another idea."

"I don't have another idea, and I may not have much time, if any. If I don't do this now, I'm going to back out. And regret it for the rest of my life."

"Okay, so what's this bad idea?"

"I don't have time to explain it. Just do me a favor, would you? Get Toby to find him, and keep him here in town for a few hours."

"Hasn't he left already?"

"I don't know." Thinking it might be too late made tears sprout to Becca's eyes, so she refused to think it. "If he has, he hasn't gotten far. Tell him and Luke to go out on patrol and find him and keep him here, somehow. Tell them if they do I'll bring fresh strudel to the courthouse every morning for an entire year."

Corinne stood up and gave Becca quick hug. "They're going to hold you to that, you know. Ahh, it's about time you needed us for something. I've needed your friendship for almost three years now. All right, girl. Get out of here and get your man!"

Chapter 14

When Colt pulled up in front of Pete's house, the family was standing out on the front porch. A blue car waited for Jeremy—his ride back to school.

Colt sensed tension in the air. Pete and Jeremy carefully avoided looking at each other. Jeremy's eyes were a little puffy, and Pete sported a suspicious-looking swell under one eye.

JoAnn hugged Jeremy. "Be careful going back. Don't let him drive too fast."

Jeremy grinned crookedly. Pete stepped up and stuck out his hand. "We'll probably get up to Abilene some time in the next week. We'll call."

Jeremy ignored the hand. "Summer school starts tomorrow. I'll be busy studying."

Pete swallowed and nodded. "Yeah, well. Maybe some other time, then."

Jeremy turned to take the door handle. He stopped, one hand on the door, his back stiff. His brows drew together.

"The week after next looks pretty slow. Call me. We'll, uh…go out to dinner or something."

He scowled and opened the door, dropping into the car without saying another word.

Colt turned to look at Pete. JoAnn was smiling widely. Pete's mouth curved cautiously. He nodded at Jeremy.

As the car pulled off, Colt turned to Bradley. "Heard you wiped out."

Bradley nodded with a grin. "She's got a lot more power than I gave her credit for." He looked at the mini-bike, resting harmlessly against the side of the house.

"I told him I was going to put training wheels on it if he does that again." JoAnn put her arm around Bradley's shoulders and hugged him briefly.

"Aw, a few stitches never hurt anybody," Colt said. "I ought to know. Pete, have you got a minute?"

The two men walked around to the back of the house. Colt looked pointedly at Pete's eye. "Walk into a door?"

Pete grinned ruefully. "I guess you could say I got what I wished for." He shook his head and laughed lightly. "I did what you said. I made him listen."

"And? Did you get anything besides a black eye?"

Pete shrugged. "I'm pretty sure he wanted to kill me. But he didn't ignore me. He didn't walk away. He got in my face and called me every name in the book. But he didn't ignore me. You were right. It was a place to start, at any rate. So, did you get the papers all signed for the house?"

Colt nodded. "It's all set. While I was there, though…" Colt squinted. "I found another house. I was in the office when the guy came in to list it. It's not in bad shape, really. The foundation's solid, the pipes are good. We could do something with it. Probably turn a pretty good profit, with some work."

"I thought you were heading out today."

"Yeah, well, maybe I'll stick around for a while."

"For a while? How long a while?"

"I don't know."

"Depends on Becca, huh?"

Colt ground a dirt clod under his boot heel and scowled. "Yeah. Depends on her."

Pete ran a tongue over his teeth, clearly wanting to pursue that line of questioning. At Colt's look, he tactfully moved on to the business at hand. "So, you're going to go into contracting full time? You're going to need some help. Got a job for me?"

Colt rubbed his jaw. "I was thinking something more on the lines of a partnership. Co-owners of the business. Fifty-fifty."

Pete snorted. "And what am I supposed to do for start-up money?"

Colt shrugged. "I put the money up front. You pay back a percentage of your profits from each job until you've bought out half."

Pete eyed him warily. "You serious?"

Colt made a face. "I guess I am. I keep trying to talk myself out of it. But it sounds like a good idea."

"I mean, are you serious about you and me, being partners?"

Colt nodded. "Yeah, that part I'm real sure about."

Pete shook his head and shrugged. "Well, hell, Bonner. I don't know what to say. It sounds like a fantastic idea to me."

"We're not going to get rich. But I think we can keep a roof over our heads, at any rate."

"I tried getting rich," Pete said wryly. "It didn't work out so great. I'll be happy if we can turn a profit."

Luke rounded the corner just then. "Hey, Colt. I thought you were heading out today."

"Change in plans" was all Colt would say. "What are you doing out here?"

"I was out at Mom and Dad's and I saw your pickup. Problems with the Realtor?"

"He's staying here," Pete said. "We're going into business together."

Luke's face split into a huge grin. "That's great, man!" Ignoring Colt's protest, he pulled him into a back-thumping bear hug. "Great. But what about Doff's record? This is your chance to break it."

Colt shrugged. "He needed it more than I do. I decided to let him keep it."

"That's true. You've got a lot more going your way than he did. That record was all he had."

Subconsciously Colt's hand went to cover the envelope in his pocket. He did have a lot more going for him, he thought, looking into the faces of his friends. A hell of a lot more. He hoped it would be enough.

Colt stepped back, feeling restless.

"Listen, I've got to go. But if things don't go so well tonight, I may need a place to bunk for a few days."

"Mi sofa es yu sofa," Luke said. "Or something like that."

"Thanks. I hope I won't need it."

"Good luck," Pete said. "If you don't mind my saying so, you look like hell. Gonna pop the question?"

"Is it that obvious?"

"Like I said, you don't look good. I remember when I asked JoAnn...I've never been so scared."

"Yeah, well, I look like this because I have an idea of what her answer's going to be. And I'm probably going to come away with a shiner to match yours."

"Small price to pay," Pete said with a grin.

"Yeah, that's what I'm thinking."

"Colt, before you go, Toby wanted you to come by the courthouse for a second," Luke said.

"What for?"

"You've got me. He just said if I saw you to send you over."

"Tell him I'll be there later. I've got to go talk to Becca."

They rounded the corner, and Colt groaned when he saw the flat tire on his pickup. "Man, I don't have time for this."

"No problem. I'll give you a ride into town."

"Nah, I'll change it here. It won't take long." He leaned over the tailgate. "Hey, where's my spare tire?"

Luke and Pete both looked. "This isn't your day, Bonner. One tire flat and the other one gone."

"You're telling me. Okay, Tanner, give me a ride into town."

"We'll stop by and see what Toby wants on the way."

"I've got to go talk to Becca first."

"He sounded like it was urgent. Don't worry, it probably won't take long."

"Why are you going so slow? The speed limit is fifty-five."

"These roads aren't in such good shape, Colt. It's really not safe to drive the posted speed."

"Well, get a move on anyway, would you? I've got things to do." He shifted in his seat and looked at the clock on the dash.

"Sorry. I'll step on it."

They drove on a few more minutes, then Luke said, "Did you hear that?"

"Hear what?"

"The engine just made a noise. I'd better pull over and check it out."

"The engine didn't make—" Colt cursed. "What are you stopping for? There was no noise."

"I heard a noise. Don't get your shorts in a bunch, it'll just take a second."

Luke pulled over to the shoulder and yanked the hood release. Whistling, he got out to take a look.

Colt muttered a few more choice words and pulled the envelope out of his pocket to study again. He thought he'd covered everything. Maybe, just maybe, if he presented everything just perfectly, she wouldn't light into him too badly. Not that he deserved to get off lightly. Not that he even deserved *her*. But maybe…

What was taking so damn long? He climbed out of the pickup and went around front to take a look. "What's wrong with it?"

"I don't know." Luke fiddled with a few hoses and stuck his hand down into the belly of the engine. "It was kind of a knocking noise."

"Probably just low on oil. Let's go into town and get a quart from Johnny."

"That's not a bad idea. We'll stop by Johnny's on the way to the courthouse."

"Whatever. Let's just get going."

"Becca? Are you there yet?"

Becca heard Corinne's voice on the answering machine as she was coming through the door. She raced for the phone and snatched it up. "I'm here."

"Toby talked to Luke, and Colt is still in town. They're masterminding a plan to keep him occupied. How long do you need?"

"At least an hour, maybe an hour-and-a-half. Do you think they can do that?"

"Are you kidding? Toby is so thrilled for you both, he'll do whatever it takes. And you know how those two are when they get to scheming. Colt'll be lucky to get away from them before nightfall."

"Thanks, Corinne. You're a great friend."

Becca hung up the phone and bit her lip, wondering

where to start. On the computer, with her new programs? Or the old-fashioned way?

She looked around the room, gauging what she wanted to accomplish against the time she had. She gathered her tools, put her largest sketch pad on her easel and set to work.

Johnny wanted to talk. Ordinarily that wouldn't have bothered Colt. But today was no ordinary day, and Luke was just too willing to waste half the afternoon shooting the breeze for Colt's frame of mind. As the other two men stood chatting over the engine of Luke's pickup, Colt snapped his fingers and tapped his feet and paced up and down in front of the gas pumps.

"Didn't you say whatever Haskell wanted was urgent?" he asked Luke.

"Oh, yeah, I did say that."

"Well, start 'er up, and I'll take a listen," Johnny told him.

Luke jumped in the cab and started the engine.

After what Colt thought was entirely too much time, the consensus was reached that there was no knocking noise after all.

"Told you," he mumbled, when they pulled back onto the road.

"What?"

"I said let's get moving. I have things to do."

Becca picked up the phone before it had finished the first ring. "Yes?"

"I thought I'd give you an update. Carla Buchanan just saw Luke and Colt at Johnny's service station and she said Colt looked like he was ready to start chewing tires."

"He's anxious to get out of here," Becca said, one hand against her stomach.

"He's anxious about something. But don't worry,

honey. Toby and Luke won't let him get away. How's your idea coming?"

Becca looked at her sketch with a critical eye. Out of necessity, it was pretty minimalist. It was a collage of Colt in different scenes—scenes that depicted what she thought of when she thought of him. There was a drawing of him as he'd been the first day she saw him again, standing on his front porch, his hand high on the porch rail, his shirt riding up. She grabbed a pencil and shaded in the shadow of toned abdominal muscles. Below that was a drawing of him wrapped in a blanket on her back porch, a dainty coffee cup clutched in one hand, his feet bare. Across from that was another scene of him hard at work, his hair slick with perspiration, a smile on his face as he pounded a hammer against a board.

The drawings were too bare, though, and didn't quite convey what she wanted. "It's going okay, but not great. If it's at all possible, I really need about another hour." She'd left the most important scene for last, and she didn't want to rush it.

"I don't think that'll be a problem. But I'll tell Toby to call me if anything goes wrong."

"You dragged me up here to help you move filing cabinets?" Colt happily would have strangled Toby just then.

"They're heavy. I needed all the help I could get."

Colt put his hands on his hips and did a slow turn around the room, giving himself time to count to ten. "I don't believe this. I have things to do, man. This can wait."

"You're forgetting that you have no transportation," Luke said, unsuccessfully trying to hide his grin.

"I'll walk."

"It'll be faster if you just help us move the stuff, then I can take you back to your pickup."

Because he knew Luke was right, Colt merely called

him a choice name and grabbed a dolly handle. "All right, where do you want them?"

"We're putting everything in cell one while we clean up in here, then we'll move it all back out."

Colt glared. "I am *not* staying long enough for you to clean this whole damn room."

"Nobody asked you to. Jeez, what got into you? Just wheel them into the cell, and we'll get them back out later."

Still glowering, Colt slid the dolly under the first filing cabinet and wheeled it back to cell one. When he came back, Luke and Toby were in deep discussion.

"You know, while we're at this, we ought to think about rearranging the office."

"That's not a bad idea. I've always kind of wanted my desk closer to the window."

"I want *my* desk closer to the window. You need to be closer to the front, anyway, since you're the sheriff."

"What goes next?" Colt asked. "This one over here?"

"What do you think, Colt? Should we put both of our desks back here by the window, and leave the front open for JoAnn's reception desk? How would that look?"

Colt stared at them, then took a deep breath. "Would you two quit being such a couple of women and help me?"

"Oh, sorry." Luke and Toby grinned at each other. "We're being inconsiderate."

"Damn right," Colt muttered as he wheeled the next filing cabinet back.

He parked the second beside the first and was turning, when he heard a *clang* behind him. He looked up to see metal bars between him and a grinning Luke.

"Now, why did you do that, Tanner?" Toby asked him.

"Sorry. My hand slipped."

"Well, get him out of there."

"Yeah, get me out of here."

"I will, I will. Man, you are uptight today. Haskell, give me the key."

"Funny, Tanner."

"I'm serious. Give me the key."

"I don't have the key and you know it."

"Yes, you do. You had it last."

"Did not. You had it when you took your nap back there last week."

"Why would I need the key then? It wasn't locked."

"Well, I don't have it—"

"One of you jokers had better find the key or I'm coming through these bars!" Colt gripped the bars, mad enough to knock their heads together if he could get to them.

"I'll find it, I'll find it," Luke said as he walked away. "It's got to be around here somewhere."

The two men moved back to the front room, and after a moment Colt realized it sure didn't sound like anyone was looking for anything. He pressed his face against the bars and peered into the other room.

Toby was lounging against his desk, grinning and tossing a Tootsie Roll from one hand to the other, and Luke was laughing so hard, albeit silently, that it was all he could do to stay in his chair.

"I knew it! What are you two up to?"

They both jumped, and Luke wiped his mouth. "Up to?"

"This isn't funny, man. I don't have time for this. Get me out of here."

"We're trying, Colt. I swear."

"Yeah, we'll have you out—" That was as far as Luke got before he collapsed back into his chair, weak with laughter.

"Get me out of here!"

"We will, we will." Toby grabbed Luke by the arm and hauled him up. "Come on, we have to go find that key."

"Yeah," Luke said as he stumbled after Toby, toward the door. "Find the key."

"Hey! Where are y'all going?"

"We're not going anywhere. Does it look like we're going somewhere?"

They left.

Colt yelled. He called them every curse word he could think of, but they didn't come back.

He couldn't believe he was locked in a jail cell on the most important day of his life. When he got out of here, the second thing he was going to do, after going to Becca, was make sure those two idiots paid. And paid.

He glared at the closed door, then turned and kicked the nearest filing cabinet.

"They put him in *jail?*" Becca wiped her eyes and reached for a tissue. Ever since she'd started this crazy drawing, she couldn't seem to stop crying. It was crazy; she hadn't cried since she could remember, and now that she'd started...

"Can you believe it? I told Toby he was going to regret it, but he said it was worth the beating he's going to get, to see the look on Colt's face."

Becca could imagine that look, and she didn't find the image particularly comforting. "He's going to be furious by the time I get there."

"He'll be so relieved to see you, he'll forget all about it."

"Let's hope so."

"How's your plan coming?"

Becca tilted her head and studied the picture. Actually, it wasn't bad. She shaded the areas between each picture and tried to calm her nerves. It said what she wanted to say—at least, to her it did. If it spoke to Colt in the same way, maybe...

"I'm about as ready as I'm ever going to be. Corinne, I am so nervous. I've never been so nervous."

"Don't think about it, honey, just do it. Go, right now, as quick as you can."

Becca lifted the pad and carefully tore off the drawing. It was now or never.

Don't think about it, just do it. Don't think about it, just do it. Becca repeated the words to herself to keep from thinking about anything else. She wasn't even sure, exactly, what she was going to say. Her hope was that the drawing would say enough for her that she could make him understand.

"Don't think about it, just do it," she murmured as she pulled up in front of the courthouse. She stared at the door to the sheriff's office. "Don't think about it, just do it." She stayed glued to her seat.

Luke and Toby were sitting on the curb around the side of the building. They stood and nodded at her, both grinning like fools. She nodded back. Her head was the only part of her body that she could move.

Okay, she was thinking about it. She took a deep breath, launched herself out of the car, and forced her feet to keep moving until she was up the sidewalk.

"The key's on the hook by the door," Toby called, as she reached the door.

She pulled the door open and practically leaped inside. Oh Lord, she was so nervous she was dizzy. But she was doing it.

"Haskell, Tanner, if you two don't get me out of here this second you will pay for the rest of your lives. The joke has gone on long enough."

Tentatively Becca stepped farther into the room, the rage in his voice adding to her nerves. "It's not—it's not Toby and Luke. It's me."

He appeared against the bars in an instant. "Becca?"

She almost wept at the relief that was in his voice. He was glad to see her, that much was clear.

"Yes, it's me." She walked to cell one and smiled at him. "Hi."

"Hi. Can you believe those idiots? They locked me in here."

"I know. I asked them to."

He narrowed his eyes. "I knew you were mad at me, but you asked them to put me in jail?"

"Oh, no. I just asked them to stall you. The jail cell was their idea. You know how carried away they get."

"Why did you want them to stall me?"

She pressed her hand against her stomach again, suddenly terrified. "I—well, I just wanted to say…" Her sweaty hands gripped paper, and she remembered the sketch in her hands. "I wanted to show you this—"

She held up the sketch like a shield.

He was still scowling, she noticed when she peaked around the edge of the sketch.

"See, it's you."

He studied the picture intently.

Okay, so maybe some explanation was necessary. She shifted the picture so that she could see it, too, and stood with her back to Colt. "See, it's you, the way I see you. That one in the corner is the first day you came back, when I talked to you on the porch. And the one in the bottom? That's the night we went up to the hilltop, and…you know, in the back of your pickup. And then this one—" She tapped the paper lightly, because her hands were shaking. "This is you in high school, right before the football game. I used to stare at you, you know. I was mesmerized by you in your football uniform."

She was afraid to look at him. He didn't utter a word, didn't even make a sound. She swallowed and tilted her head to look at him.

"And in the middle?" he asked, his voice strained.

"That's…well, that's you, too." She smiled at the drawing in the middle. She'd gotten a little carried away, drawing Colt in a suit of armor, his chest valiantly thrust out and his face turned into the wind, standing on a hilltop. He held a sword in one hand, and a white horse pranced in the background. "Um…as Prince Charming." She took a deep breath and turned back to him. "I know you don't see yourself that way, but I do, Colt. I really do. All the qualities that are important to me—honesty, caring, respect—you have them all. You are a Prince Charming, whether you know it or not."

He peered at her. "Becca, have you been crying?"

She lowered her face self-consciously. Her eyes were probably red, her face blotchy. She should have given some thought to her appearance before she dashed out the door. "Yes," she said. "I was crying because I was thinking of everything you mean to me, and wondering how I could make you see that. Because I don't think anyone's taken the time to point out all the goodness inside you, the way you have for me. You helped me believe in myself, Colt, and stood by me. You supported me in my dream. You even pushed me to pursue it. No one's ever done that for you. And that broke my heart. So I cried, because I needed so much to make you see yourself the way you really are."

He swallowed, then said softly, "Is there any way you can get me out of here?"

She jumped, then ran for the front door. "I'm so sorry," she called over her shoulder. She came back with the key and turned it in the lock. "Toby told me where it was, but I was so nervous I didn't even think about—"

Colt had no sooner cleared the door than she was in his arms. "Oh, Becca." He kissed her, bone-meltingly deep. When they finally came up for air, he said, "Marry me."

She froze. "What?"

"I said, marry me. Please. Here, I'll get down on one knee."

She stopped him. "You don't have to do that."

"It's no problem." He moved to kneel.

"No, I mean you don't have to propose. Just because I did something nice for you, you don't have to—what's that?"

He'd pulled the envelope out of his shirt pocket and handed it to her.

"Open it. I got it this afternoon."

She opened the flap of the envelope and pulled out a piece of cardboard. "Is this a plane ticket?"

"Several plane tickets. See, I thought—" He took the envelope back, excited once again with his plan. "I thought about a big ring, but then I thought you'd really like this as a proposal a lot better. First, we'll spend two weeks in New York City. Go to that museum you were always talking about. See a few Broadway shows. I don't have the faintest idea which ones are good, so you'll have to decide that. From there, we'll go to Paris. For six weeks. I mean, we'll have to leave soon if you want to get back by the time school starts. And I'm sorry, but that means a small wedding. Unless you want to get married on the honeymoon, which would be—"

"Wait a minute!" Becca put one hand on her forehead and the other on the bar of the cell to steady herself. "Are you actually proposing?"

"That's what 'marry me' generally means. And, I'm trying to show you why you should say yes."

"Why I should say yes," she repeated faintly.

"Yes. See, I've worked it all out. I'm staying here, in Aloma. Pete and I are going into the construction business together. And you and I…can get married."

"Get…" Becca stared at the tickets in his hand, then at the ground, then up at him. Tears welled once again.

"And what about you? Aren't you going to ride any-more?"

"No, I'm through."

"The doctor said you could do anything you want."

"I am. This is what I want. I want to stay here. I want to go into business with Pete. And I want to marry you."

"And that's why I should marry you? Because you have it all worked out? What about how we feel about each other?"

"Becca, you know how I feel about you."

She shook her head. "No, Colt. I've spent my entire life settling. I've compromised everything because I felt like that was all I deserved. I'm not going to settle for marrying you because you think it will fit in your new plan. Two months ago—two *weeks* ago, even, I would have accepted your offer. But I don't want close enough anymore. You've taught me I don't have to settle for that. I want the real thing." She took a deep breath and slowly, slowly let it out. "Now, try again. Why should I say yes?"

"Because..." His voice was gruff, and he had to swallow before he could continue. He took her hand in his and squeezed, hard. "Because I love you. Because I can't imagine how I would ever go back to living without you. Because I want to spend the rest of my life giving you everything you deserve, everything you and I both missed. Because—"

He stopped when Becca covered his mouth with hers. Tears ran down her face, wetting both their cheeks.

"Yes," she said against his lips. "Yes, I'll marry you. Promise me you'll say that to me, every day, for the rest of our lives."

He gathered her in his arms, holding her as tightly as he'd ached to for so long. "I promise."

* * * * *

I N T I M A T E   M O M E N T S™
is proud to present

Romancing the Crown

*With the help of their powerful allies,
the royal family of Montebello is determined
to find their missing heir. But the search for the
beloved prince is not without danger—or passion!*

**This exciting twelve-book series begins in January and
continues throughout the year with these fabulous titles:**

Available at your favorite retail outlet.

Silhouette®
Where love comes alive™

Visit Silhouette at www.eHarlequin.com   SIMRC

CALL THE ONES YOU LOVE OVER THE HOLIDAYS!

Save $25 off future book purchases when you buy any four Harlequin® or Silhouette® books in October, November and December 2001,

PLUS

receive a phone card good for 15 minutes of long-distance calls to anyone you want in North America!

WHAT AN INCREDIBLE DEAL!

Just fill out this form and attach 4 proofs of purchase (cash register receipts) from October, November and December 2001 books, and Harlequin Books will send you a coupon booklet worth a total savings of $25 off future purchases of Harlequin® and Silhouette® books, AND a 15-minute phone card to call the ones you love, anywhere in North America.

Please send this form, along with your cash register receipts as proofs of purchase, to:

In the USA: Harlequin Books, P.O. Box 9057, Buffalo, NY 14269-9057
In Canada: Harlequin Books, P.O. Box 622, Fort Erie, Ontario L2A 5X3

Cash register receipts must be dated no later than December 31, 2001.
Limit of 1 coupon booklet and phone card per household.
Please allow 4-6 weeks for delivery.

**I accept your offer! Enclosed are 4 proofs of purchase.
Please send me my coupon booklet
and a 15-minute phone card:**

Name: _____

Address: _____ City: _____

State/Prov.: _____ Zip/Postal Code: _____

Account Number (if available): _____

---

097 KJB DAGL
PHQ4013